"Why did your sister not come to be my bride?"

"Because she has entered a convent. Besides, since money is of such importance to you, I have the larger dowry."

Sabina stood face-to-face with the seigneur now, and they glared at each other like a pair of angry dogs.

"With your low opinions of us Bretons, I wonder that you agreed to come." Ronan Guennec's voice was close to a snarl.

"I did not come willingly! My father threatened to carry me bodily to the ship himself. He said I'd been a plague to him for seventeen years, and I could now come and plague you!"

"He did, did he? Well, he'll find himself mistaken, for I'll not have you! As soon as the gales subside and the ship can sail you will be on board heading back to England!"

"So much for the sanctity of betrothal vows! All the same, I cannot leave this wretched place fast enough! My one regret is that I won't be able to hear the laughter when the story gets around how you were fooled by Giles and nearly got palmed off with the wrong bride!"

THE RANSOMED BRIDE

ELIZABETH LOWTHER

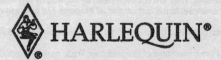

HARLEQUIN®

TORONTO • NEW YORK • LONDON
AMSTERDAM • PARIS • SYDNEY • HAMBURG
STOCKHOLM • ATHENS • TOKYO • MILAN • MADRID
PRAGUE • WARSAW • BUDAPEST • AUCKLAND

ISBN 0-373-30379-3

THE RANSOMED BRIDE

First North American Publication 2001

Visit us at www.eHarlequin.com

Printed in U.S.A.

ELIZABETH LOWTHER

was born a Geordie, though for most of her life she has lived in Devon. For a while she was a teacher, then began writing to take her mind off a bout of jaundice. The jaundice went, the writing bug remained! She has since published many stories, articles and books, but historical novels are her favorites. She admits to getting hooked on research. Sensibly she married a man who could correct her spelling, and lives in Devon with him, their two daughters and that obligatory writer's companion, a black cat.

Chapter One

1405

The litter gave a violent lurch, causing Sabina to clench her teeth. Already its erratic swaying was reminding her forcibly of the stormy Channel crossing she had just endured, and the musty smell of its interior was doing nothing to settle her stomach. Pulling back the leather curtains, she called to her brother, "Giles, I beg of you, can't we halt for a spell?"

Giles Corbyn reined back his horse so that he was level with his sister. A scowl darkened his splendid features.

"Where do you suggest we stop?" he demanded. "Here by the road, to get soaked, or in one of the miserable peasants' hovels?"

"There must be somewhere!" Sabina pleaded.

"If you can see a fitting spot we'll go there, else we keep moving."

Sabina looked about her, but all she could see was the empty Breton landscape blurred by mist and rain.

"Then at least let me ride on horseback!" she insisted.

"In this weather? And have you arrive at the Château de Plou-Aven looking like a drowned rat? Certainly not!"

The impatience in Giles's tone was too much for Sabina. "I could have hoped for more sympathy and kindness from you," she retorted angrily, "seeing that my dowry is paying most of your ransom! In the circumstances I wonder you have the nerve to look me in the face!"

"And I wonder at that tongue of yours!" answered Giles. "I'd forgotten what a shrew you are. I hope the Seigneur beats the waspishness out of you—he's not a man to stand any nonsense."

"He's put up with you for nigh on two years," rejoined Sabina. But she was talking to the rain-laden air. Giles had driven his spurs into his horse and galloped ahead.

Sabina fell back against the cushions, anger and resentment overwhelming her nausea. It was being treated like a parcel of goods that infuriated her the most. She might have been a bale of wool, or a bundle of cowhides, the way in which she had been packed off across the Channel. And she was expected to feel grateful! "Such news! The Seigneur de Plou-Aven has agreed to take your dowry as part of your brother's ransom," her mother had informed her delightedly. "A husband for you, and release for Giles. Isn't that a fine thing? Otherwise I'd no idea how we'd raise the full amount!"

No one had asked Sabina if she'd wanted to go. Her parents' only concern was to get their darling son and heir back home again.

"But, what's he like, this Seigneur de Plou-Aven?" Sabina had cried. "Is he young or old? Is he a good man?"

"He's a widower, and seems to be treating your brother well enough." Her mother had been unconcerned by her fears.

"Surely you know more than that?" Sabina had implored.

"He is of good birth. He speaks no English so you will needs converse with him in French, but that is unimportant. What more is there to know?" Her mother's tone had firmly implied that the conversation was at an end.

On such meagre reassurance she was condemned to a lifetime's exile from her beloved Devon, all because her eldest brother had taken part in an ill-conceived raid on the Breton coast and ended up a prisoner of the Seigneur de Plou-Aven.

Suddenly the cavalcade came to a halt, and for one dread moment Sabina thought they had arrived. When she looked outside, however, she saw that they were in a wood. Giles came hurrying up.

"Another mile or so and we're there," he said. "Perhaps you had better do something to your appearance. I'll send your tiring-woman to you."

"Let poor Alice be," said Sabina. "She was more unwell on the crossing than me. I'll manage for myself."

"Are you sure you can?" Giles was doubtful. And beneath his doubts she sensed a strong measure of unease. "Can't you put some colour into your cheeks? And your hair—do something about it, it's sticking out of your crispinette." He peered more closely at her. "It's so dark, too, when it used to be so golden. And you're quite sallow-faced. I can't believe how much you've changed; you used to be such a pretty little thing.''

''That was our sister, Blanche,'' Sabina said flatly. ''You always did confuse us, though only the blessed saints know why, we're not at all alike!'' An alarming thought occurred to her. ''You weren't expecting Blanche, were you?'' she demanded. ''You didn't describe me to the Seigneur de Plou-Aven as a golden-haired angel, did you?''

''I merely told the Seigneur that I had unmarried sisters enough and to spare. There are so many of you I can't be expected to bother about which is which!'' The scorn in Giles's voice did not quite mask his anxiety.

Sabina groaned. She had thought her spirits low enough already but now they plummeted further. She was used to being compared unfavourably with the rest of her numerous and beautiful family, and much of the time she managed to persuade herself she didn't care, but this was a very different matter.

''You mean the Seigneur is expecting a bride of great beauty?'' she cried. ''What will he do when he sees me? He'll think you've deliberately deceived him.''

''How was I to know which sister you would be? Blanche, Joan, Katherine, Sabina! You're all one to me!''

''But not to the Seigneur! Blanche, Joan and Katherine are beautiful. I'm not! We must pray that having had you under his roof for two years the man knows you for a fool!''

''That tongue of yours will bring you trouble!'' Giles tried to sound stern, but failed, overcome by his own misgivings. "Well, it's too late to do anything about it now," he added. "Do what you can to make yourself tolerable. But be quick."

Left alone Sabina set about repairing the damage caused by the long hours of arduous travel. Looking at herself in her polished metal mirror, she noted her pallid complexion and the shadows beneath her hazel eyes. Even at her best she knew she was no beauty, and she was far from at her best now. For the first time she wished she had some face paint; normally she never bothered about such fripperies. She regretted, too, that she was still dressed in homespun kersey; she had intended to change into something more grand for the first meeting with her future husband. A gown of blue Flemish cloth had been packed for the purpose, but what with the crossing being so stormy and she and Alice being so ill, somehow she had not had the heart to go rummaging in her boxes for it. Upon consideration, she wished she had managed to rouse herself more but, as Giles had observed, it was too late now. All she could do was to repin her mouse-brown hair under her crispinette and brush the worst of the travel stains from her long skirts.

Typically, Giles did not bother to enquire if she was ready. As she was attempting to pinch a little colour into her cheeks the litter swung abruptly into motion, and they were on their way once more.

Soon they had left the woods behind them and they were travelling through what seemed to be wild moorland, though in places the scrub had been cleared for cultivation. Peering through the curtain, she noticed small cottages scattered about the countryside, their stone-built walls merging with the landscape so well they seemed to be growing out of the earth.

Despite the rain, peasants toiled in the fields, and they paused from their labours to watch the travellers pass, their wooden clogs sunk deep into the mud, their faces sullen and unsmiling. Sabina hoped fervently that she would get a warmer welcome from the Seigneur.

The château loomed ahead with alarming suddenness. It was smaller than she had expected, yet, for all that, its stone walls seemed stark and forbidding. On its hilltop perch it dominated the countryside, its rounded turrets piercing the mist, their slate roofs gleaming in the wet. This was a fortress, dour and impenetrable. It was also to be her home until the end of her days, and she could not restrain herself from swallowing nervously at the daunting prospect.

Sheer anxiety made Sabina drop the curtain and huddle in the comforting darkness of the litter, so that she was only vaguely aware of the flaring torches lighting the dark gloom of the gatehouse and the excited bustle of the servants as they rode into the inner bailey. The horses' hoofs clattered and slipped on the stony courtyard—then they came to a halt. She had arrived at the Château de Plou-Aven!

The curtain of the litter was pulled aside and Giles's face peered in. He looked increasingly wet and anxious.

''The Seigneur awaits,'' he said brusquely, thrusting out a hand to help her down.

Stiff and cold with nerves and fatigue, Sabina stepped out. Ahead of her a short flight of steps led up to a great arched door. It stood open, letting light flood out on to the puddles in the courtyard. There seemed to be many people crowded into the doorway, but before she could determine which one was the Seigneur Giles seized her arm and hustled her forward, forcing her to trot to keep up with his long stride. As she did so a swirling gust of wind caught her crispinette, tearing it half off her head. She was still trying to pin it back with her free hand when they reached the top of the steps and Giles said in French, "Seigneur, may I present my sister, Mistress Sabina Corbyn?"

The man confronting her stood four-square, his legs planted firmly apart, his hands on his hips. Giles was taller than him by some inches, and more handsome, yet he paled into insignificance beside Ronan Guennec, the Seigneur de Plou-Aven. The Breton emanated vigour and energy; the dark brown eyes that glared at Sabina were shrewd and proud.

Sabina glared back. She should have noticed that he was far from old—not more than eight-and-twenty—and that he stood straight-backed and was not at all ill-favoured. She should have noticed the slight curling of his dark hair, the strong hawk-like curve of his nose, the tan on his cheeks which spoke of much time spent out of doors. But she saw none of these things. She saw only the expression, on the Seigneur's face. It was one of disappointment, dismay, and growing anger.

"This is your sister, you say?" he demanded at last.

"Aye, my sister, Sabina." Giles shuffled uncomfortably.

"This cannot be so! You said she was a beauty!"

"Sire, you must allow for my partiality towards

my own sister. I—I may have exaggerated a little,''
stammered Giles.

"Exaggerated! You exaggerated to the point of
lies and deceitfulness!" The Seigneur's voice rose to
a roar which echoed round the great hall.

"Seigneur," protested Giles, growing more and
more agitated, "i-it is some years since I have seen
her. Sh-she has changed... She was but a child when
last I—''

"A slender form, a cheek like a wild rose, and
hair spun from pure gold—that was what you promised me!" bellowed the Seigneur. "Tall and golden
like an angel, you said. Look at her! She's a little
mouse of a thing! And she's brown! All brown!"

This last insult was too much for Sabina.

"Then it's a pity the Seigneur did not order his
wife by size and colour, as he might a mantle or a
gown," she snapped.

A shocked silence fell upon the hall, broken only
by an anguished groan from Giles.

The Seigneur stared at her in hostile disbelief.
Sabina stared back, her jaw jutting belligerently...
Then it all proved too much for her; to her horror
she felt a single tear begin to course its way down
her cheek. Angrily she scrubbed at it with her sleeve,
biting her lips and sniffing to make sure no other
followed it.

The Seigneur muttered something incomprehensible, then growled, "I won't have her!"

"Good!" retorted Sabina. Picking up her skirts,
she made for the open door.

"Where are you going?" he demanded.

"Back to the ship, before it sails, and thence to
my father's house!"

"No! I am not having my horses go out again in this weather!" Ronan Guennec muttered to himself once more, then barked in exasperation, "We'll talk tomorrow." Turning on his heel he stalked out of the hall, scattering the servants, dogs and floor rushes out of his way as he went.

Sabina stood very still, steeling herself for the tirade that was certain to follow from her brother.

But Giles had apparently been struck dumb by the scene he had just witnessed. As she made to follow a servant towards her chamber for the night he recovered enough to wail, "Now I shall never get home—and it's all your fault!" A remark that Sabina did not think worthy of a reply.

She climbed the turret stairs in the wake of the servant, too appalled by her encounter with the Seigneur to notice the room in which she was to sleep or the food which was brought to her. A tearful and decidedly unwell Alice helped her undress, and she collapsed into bed. Things could scarcely have gone more disastrously...

Anger and humiliation took hold of her. "Who does he think he is?" she muttered to herself in the darkness of the big, caved bed. "So, he won't have me because my hair is brown and my skin is sallow. Well, that pleased me, because I'll not marry such an ill-tempered devil! I'll have the first scurvy beggar that comes along before I'll have the Seigneur de Plou-Aven!"

"Does this mean we're going home, mistress?" asked Alice plaintively.

Sabina realised that she must have been speaking aloud.

"Aye, first thing tomorrow, hopefully."

"Oh, the blessed saints be praised! To be out of this God-forsaken country!" Alice's voice betrayed exactly what she thought of Brittany. "But, mistress, your honoured parents! They'll not be at all pleased—especially if you have to leave poor Master Giles behind!"

Similar thoughts had been creeping into Sabina's mind. The ignominy and humiliation of having to return home because the Seigneur did not consider her fit to be his bride would be bad enough, but her parents' fury at not having their darling Giles returned to them would be even worse. Of their many children, they had always considered her to be the most troublesome and difficult—and now, seemingly, she could not even manage a simple matter like getting herself married to a Breton. She would get no welcome back at Corbyn Manor.

"I seem to be in a pretty fix," she whispered in some distress. "The Seigneur won't wed me and my parents won't have me home. What am I to do?"

No answer came from Alice, who had settled herself in the little *couchette* bed at Sabina's feet, only the heavy, rhythmical breathing of a sound sleeper.

Sabina pulled the coverlet closer about her ears, convinced that her predicament and the anguish of her encounter with Ronan Guennec would keep her wide awake. But the feather mattress was comfortable and she was exhausted; oblivion claimed her almost immediately.

When she awoke, the unfamiliar dimness struck cold, and a strong wind whistled and howled through the narrow slit windows. The reality of her situation flooded back to her, and she had to struggle hard to conquer the wave of panic which suddenly beset her. Somehow she managed it, and stretching a bare foot out of the warm covers she prodded her maid's still sleeping form.

"Stir yourself, Alice, and get me ready," she commanded. "I've no wish for the Seigneur to think I'm a sluggard."

"Are we truly going home today, mistress?" asked Alice, pulling on her gown.

"We'll have to see."

"But, mistress, you said—"

"No doubt I did!" Sabina cut short the maid's wail. "But it isn't up to me. We must see what the Seigneur has to say on the matter. Now set to, else we'll be here all day."

"But your clean linen's still packed in your boxes. And I don't know where to fetch the water from—"

"You never will unless you make the effort. I'll find fresh clothes while you go and look. And don't appear so terrified. No one is going to murder you!"

The maid left the room looking far from convinced. But she was back soon with a brimming ewer. As Alice helped Sabina to dress a manservant arrived bearing a platter of wheaten bread, honeycomb, and a goblet of wine. Sabina looked at it appreciatively.

"Pardon, *ma demoiselle*, but the Seigneur asks that you join him in the solar when you have eaten," said the servant as he departed.

For a moment Sabina thought that his words had dulled her appetite, but once her teeth dug into the fresh crust she began to realise just how hungry she was. At last she could eat and drink no more, and she knew she could no longer put off her meeting with the Seigneur.

The servant was waiting for her outside the door. As she followed him down the spiralling stairs she was thankful that this time she would face Ronan Guennec looking presentable, at least. The gown of Flemish blue cloth was not new, it had been a gift from Giles's wife, but, though it was too big and did not fit closely to her figure as a fashionable cote-hardie should, it was of a fine quality. Alice had plaited her hair and twisted it up under a blue net held on by a narrow fillet of silver about her brow. When she reached the solar, the private family room above the great hall, she knew that her appearance was an improvement upon the previous day's, but her looks still fell far short of the golden angel the Seigneur had been promised.

Ronan Guennec was facing the door as she entered. He looked imposing in his calf-length gown of russet velvet edged with fur. Again he was standing with his feet apart, his hands on his hips, as though ready to deal firmly with anything or anybody who dared to cross him.

Sabina refused to be intimidated. "Good morning, Seigneur. I understand you wish to speak with me."

"Indeed I do…er…I hope you slept well?" His manner changed from belligerence to unease, and he dug his hands deep into his belt.

"Yes, thank you." Sabina regarded him steadily. It was he who looked away first.

"I must beg your pardon," he said at last. "The welcome I gave you last night was a rough one…I am sorry. I should have made allowances for your arduous journey. You look a deal better now you've dried out. Not that it makes any difference to my decision. Your brother deceived me about you—you aren't the bride I agreed upon—so you can go back to your father as soon as you please.''

Sabina was not sure whether to be amused or angry at this speech. Finally her sense of justice won. ''My brother didn't really intend to deceive you, Seigneur. The fact is, he confused me with our sister, Blanche, who really is a golden beauty.''

''You are saying that he cannot tell his sisters apart?''

''We are a large family,'' Sabina explained. ''Twelve of our parents' children still live, and, of those, eight are girls. Giles is the eldest child, and has spent much time away from home. He has had little contact with us younger ones. Besides, he has never been one to show an interest in babes and such; his wife complains constantly that he takes little notice even of his own.''

''But not to know which sister is which! Still, having been acquainted with your brother these two years, I accept that such a thing is possible. All the same, it was your sister—Blanche, did you say her name was?—who was described to me.''

''Maybe. But it was me, Sabina, you agreed to marry. Why?''

''Why?'' Ronan Guennec looked startled by the directness of the question.

''Yes, why would you have an English wife when surely there are Breton and French brides in plenty to be had?''

''Our late Duc, Jean de Bretagne, took an English wife. I was merely following my lord's example.''

''You don't appear to me to be a man who would

follow someone else's example,'' said Sabina bluntly.

''Oh... If you want the truth—your brother has been under my roof, living at my expense, for two years—I would be rid of him. But every demand for a ransom I sent to your father met with the same reply, 'I am trying to raise the money but I am a poor man. Give me more time'. Then, just when I feared I must have charge of him till the end of my days, there came a message from your father saying he could find the money if the dowry of one of his daughters was included. I needed a wife; the description given by your brother was favourable—and I would be rid of him into the bargain—so I said yes.''

''If you found the company of Giles so irksome you could simply have sent him home and made no demands for money,'' said Sabina.

The Seigneur greeted this suggestion with a look of utter contempt. ''It was the English, your brother among them, who invaded my land,'' he said. ''I am entitled to compensation.''

''And why did we attack you? As a reprisal for you Bretons burning Plymouth earlier that year!'' Sabina was incensed. ''They say nearly half the city was destroyed. We could see the glow from the fires reflected in the sky even at Corbyn... You didn't fare so well at Dartmouth, though, did you? You were truly routed there!'' she taunted.

The Seigneur glared at her angrily. She expected a stinging reply; instead he chose to change the subject. ''I still do not understand... Why did your sister not come to be my bride?''

''Because she has entered a convent. Besides,

since money is of such importance to you, I have the larger dowry."

"Your father doesn't treat all his daughters alike? Surely that is strange?"

"Marriage portions for eight of us have been a sad drain upon his resources. However, my mother's brother, who is my godfather, paid mine."

"The pity is that your uncle did not agree to pay the balance of your brother's ransom," growled the Seigneur.

"He wouldn't do that! He said he was providing for one of his sister's brood, and that was enough. In his view Giles got his just deserts being held prisoner by you, he deserved no better for allowing himself to be captured by a pack of scurvy Bretons!"

Sabina stood face to face with the Seigneur now, and they glared at each other like a pair of angry dogs.

"With your low opinions of us Bretons I wonder that you agreed to come." Ronan Guennec's voice was close to a snarl.

"I did not come willingly! I was beaten black and blue first! My father threatened to carry me bodily to the ship himself. He said I'd been a plague for him for seventeen years, and I could now come and plague you!"

"He did, did he? Well, he'll find himself mistaken, for I'll not have you! As soon as the gales subside and the ship can sail you will be on board heading back to England!"

"So much for the sanctity of betrothal vows! All the same, I cannot leave this wretched place fast enough! My one regret is that I won't be able to hear the laughter when the story gets around how you were fooled by Giles and nearly got palmed off with the wrong bride!''

The Seigneur opened his mouth to make an angry retort, but closed it again with a snap as Sabina's words sank in.

"You said your brother was not deliberately trying to play me false," he pointed out.

"Nor was he. You and I know that, for we know he is a fool. But the rest of the countryside will think he cheated you."

The Seigneur scowled at her.

"Of course," Sabina went on, "we could go ahead with the ceremony and when we get to the altar I could refuse you. Perhaps it would save your pride a little."

"It would not, as you very well know!" he snapped. "I have made up my mind. I won't have the Guennec name held up to ridicule, particularly not at the hands of the English, nor will I have anyone accusing me of breaking my betrothal vows, even though they were given by proxy. I need a wife, you're of gentle birth, and seemingly come from a line that is both robust and fertile—you'll have to do!''

"Do you mean that you will wed me after all...?"

"I said so, didn't I? But watch that tongue of yours; if there's one thing I cannot stand it is a shrew!"

At his words Sabina could not hold back a slight sigh of relief.

The Seigneur heard it. "You want to marry me?" he asked incredulously.

"No," she replied frankly. "But what will happen to me if I return home in disgrace? I'll be beaten again, then rushed into some other marriage. I had another suitor who was older than my grandfather and bent double with rheumatism. I don't relish being your bride, but at least your back is straight and both your legs seem to be the same length. I've no wish for a husband too frail to reach the altar unaided.''

''It sounds to me as if you have no wish for a husband at all. I wonder that your father did not pack you off to the convent with your sister.''

''He did,'' admitted Sabina. ''But the mother abbess sent me home again. She said I was a disruptive influence.''

''*That* I can believe,'' said the Seigneur with feeling.

She glanced up at him, and for a moment thought she detected the corners of his mouth twitching, as though he were struggling to suppress a smile. But when she looked again his face had assumed its original scowl.

She gave another sigh. ''You don't want to marry me and I don't want to marry you,'' she said. ''The prospects for our future together do not seem too good, do they?''

The Seigneur did not contradict her.

''We'll be wed tomorrow,'' he said. ''Be ready!''

If Sabina had expected the Seigneur or her brother to entertain her that day then she was disappointed. At the end of her encounter with Ronan Guennec he had shown her to the door, clearly leaving her to her own devices. Of Giles there had been no sign. For a while she returned to her bedchamber, but found it too cold and gloomy to remain long. Besides, Alice was there unpacking, and the tiring-woman had taken

the news ill that they were not to return to Devon—
Sabina was in a black enough mood already without
having to listen to her woman's continual sobs.

A sense of isolation beset her, along with more
than a touch of homesickness. Her initial relief that
the Seigneur was going to marry her had dissipated
and now she was in a fret of anxiety in case she had
made the wrong decision. Perhaps she should go
back to England after all, and face her parents' wrath.
She longed for someone with whom to discuss her
problems, *even* her brother would do. To this end she
set off in search of him.

She did not find Giles, but several times her path
crossed that of the Seigneur.

"*Ma demoiselle,* are you seeking me out?" he demanded eventually.

"Indeed no, Seigneur," she replied sweetly. "It is
my brother whom I seek. I can't find him anywhere.
Do you keep him locked up?"

"I do not!" He was indignant. "He's allowed the
freedom of my estates, provided he goes accompanied by two servants."

"I'm surprised you aren't afraid he'll try to escape."

"Even your brother is not fool enough to attempt
that! I suspect he is now probably doing the only
sensible thing he has ever done in his life—keeping
out of my way!"

"Oh…" Sabina was disappointed. She had no particular love for her brother, but at that moment a
familiar face would have been very welcome.

"Your pardon, *ma demoiselle.* I've much to attend
to today." The Seigneur's leave-taking was brusque,
but at the door he stopped and said, "I will send

Zacharie Le Godet to you—my seneschal—he can show you round and tell you about the domestic arrangement and such. Wait here.''

Sabina was about to protest that she did not want to be escorted round the château by his servant, but she changed her mind. Any activity was better than aimless wanderings, that gave her too much time to think.

Zacharie Le Godet proved to be a small stick-thin man with sparse grey hair, and such meagre shanks that the cloth of his hose hung in wrinkles about his ankles.

''*Ma demoiselle.*'' He greeted her with a low bow. ''Let me first offer my humble welcome to you, to our new Dame de Plou-Aven. You have no idea how we need your gracious presence to create order where now there is only chaos and...''

Sabina began to wonder if this effusive greeting and ingratiating speech would ever end. She regarded the little man with caution—despite his protestations she had come across no signs of disorder or chaos at the château. Moreover, she detected a certain wariness in his eyes, along with a stronger emotion which might have been resentment.

''I am pleased to make your acquaintance, Zacharie Le Godet,'' she said, breaking into his flowing speech. ''I shall doubtless need to rely heavily on your knowledge and experience. You have been at the château a long time?''

''Twenty years come Martinmas, ever since the time of Dame Yolande, the present Seigneur's mother. From her death, fifteen years ago, the running of this establishment has been solely in my unworthy hands.''

"But surely the Seigneur's wife...?"

"Dame Marianne was a very delicate lady, too delicate to be concerned with matters of housekeeping; she did me the honour of leaving everything to me."

Now we have it, thought Sabina. She knew the seneschal was waiting to hear her say, "And I shall do the same." But she did not. Most of her life to date had been under the rigid control of others and a rebellious streak in her longed to have some freedom, be it only the right to order her own household. No, she would not follow the example of Dame Marianne.

"Perhaps we should begin our tour of the château," she said.

Le Godet's brow wrinkled with annoyance, but he was too good a servant to show his disapproval more openly.

"If the *demoiselle* will graciously follow me...?" He bowed and led the way from the room.

He moved surprisingly swiftly, going from room to room, from hall to bailey, from stable to cider press; anyone less nimble than Sabina would not have kept up with him. He was certainly well informed about the château and he spared no detail. She knew that he was only stressing his self-importance in front of her, and she might have sympathised with him if he had not infuriated her so. It was the way in which he answered her questions— it did not matter what she asked about, Le Godet always ended his replies in the same way:

"But, *ma demoiselle,* you have no need to concern yourself with that. I will see to it all."

Sabina began to realize that there would be precious little left under her control if she did not watch out.

"You are leaving me nothing to do!" she cried.

"But you will be the châtelaine of this household." He feigned bewilderment. "Everything will be as you order it. I will merely be your humble servant and intermediary."

Just how much of an intermediary she soon found out. They had finished looking at the larder, pantry, and buttery when Sabina noticed a building standing a little apart.

"What is that?" she asked.

"Merely the kitchen, *ma demoiselle.*'

Le Godet led the way and flung open the door, letting out a wave of heat and cooking smells. He was about to close it again when Sabina said, "No, I wish to go inside."

"But they are busy preparing the wedding feast..."

"I do not intend to interrupt them, but I feel I should at least meet the cook."

Sabina stalked forward to the interior of the kitchen, leaving Le Godet no option but to follow her. A surprised silence greeted her entry, and a dozen pair of eyes gazed at her in astonishment.

"Good day," she said. "Who among you is the head cook?"

No one moved.

"The head cook," she repeated. "Is he not here?"

The kitchen servants shuffled uncomfortably and looked at one another in bewilderment.

"This is foolishness!" she exclaimed irritably. "Why does no one answer?"

A discreet cough came from Le Godet. "I fear

they do not understand, *ma demoiselle*. They do not speak French, just their own outlandish tongue.''

"They don't speak French…?" Sabina said in dismay.

This was the first time she had come across a language barrier. She had heard the servants talking to each other in their native Breton, but those who had served her at meals had at least understood French. It had never occurred to her that she would not be able to communicate with most of them.

Le Godet knew, though. It took considerable self-control not to give him the sharp edge of her tongue. But she managed to say calmly, "I presume, therefore, that every command I give must be interpreted by you."

"Indeed so, *ma demoiselle.*'

"Then the sooner I learn Breton the better."

"Learn Breton!" Le Godet was shaken out of his self-satisfaction. "*Ma demoiselle,* it is not a language fit for ladies of gentle birth!"

Sabina ignored his shocked comments. "In the meantime," she said, "would you be good enough to ask the head cook to come forward?"

The seneschal rapped out an order, and a sturdy, middle-aged man stepped forward and bowed.

"This is the head cook, Alain," said Le Godet, unable to keep the disapproval from his voice.

"If you please, tell him he need not look so alarmed," said Sabina. "I merely wish to make his acquaintance. I have a hearty appetite, and shall take a keen interest in his skills. We will talk more another time when he is less busy."

She meant the words to put Alain at ease, but the anxious frown on his face did not lessen; she suspected that Le Godet's translation had not been strictly to the letter.

The cook said something which Le Godet repeated as, "He is honoured by your visit, *ma demoiselle.*" But there was more relief than honour on the man's face when Sabina dismissed him and left the kitchen.

"Did Dame Marianne speak Breton?" Sabina asked.

"Certainly not, *ma demoiselle.* She had no need. The upper servants understand French even if they don't speak it well."

"But how did she communicate with the lower servants?"

"Dame Marianne had no contact with the lower servants." The seneschal sounded shocked at the idea.

Sabina said no more. Her view of her new life was becoming increasingly gloomy. It would be hard enough having to deal in French all the time, but at least she knew sufficient to be able to manage the day to day affairs. To be unable to speak to most of the servants was a blow she had not anticipated. She did not relish the idea of being so completely in Le Godet's power—she was going to have to struggle to assert herself. This, coupled with her growing sense of isolation, did nothing to ease her misgivings at the prospect of her coming marriage.

At last Le Godet begged to be excused, on the reasonable excuse that there was still much to do for the festivities. Sabina felt she had suffered enough of his presence for the time being and was glad to see him go.

The rest of the day dragged on. Guests were beginning to arrive for the wedding, but, of course, she knew none of them, and she felt reticent to join them.

Shortly before supper Giles put in an appearance.

"Thank you for your support and comfort on this, the day before my wedding, brother dear," she said witheringly.

"I only rode in the woods with my dogs and hawks for a little sport," he protested.

"Dogs and hawks? I can see your enforced stay here has been very arduous!"

Giles ignored his sister's sarcastic comment. "Your wedding-day? You mean the marriage is to go ahead? That is good news!"

"No thanks to you! You didn't exactly put yourself out to smooth over the harm you had done!"

"I was confident you would cope much better without me. I knew you would swing things around—you always were my favourite sister, you know."

"If only you could remember which one I am! Oh, Giles, don't be a bigger fool than you can help!"

Giles glared at her and would have replied, but at that point a servant arrived to call them to table.

The Seigneur was waiting for them. At the sight of Giles his face darkened. "I would have thought you could have given some of your time to your sister today instead of skulking off," he said. "Though by the look of you it is my guess she's already had something to say on the subject."

"Seigneur, I simply—"

"Let us consider the matter closed," said the Seigneur firmly. He held out his hand to Sabina. "*Ma demoiselle,* let me lead you to your place before the food gets cold."

When he does this tomorrow, I'll be his wife, thought Sabina—then spent the rest of the meal trying to dispel the chill agitation the notion aroused in her.

More wedding guests had arrived. The wine flowed freely, and there was music and laughter; in any other circumstances Sabina would have enjoyed herself. As it was, she had to struggle to maintain polite conversation with her neighbour. From time to time she glanced at Ronan Guennec under her lashes. When caught unaware his expression sometimes held an intense sadness that was at variance with his normal brusque manner, and she wondered what sort of a man he really was. He had a temper, that much she knew, other than that... If only I'd had time to get to know him or talk to him properly, she thought—but it was too late for that.

Eventually the wine flagons ceased their rounds and most of the guests, Giles included, made their unsteady way to bed, supported by servants.

"If you please, Seigneur, I would withdraw now," said Sabina.

"Doubtless you are weary. I know that I am."

Sabina watched as he set down his wine goblet. "You are an abstemious drinker, sire."

"I am tonight. You said you wanted a bridegroom who could reach the altar unaided, didn't you? Well, that's what you will get!" His tone sharpened as he said, "We should have spoken alone more today. There are things which should be said. But I've had much to do. If I may, I will attend you in your chamber in a few minutes."

"But, Seigneur...!"

"The Devil take properties! We'll be wed tomorrow!"

"Very well, sire, if that is your wish."

Ronan Guennec eyed her warily. "I'd not expected to hear such a meek tone from you," he said.

"I'm so fatigued I can scarce stand!" retorted Sabina with as much vigour as she could muster.

"I suppose you must be. I promise I will not keep you long."

Sabina climbed the stairs to the turret room, full of misgivings as she wondered what the Seigneur wanted to discuss so privately. She did not have to wait long, for, true to his word, he arrived at her door soon after her.

"Leave us, Alice," she ordered.

The tiring-woman looked scandalised and made no move until the Seigneur bellowed, "Out!" and slammed the door after her.

"You should be better attended," he declared angrily. "That snivelling wretch is not sufficient! Why didn't you bring more women with you? One of those numerous sisters I keep hearing about? Did you expect me to provide everything?"

Sabina was both startled and confused by his outburst.

"I don't understand, Seigneur," she said. "Alice is very competent. I've no need for another woman."

"I'm not talking about a servant, but someone to keep you company. With my first wife the place was full of her female relations for weeks. You should have someone. It is no use relying on me, I have few female kinsfolk."

Although she was well aware of the sparsity of her

retinue, Sabina's pride was stung that he should find her wanting.

"You are kind, Seigneur, but you have no need to worry. I am quite used to managing by myself."

"It seems a ramshackle way of going about things. My wife—my first wife—was much better attended. Still, I didn't come to talk of such matters. I came to ask if you have all you need."

"Yes, thank you, sire."

Sabina waited expectantly for the Seigneur to leave. But he did not. He just stood looking about the dimly lit bedchamber, his jaw gradually tightening, his lips compressing until they become a straight line.

"She stayed in this room before her wedding, too," he said.

"Who?" asked Sabina in surprise.

"My wife... She died in childbed." There was no brusqueness in his tone now, just an anguish which he fought unsuccessfully to conceal.

She could not fail to recognise the depth of his feelings. "It was a love-match, your other marriage?" she asked quietly.

"Aye, we were the talk of the country." The pain in his voice was swept away by bitterness. "The local minstrels and bards excelled themselves singing the ballad of 'Ronan and Marianne'. The pity was that it had so few verses—she died within the year."

Sabina stood in silence, not certain of what to say.

"The prospect of tomorrow must revive painful memories for you," she said eventually.

"I hadn't anticipated quite how painful... For myself, I'd never wed again. But I thought that after five years..." He seemed to recollect himself suddenly. "Your pardon, that was not a seemly thing to say to you, of all people."

"You were being truthful. There's no need to apologise for honesty."

"All the same," the Seigneur returned swiftly to his brusque manner of speaking, "what I wanted to say is that you need not worry I'll trouble you unduly. Plou-Aven needs an heir—when that is assured you will likely see little of me, which should be of some comfort to you."

"Indeed it will," returned Sabina. "Though I fancy the comfort will not be all on my side. I assure you I'll do my duty to the best of my ability so that we may both be free of our more odious obligations."

"So be it." The Seigneur fairly rapped out the words. "I'll bid you goodnight."

After he had left the room Sabina sat down on the bed and slowly began to unbraid her hair. She could not prevent herself from contrasting the way he had outlined their future relationship with the way in which he had spoken of his first wife. What was it like to be so loved, she wondered, to be so adored that even death failed to lessen the emotion? A sudden envy for poor dead Marianne swept over her. Marianne had experienced more love in that one short year than she could anticipate in her whole lifetime.

That dismal thought stayed with her half the night and it was the first thing which sprang to her mind when she awoke on the morning of her wedding.

Chapter Two

As she lay in the turret room, the hubbub of arriving guests and bustling servants reached Sabina. From the moment she finished breaking her fast it seemed to her that she did not have a second to herself. The Seigneur had clearly ignored her assertion that she needed no female company, and had prevailed upon the wives and daughters of neighbours to come to her aid. In no time at all the room was packed with ladies she had never seen before, each intent upon advising her in accented French she could barely understand, and ordering the servants about.

By the time she was bathed in lavender-scented water and clothed, Sabina's head was spinning. And when half a dozen hands reached out simultaneously to dress her hair, she began to wonder if she would have a single lock left adhering to her scalp. Fortunately, a plump matron dressed in plunket-blue silk realised her predicament.

"Step back, all of you!" she commanded in a voice which brooked no argument. "Can't you see the poor child can hardly draw breath? Her tiring-woman and I can manage well enough."

The others moved away, but remained close enough to offer a stream of advice and criticism. When at last Sabina was dressed a chorus of approval broke out.

Alice sniffed tearfully. "You look lovely, mistress," she said.

Sabina had her doubts. Her dress was fine enough, for it was of pink velvet edged with ivory satin, but the cloth had been bought originally for one of her elder sisters—its delicate rosy tint was perfect for one of the fair Corbyns, but it made her look washed-out. Nevertheless, she decided that the best had been made of a bad job.

With her brown hair loosed from its braids and sleekly brushed, Sabina allowed a chaplet of spring blossoms to be placed on her head. The skirts of her gown were tweaked into order, and perfumed oil was rubbed into her hands. Then she was suddenly tired of all the fuss and bother. She wished heartily that the wedding were over. It was not as though she expected any joy from her coming marriage. There was no happiness in her heart as she realised that in less than an hour she would be the wife of Ronan Guennec.

The arrival of Giles to escort her to the ceremony was a signal for the ladies to leave. The matron in the blue silk was less easily dislodged, however. She took one of Sabina's hands in both of hers and leaning close whispered, "Since your mother is not here I must ask you... Do you know what the Seigneur will expect tonight?"

"Yes, thank you, *ma dame*," replied Sabina.

"Good. I'd not like to have you go to your marriage-bed uninformed." The matron patted her hand.

"The menfolk consider it important, but it's not so bad really. Take my advice, have your woman bring you a cup of *eau-de-vie* before you retire. It will make things easier… Oh, and some young men these days can behave most improperly when they try to seize the bride's garter for good luck. Be forewarned! Wear yours well below the knee!"

"Thank you, *dame*. I will." Sabina was touched by her kindness and wished the motherly woman could stay with her longer. She felt sadly in need of comfort and reassurance.

Giles, however, was waiting. He regarded her critically, "You look tolerably fair," he said.

"That comment was more honest than tactful," said Sabina.

"Not at all. You look better than I'd dared to hope. If you had more skill with the womanly arts I think you could look quite reasonable. But we've no time to be gossiping. Have you everything you need?"

"Don't you think it's a mite late to ask me that, with my bridegroom waiting for me downstairs?" enquired Sabina drily.

"I just thought I'd ask… Oh, come along! It's time we were going."

He headed for the door but Sabina stood still.

"Giles, what sort of man is the Seigneur?" she asked, fighting to quell a sudden fit of panic.

"What sort of man?" Giles looked at her in astonishment. "But you've met him!"

"Aye, but not for long enough to get to know him. He'll have complete power over me—there will be no going home for me after *my* ransom is paid. I would know what sort of future lies ahead of me."

Giles thought hard. "He's a good enough sort of

fellow—for a Breton. He's one of the best horsemen I've ever seen. As for boar hunting, his bravery is—''

"Giles!" cried Sabina in protest.

"Well, what would you know about him?" Giles demanded. "He's good to the poor, and the peasants seem to hold him in high esteem. From what I've heard he's not one to ill-treat a woman—though, mind you, he dearly loved his last wife, so perhaps that doesn't signify. Your marriage to him will be a very different matter, won't it? And so for—''

"Never mind," Sabina cut in, "that will do for now."

She had been a fool to expect any kindness or consolation from her brother. She would find out soon enough what sort of man she was about to marry.

By Giles's side, and accompanied by a bevy of young girls, not one of whom she could recognise, Sabina went downstairs. She had never missed her sisters so much, or so longed for a familiar face or two—her brother hardly counted. Characteristically, the grasp of his fingers on hers was light and insubstantial, as if to stress that she could expect no support from him. She knew she had only herself to rely on, so she raised her head proudly, in spite of the fact that it only came up to Giles's shoulder.

Her knowledge of the wedding procedure was hazy; she knew only that the ceremony was to take place in the little chapel dedicated to Saint Jehan which stood outside the château walls. She fully expected to have to walk there, so she was surprised, upon leaving the great hall, to find the Seigneur already mounted and waiting for her in the inner bailey. Grave and pale, he sat astride a huge bay stallion, his fur-trimmed mantle covering the horse's dark rump in a swathe of blood-red velvet. At the sight of Sabina he doffed his cap to her and bowed low.

"I greet Mistress Sabina Corbyn, soon to be the Dame de Plou-Aven," he said, and bowed again.

Not sure what to reply, Sabina sank into a curtsy. As she rose a groom came forward with a palomino mare, whose fine trappings of blue and cloth-of-gold matched the stallion's. So, this animal was to transport her to her wedding! She waited expectantly for Giles to help her into the saddle. But he did not move. An impatient snort from the Seigneur and a discreet but sharp kick in the shins from his sister reminded Giles of his duty. He lifted her up, gingerly, so as not to risk soiling his elegant tunic of particoloured black and red.

The Seigneur looked at Sabina, raised his eyebrows and pulled a face to show how exasperating he found her brother. She smothered a giggle at this unexpected show of sympathy. Then the brief moment of compatibility was over and they were once more strangers.

At an unseen signal the bagpipe drone of a *biniou* began, swelling into a jaunty tune which was taken up by the wailing voice of a *bombarde* and the steady beat of a *tambour*. The little group of musicians led the way, playing for all they were worth, and the wedding procession followed them down the steep path to Saint Jehan's Chapel.

The chaplain, Père Martin, was waiting for them in the chapel porch as they dismounted. With nerves as taut as bowstrings Sabina felt the Seigneur take her hand as they approached the doorway. His grasp was firm, in marked contrast to her brother's, and she interpreted it as a sign of how tightly he held on to what was his.

They came before the priest. Père Martin, the gold wedding-ring balanced on the open prayer-book before him, began the formal interrogation in his soft, dreamy voice. Were they of age? Had the banns been published...? As if in a dream Sabina heard the Seigneur's replies and then her own. Everything assumed a vague and unreal quality—until the gentle chaplain asked the next question:

"Do you both freely consent to this marriage?"

Sabina took a deep breath. She had a mad impulse to cry out, Of course I do not freely consent to marry a man I do not know! But then the Seigneur's fingers tightened on hers and she glanced at him. He did not look at her but stared steadfastly ahead. His already pale face had lost the last vestige of colour and his mouth was grim. She was not sure whether the painful pressure of his grasp was a warning not to make a fool of him before his guests, or whether it was the result of a stronger emotion as he recalled the last time he had stood before a priest like this. Either way, it made no difference. Her answer was a foregone conclusion. "I, Sabina Mary, do freely consent to this marriage," she said quietly.

The formalities over, Père Martin began his homily, his blue eyes bright with enthusiasm. It was on the joys of matrimony and how close they were to heavenly love. Sabina noted he made no mention of what joy you could expect if your marriage had been arranged as part of a ransom settlement.

Now it was time for the blessing of the ring. Taking it, the Seigneur slipped it in turn on to each of the fingers of her left hand.

"In the name of the Father, and of the Son, and of the Holy Ghost," he said. And as he put it on her third finger he said clearly, "With this ring I thee wed."

There was a finality about those words that made Sabina's heart chill within her, and suddenly the narrow band of gold seemed to weigh heavily indeed upon her hand. As they left the porch and followed Père Martin into the chapel for the wedding mass she wondered if she would ever grow accustomed to wearing it on her finger and if she would ever grow accustomed to the new life that lay ahead of her.

Finally their vows were said and the ceremony was almost over. Only one more thing remained—for the groom to kiss the bride. The Seigneur's lips barely touched Sabina's cheek as he murmured formally, "*Ma chère femme.*" His words were simply part of the ritual, nothing more. She might now be his wife, but she knew she was certainly not dear to him.

As they turned from the altar to leave the chapel Ronan Guennec once more took her hand in his iron grip.

"Sire, you are hurting me," protested Sabina in a whisper.

"I am? *Pardon!*" He sounded surprised, as though he had been quite unaware he was crushing her fingers, and also apologetic. She began to suspect that, despite his grave, almost dour, exterior, he was finding the wedding ceremony every bit as arduous as she was.

When they left the chapel cries of "Good luck" broke the tension.

"Come, we must run to the horses!" the Seigneur cried.

"Run...? Why?" asked Sabina.

She soon found out as the guests and bystanders began pelting them with a veritable hail of nuts.

"They are to bring us luck and fertility," the Seigneur explained as they dodged the onslaught.

"And bruises!" added Sabina, rubbing the spot where a carelessly thrown hazelnut had caught her on the nose.

"Yes, those too!" For the first time the Seigneur almost smiled.

The procession back to the château was more informal than the previous one, with much laughter and chatter. The band of musicians caused a great deal of amusement, for the unfortunate wind-players found the steep path to the gatehouse hard going, and each missed note or wavering phrase earned a good-humoured cheer. The perspiring minstrels were clearly relieved when a tangle of brambles on the path forced them to stop.

Sabina was intrigued to see that the briars had been plaited into a rough garland to obstruct their way, and when a horde of beggars emerged from the undergrowth her curiosity changed to unease. The Seigneur seemed to expect them, however, and taking a handful of coins from the purse at his belt he scattered them on the ground. As the prickly barrier was removed he said something to them in Breton.

"What did you say to them?" she asked as they rode on.

"I told them there would be food in plenty for them at the château tonight."

"There's a great number of them," she said, looking over her shoulder at the beggars.

"No matter. I will not have anyone on my land starving while I feast."

Sabina was surprised into silence. Such generosity was not a quality she had expected to find in him.

The beggars were not the only ones to swell the ranks of the guests at the wedding feast; it seemed that every tenant, every peasant, and every vassal of Ronan Guennec had come along to join in the celebrations; improvised tables had to be set up in the inner bailey to cope with the numbers. The main banquet was to take place in the great hall. The huge room smelled of new-cut boughs from the garlands which decked the walls and fresh-strewn rushes which covered the floor, and the scent of green sap intermingled with the savoury odour of food. The Seigneur led Sabina to her place at the high table, raised on a dais above the rest. At first she was too absorbed by the scene in front of her to think about eating, for there were row upon row of trestle tables, spread with crisp white cloths, which threatened to collapse under the weight of food. Père Martin barely had time to finish grace before the mountain of food began to disappear, consumed by hungry guests, and the wine jugs carried by an army of servants were quickly in demand.

"You aren't eating." Her husband's voice made her jump. "Is there nothing on our table which pleases you? Shall I send for something else?"

Sabina looked down at the flat trencher of bread set before her; it was intended to serve as a platter for her meat, but no slice of beef, no portion of mutton, no dribble of gravy had so far marred its crisply baked surface.

"No, thank you, I have no appetite," she replied.

"That will not do. I cannot have my bride fainting on her wedding night from lack of nourishment."

He seemed to have thrown off the gloom that had assailed him during the ceremony, and was almost jovial as he cut a slice of breast from the roast capon in front of him and laid it on Sabina's trencher.

"Really, sir, I'm not—" she never uttered the word "hungry", for the Seigneur had taken the rejected morsel of capon and popped it into her mouth, as he might have fed a titbit to his dog.

Caught unawares, she gulped, causing it to go down the wrong way. Her coughing and spluttering provoked much merriment among the guests, especially when the Seigneur began to thump her forcibly on the back.

"Isn't it enough that you try to choke me before we're wed ten minutes without trying to break my spine into the bargain?" she gasped, when she had recovered.

"Good." The Seigneur gave an unexpected grin that lit his face in a way Sabina had not seen before.

"What is—that I haven't dropped dead during the wedding feast?" she demanded.

"No—your tongue has recovered some of its sting. You have been so quiet since our wedding that I feared you were sickening for something. There's no need to look so worried, you know. You have nothing to fear from me."

"I'm not afraid of you," retorted Sabina. "It is simply that I find all this festivity overwhelming. I'm not like you—I've not been married before."

A shadow flickered across his face. "I had not forgotten," he said sharply. "Nor have I forgotten that my first bride wed me willingly, while you did not!"

Sabina had not intended to provoke him, nor touch a wound that was obviously still tender. She wanted to apologise, but his expression had grown so stern she kept silent. When she did glance in his direction she saw the pained, wistful look in his eyes she had come to recognise. She guessed he was remembering that other, happier wedding feast, when it had been his beloved Marianne who had sat at his right hand, instead of a plain girl from Devon who had come to him as part and parcel of her brother's ransom.

It was a relief when the tables were cleared away and the benches pushed back against the walls, for this was a sign that the entertainment was due to begin. There was such a variety that she wondered where they had all come from—her favourite was the minstrel who played on a harp made of willow, the same type of instrument, or so he claimed, that Merlin had used to make his magic music. Hearing the sweet, unearthly tunes, Sabina could well have believed that both the strings and the fingers which plucked them were enchanted. She was so absorbed by the plaintive melodies she was quite taken aback when Zacharie Le Godet, who was acting as master of ceremonies announced, "Seigneur, *ma dame,* the musicians will play for your delight. The dancing will begin, if you, sire, and Dame Sabina will honour us all."

"I do not dance," she whispered in horror as the Seigneur rose and offered her his hand.

"Come, everyone can dance," he insisted.

"I can't! I don't know the steps!"

"I will teach you. You must do it. If we do not begin the dance everyone else must remain seated." He sounded stern. But it was not the sharp note in his voice which made Sabina accompany him on to the floor, it was the faces round about, all bright and eager for more enjoyment. She could not bear to disappoint them.

Convinced she would make a fool of herself, Sabina flung back her head in her customary defiance, as if daring anyone to laugh at her. No one did; there was no need. The steps of the dance were simple and repetitive, and with the Seigneur's firm grip on her hand giving her an unexpected confidence she acquitted herself creditably. At a signal from the Seigneur the other guests joined in the stately dance, the long line following his lead like a good-humoured serpent. When the music stopped it was Sabina who called loudly for more.

"I thought you had no fondness for dancing," remarked the Seigneur.

"Normally I have not. But I'd be a poor creature not to dance at my own wedding," she replied.

"So be it. Musicians, play on," he ordered. But the look he gave Sabina was half amused, half disbelieving.

She wondered if he had guessed the truth—it was not that she really wished to prolong the dance, it was that she wished to delay her wedding night. She did not fear the marriage-bed; what she had not learned from her mother and her married sisters she had gleaned from the outspoken village women, so she knew pretty well what to expect. No, what distressed her and made the whole process abhorrent was that it would be governed by cold, impersonal duty, when a persistent instinct told her it should be something much more.

The dancers and musicians had their limitations, she knew, and the time finally came when one of the groomsmen called, "Enough of this merrymaking. There are more serious matters to be dealt with tonight." This was greeted by a great cheer, and Sabina felt herself go hot with nerves and embarrassment.

A procession carried the Seigneur and her up to the bridal chamber, led by the minstrels and accompanied by a deafening cacophony on improvised instruments. At some time on the short but hazardous journey up the stairs her embroidered garter was seized and waved aloft by a young man. As the victor tied his prize around his arm Sabina breathed a silent thank you to the friendly matron who had advised her to wear her garter low. Until they reached the bedchamber the procession had been noisy and decidedly bawdy, but then a hush descended, and the guests looked at one another.

"The bed! Who's to search the bed?" asked one voice.

"It should be the bride's mother," replied another.

"And what is the new Dame de Plou-Aven to do, since she has no female kinsfolk with her?" It was the plump matron who spoke. "Wait here still a maid while a ship is sent to England?"

All eyes were upon Sabina now. "*Ma dame*," she said to the plump matron, "since I need someone to stand proxy for my mother, and you have already shown me such kindness...?"

She did not need to finish her request. The matron

beamed proudly and said, "Of course I will stand for your mother!"

"*Ma dame,* I ask you this favour yet I don't know your name."

"So you don't!" The matron chuckled, her rounded cheeks rosily gleaming. "I am Morgan, the Dame de Saint-Léon. Our land marches alongside Plou-Aven."

"So you are our neighbour." The idea that this kindly lady would be close by was comforting to Sabina.

"Indeed I am. Should you ever need help or a little female gossip, remember I am no distance away. Now, though, I am pleased to perform this most important duty, without which the wedding night could not continue."

To Sabina's surprise she began to strip the neatly made bed, keeping up a running commentary in a loud voice, presumably for the benefit of the many guests who could not get into the chamber and who were squashed on the stairs.

"That's the coverlet off," she declared. "There's nothing there! Now the top sheet... All that's left is the under-sheet... No, nothing mischievous there... The bed is safe from evil charms! There's nothing to blight this marriage!"

Her announcement was greeted by a cheer, and Sabina felt herself propelled into the centre of a group of women who proceeded to help her undress down to her linen smock. She presumed the Seigneur was suffering similar treatment at the hands of his groomsmen at the other side of the room. She kept her eyes delicately averted, though, in truth, she was too well shielded by her temporary handmaidens for any immodesty. Speechless with embarrassment, she slid into her side of the bed, conscious that the Seigneur was climbing in too.

Amid much laughter and earthy advice a silver loving-cup filled with the wedding posset was handed to the newly wed pair, with instructions that they were to drain every drop. Noting the size of the cup and the amount of wine she was expected to drink Sabina reflected it was probably just as well she had forgotten Dame Morgan's advice about the *eau-de-vie*. There were cries of "Good luck" and more advice of an indelicate nature, then all at once the bedchamber door was closed on the last departing guest, and she was alone with the Seigneur.

Not certain where to look or what to do, she stared steadfastly at the bed-curtains, vaguely conscious of movement beside her.

"Do you intend to sleep clothed, *dame?*" the Seigneur asked. "That is a curious English custom indeed."

"Of course I do not!" she replied, her voice a pale imitation of its usual self. Then, because she was nervous, she continued, "Sleeping clothed! Whoever heard of such a thing!"

Clasping the coverlet up to her chin with one hand, she endeavoured to wriggle out of her smock using the other. It was a surprisingly difficult manoeuvre, and she was mortified when the Seigneur reached out and finally tugged the garment over her head, leaving her naked. She dived under the bedclothes, with scarcely her nose showing, then lay there, feeling every muscle in her body go taut with nervous anticipation.

"I hope you don't intend to suffocate yourself," remarked the Seigneur.

He attempted to pull the coverlet lower. Sabina resisted, clutching the quilt with both hands.

"Well, let's do what must be done," he said briskly. "It won't help anything to wait, will it?"

"No, sire." Sabina could hardly utter the words.

"Let go the cover, then. You're grasping it like a drowning woman. And move closer to me! I cannot reach you if you lie on the edge of the bed in such a way!"

Obediently Sabina loosened her grip and moved a fraction nearer to him. With a grunt the Seigneur rolled on to his side and, propping himself up on one elbow, pulled the coverlet away from her. She bit her lip at this exposure of her nakedness, then flinched at the touch of his hand as it caressed her bare flesh. She lay rigid, staring up into the shadows of the bed canopy, not wanting to look at this man who was claiming his rights to her body. She longed only for the next few minutes to be over as swiftly as possible. He bent and kissed her on the mouth; his lips, soft and warm, travelled along her throat to the soft curving swell of her breasts. But still she lay as though carved from marble. She steeled herself for his final possession of her. Instead, he fell back with an exclamation of irritability.

There was another silence, then Sabina asked hesitantly, "Is—is there something wrong, sire?"

"Yes, there is!" He sounded angry. "To put it bluntly, I've never lain with a woman who was unwilling and I find it far more difficult than I'd imagined."

"Oh..." Sabina almost asked him how many

women he had lain with but stopped herself in time. "I—I fear the fault is mine, Seigneur," she said.

"No, not yours. You are nervous and weary and alone among strangers. It is understandable." His words were kind but his tone was sharp. "I expected too much. I thought we could deal dispassionately together, then go our separate ways. But I see this marriage will not be so simple."

Sabina was suddenly contrite, conscious that she had committed herself to him, made her vows to him, and that now she was not fulfilling her obligations.

"I'm sorry," she said.

"For pity's sake, don't apologise! That's the last thing I want!" He pummelled the pillow with unnecessary vigour.

"I swear I'll do my duty without complaint."

"That," he said vehemently, "is no help at all!"

"What do you want, then?" demanded Sabina, sitting up abruptly, all contrition evaporated. "I say I'm sorry, but you don't want that! I say I'll do my duty, but you don't want that, either! There's no pleasing you! We've been in bed less than half an hour and because all has not gone well you are in a temper! I suppose you wanted me to drag you to bed like some painted whore and behave like a wanton!"

"I most certainly did not!" the Seigneur exclaimed indignantly. "And how did you come to know of such things?"

"Do you think I've spent my life locked in a closed tower? I have eyes and ears and I use them. Our village had a whore, Susanna Gill, who plied her trade behind the tavern."

"I am surprised at your mother allowing a gently

bred girl like you come into contact with such low women.''

"You can't blame my poor mother!" Overwrought nerves were causing Sabina to rattle on inanely. "Whenever I was in disgrace I would escape over the park wall and take refuge in the village. That way I learned much that was denied to my sisters.''

"So I can imagine," said the Seigneur drily. "And were you often in disgrace?''

"I fear so. And once I'd made my escape everyone was so relieved to be rid of me they seldom bothered to seek me out.''

" 'A disruptive influence' was the term used by the abbess, I think you said.''

"It's not that I try to be provoking, it just happens. And you needn't think Susanna corrupted me. The poor soul wasn't quite right in the head, and she couldn't have been very good at her trade for if she hadn't kept pigs she would have starved. Though, perhaps, if she hadn't kept pigs she'd have earned more money by other means, because you could smell the stink of those pigs a mile off, and Susanna also— Now what is the matter?''

She turned and saw that the Seigneur was laughing. "Did I say something funny?" she asked.

He nodded. "I don't know what other folk talk about on their wedding night, but I doubt if the village whore and her pigs often enter the conversation.''

"Perhaps it was not a very proper topic. I am sorry if I have been immodest. I think I was talking so because I am anxious. At least you aren't angry any more.''

"No, I'm not angry any more.''

He smiled at her, and Sabina was conscious of a feeling of relief. She was conscious, too, that her husband was pleasing to the eye. The flickering candles shed a soft mellow glow over his skin, emphasising the compact curves of the muscles on his arms and shoulders. His black hair was in disarray, and dark stubble was beginning to shadow his chin, contrasting sharply with the white gleam of his strong, even teeth. He looked younger, less forbidding. She could not help comparing him with the frail, senile suitor who would have been her fate had she returned to England. Anything was better than that, even a lifetime's exile in Brittany.

"Come, lie down." The Seigneur patted the pillow. "We will sleep now. We've both had a long day. The getting of an heir for Plou-Aven can wait for another time. There is no urgency."

"But what of the bride-sheet? If there is no blood everyone will say I was not a virgin!"

"If I declare myself satisfied then no one else will dare object. Settle beside me now, you must be weary."

Sabina did as she was bid, thankful to relax and feel the anxiety drain from her. She barely had time to say "Goodnight, sire" before her eyelids closed and she fell asleep.

When she awoke the candles in their sconces had long since spluttered themselves into extinction. Drowsily she could just make out the shape of a narrow window, hardly lighter than the impenetrable darkness of the room. Dawn was still a long way off, and she snuggled into the warm softness of the feather bed. Half asleep, she felt the weight of the Seigneur's arm across her, but she was too comfortably drowsy to wish to move it. Then, almost imperceptibly, she felt him draw closer, so that she was pressed against him. His fingers began to caress her, moving across her skin with surprising gentleness.

"You are not afraid of me now?" he asked softly, sensing she was awake.

"No," she whispered.

"Nor are you unwilling?"

"No..." What else could she reply? She had no right to refuse him.

"Good."

His touch was becoming more insistent now, exploring her body in a way she found oddly disturbing. As his passion increased she was surprised to find herself having to quell her response to his questing fingers. With difficulty she kept herself under iron control, submitting to him, doing her duty—but nothing more. Then his weight was on her, crushing her to the bed. She was startled and surprised by his vigour and energy; she had not expected such intensity. But she did not cry out—she was quite proud of that. Even when she felt the hot stab of pain she just lay very still, biting her lip until his need of her abated and it was over.

"That was not too bad, I trust?" he asked solicitously. "I didn't hurt you too much?"

"No, sire, I thank you," she replied almost primly, as if he had asked her if she had spent a pleasing morning.

"Good," he said again.

Soon she heard the deep rhythm of his breathing and knew he was asleep.

She lay awake, staring sightlessly up into the darkness, thinking of the changes that had happened so swiftly in her life. This man she had married was still a stranger to her, but she knew now that he was kind. He had shown her more consideration than she had dared to expect. It was an important quality in a husband, more vital than wealth or power or anything else. She should have felt grateful and relieved to have made this discovery—but she did not. As she lay there in the sleepless dark she could only feel such a great sadness that tears began to soak her pillow, and she did not know why.

Ronan Guennec was in a good mood next morning. Sabina heard him whistling softly to himself before she had opened her eyes. He was sitting on the edge of the bed, dressed only in a brown woollen chamber-robe.

"Good morning, *dame*," he greeted her cheerfully, when he saw that she was awake. "You slept well, I trust?"

"Yes, thank you, sire." Sabina stretched drowsily, then realised that in doing so she had pushed back the bed-clothes to below her waist. Blushing furiously she hauled them back, swiftly covering her nakedness.

The Seigneur noted her action. "There is no need for that," he said. "We committed ourselves well enough last night, so we can forget such matters for a while, eh?"

So that was the reason for his good humour—the fact that he did not need to touch her again so soon! She was thankful he was going to keep his word and not pester her unduly. All the same, illogical indignation stabbed at her that he should find her so totally undesirable.

"Of course, we must continue to share the same bed," he said.

"Of course. We'd be the talk of the district, else. And we don't want that," said Sabina, so demurely that he looked at her dubiously.

"You have no need to fear I'll keep you constantly with one babe in the belly and one at the breast, like so many husbands," he continued.

"For which I thank you, Seigneur," said Sabina, her eyes modestly cast down. She felt that he was emphasising the point a little too forcibly for her self-esteem.

They breakfasted in the bedchamber, but in spite of—or perhaps because of—the intimacy of the situation, the conversation was stilted, with many long awkward pauses. Sabina had wished to know her husband better by talking to him, but she learned nothing more of his character that morning. It was a relief to go down to the great hall where the guests awaited them. Their appearance was greeted by cheers. There were also ribald remarks in plenty, but she pretended not to hear them.

"I propose we all ride this morning," declared the Seigneur. "A good gallop will clear our heads of last night's wine and prepare us for even more, eh?"

There were more cheers at this remark, and the entire party went out to the inner bailey. The Seigneur mounted his bay stallion, and the guests each claimed his or her own steed. Sabina hung back, for she had no horse.

"Which animal am I to ride, sir?" she asked.

"That one, of course!" He pointed with his whip to where a groom was bringing forward the palomino mare she had ridden to her wedding.

Sabina stroked the soft golden nose, pleased to renew her acquaintance with the gentle creature.

"Why do you not mount?" asked the Seigneur. "Does the beast not please you?"

"Of course she does! I'd be hard to please if I did not delight in riding such an animal!"

She allowed the waiting groom to help her into the saddle, so that now she was almost on a level with the Seigneur.

"I'm glad to know it. I'd be disappointed to learn that the horse I'd bought for you did not suit."

He put his heels to his stallion's flanks and began to move away, leaving Sabina not certain she had heard him correctly. She urged the pretty mare after him and demanded, "Did you say you had bought her for me?"

"I did."

"She is my mare?"

"Must I repeat it? Of course she is your mare! Does she look the sort of creature I would ride? Now, *ma dame,* I've had enough of this gossiping. I would ride out." His words were clipped and he stared ahead of him as if eager to be away.

"I don't know how to thank you, sire," she said. "She is beautiful!"

But the Seigneur was determined not to accept thanks gracefully. "If you are content with your mare I suggest you let us begin our ride so you can try her paces." He was having difficulty in keeping his tone impatient, and sounded almost concerned when he asked, "You like to ride astride? Or would you prefer one of these new side-saddles? It can be arranged."

"No, thank you. I prefer astride. It gives me greater control."

The Seigneur gave a snort. "Hm! I should have guessed it!"

Sabina grinned, but it was to his back for he had ridden on ahead. She patted the creamy mane in front of her, thinking, without regret, of the bad-tempered, sway-backed pony that had usually been her lot at Corbyn. Then she was caught up in the tide of the other riders and swept out into the countryside.

Perhaps it was her new mare, perhaps it was the sunshine—Sabina found Brittany much more to her liking than she had first thought. Her early impressions in the rain had been misleading. It was a wilder landscape than she was used to, with dramatic outcrops of granite and stretches of moorland interspersed with stone-walled fields and patches of grazing. The harsh grey of the rocks was softened by splashes of golden lichen edged with delicately unfurling fronds of bracken. The sky seemed vast, shedding a brilliant quality of light she had never experienced before. Filling her lungs with air heavy with the scent of blossoming gorse, she was conscious that this land had a beauty which was both savage and unexpected.

Again she glanced towards her new husband. Giles had been right—he was an excellent horseman. He rode his mount with an effortless skill that made all about him seem clumsy and inept. He was laughing at something said by one of his companions, but when the joke was done and the laughter faded from his face Sabina noted that for a moment his expression regained the bleak sadness she had seen before.

Then another guest claimed his attention, he smiled again, and she returned her gaze to the countryside.

Such a procession of gentry was clearly a novelty in the district, for the peasants turned out in force to watch them ride by. Sabina noticed that the Seigneur frequently stopped to talk to them in fluent Breton. However, when she approached the peasants they shuffled awkwardly and looked away.

"They are just wary of foreigners," remarked one of the guests who rode alongside her. "They will soon get used to you."

But how, if I cannot talk to them? wondered Sabina. And how long will it take?

"You ride well," remarked the Seigneur when they had returned to the château.

"Thank you, sire." Sabina observed silently to herself that they were the first words of praise she had heard from him.

"I am glad I chose a horse as your gift. It is one I fancy you will use often."

"Indeed I will—as often as *mon Seigneur* permits. I love to ride!"

"There is no need to wait for my permission. The horse is yours; you are the Dame de Plou-Aven. You may please yourself when you ride out and where you go."

"Any time I please?"

"Yes. All I ask is that you never go unaccompanied. You do not know the country yet, and I fear we have our fair share of thieves and robbers."

"And I can come and go as I please?" Sabina still could not believe that she could have such freedom.

"Have I not said so? But no climbing over walls here, as you tell me you were wont to do in England.

Such behaviour would be unseemly for the Dame de Plou-Aven. You will use the main gate like everyone else!'' His words were stern but there was a spark in his eyes that might have been humour.

"I only climb over walls when I feel there is a need to escape," grinned Sabina.

"Then we must make sure that such a circumstance does not arise," replied the Seigneur, the light fading abruptly from his eyes. "For make no mistake, if I tell you to stay within the confines of the château then you will stay!"

Having established that he was the master and would be obeyed, the Seigneur walked off to talk to his guests, leaving Sabina alternating uncomfortably between furious rebellion at his words and grateful pleasure at his generous gift.

Chapter Three

While the wedding celebrations continued Sabina had neither the time nor the need to try out her new-found freedom, for the hours were taken up with the festivities. Rather to her surprise she found herself enjoying her first days as a bride. It was a novel situation for her to be the favoured centre of attention. She knew she owed some of the pleasure to the fact that each night she fell into bed agreeably tired, to sleep undisturbed by the more distasteful of her wifely duties.

The festivities could not continue for ever, though. Soon the guests had ridden away, and the last minstrel had packed up his instruments and trudged down the track from the château gate. It was then she began to find time on her hands. In normal circumstances this would have been the moment when she picked up the reins of the household, but Le Godet still held those reins tightly in his grasp. She soon discovered that, meticulous though he was about consulting her on the running of the household, where her opinion differed from his it was he who won.

At first Sabina thought to complain to her husband—but about what? The household was well run. It was just that she had no part in it. She might as well have not been there. Upon consideration she held her tongue. Apart from anything else she was reluctant to bother the Seigneur with trivial domestic matters for, by contrast, he had much to occupy him. The Seigneur de Plou-Aven was not a man who left the running of his estates to others. Every day he rode out to attend to estate matters. When he was home he spent long hours closed with his stewards and account books.

This is what he meant when he said we would lead separate lives, thought Sabina one day when she had not seen her husband since dawn. Well, it pleases me!

The trouble was that she did not seem to have a life of her own to lead. A daily ride and her embroidery were insufficient occupations for someone who thrived on activity. Matters were not improved by Giles being in a constant state of misery. He should have left Plou-Aven for England immediately after the wedding, but the winds were contrary and no ships could leave port.

"I don't believe it!" he kept saying, when there had been no change in the weather for a week. "That scurvy captain has got too comfortable a berth in port, you mark my words! Or else it's a plot to keep me here longer!"

He was unwise enough to voice his views at supper one evening in the presence of the Seigneur.

Ronan Guennec looked at him coldly. "I assure you, sire, I will be most happy to see the back of you," he said.

"That fool of a captain's too cowardly to sail on anything rougher than a millpond," blustered Giles. "I'd soon stir him out of his cosy harbour!"

"You'd have to walk there if you did," stated the Seigneur. "I'll not spare my horses to carry you nor my servants to attend you. You go on your own two feet or you stay here until we get word from the captain. Which is it to be?"

"You leave me little choice, sire," glowered Giles.

"Surely you can persuade your husband to let me go?" he said to Sabina later.

"It's no use expecting me to persuade the Seigneur to do anything. I have no influence over him," she replied.

"You talked him into marrying you easily enough!"

"That was making the best of a bad job, putting right the terrible botch you had made of things, as usual!" Sabina snapped. "Believe me, it wasn't easy!"

"You don't want to try, that's your trouble. Well, I'm glad you turned out to be the wrong sister because you and Ronan Guennec are well suited! I hope you make each other thoroughly miserable!"

With that Giles stalked from the room.

His words sounded so uncomfortably like a prophecy that Sabina suddenly felt uneasy. It would be just like Giles to ill-wish her out of spite. As a precaution she crossed herself and uttered a speedy prayer.

"That brother of yours is a fool," remarked the Seigneur as they settled into bed that night.

"He's eager to be home," said Sabina.

"No more eager than I am to be rid of him!"

Thoughts of home brought a rush of longing to Sabina. She felt a sudden need for a little human warmth and sympathy.

"You could send me back with him. No one would blame you," she said, and waited. She wanted the Seigneur to say something approving about her, perhaps that he was well pleased with her as a wife or that he did not want to let her go.

Instead he said, "I can't get an heir with the Channel between us, can I? You had best stay."

The words were no comfort to Sabina. They put her firmly in her place—as a breeder of heirs. She might as well have been a brood mare. Her homesickness turned into resentment. Why should she find herself in such a situation simply because she was a female? Surely she should have some right to determine her own life? But it was too late now. She was bound to Ronan Guennec, and her discontent focused on her sleeping husband. Her last thought before sleep claimed her was, I'm sure he never turned his back on Dame Marianne as he has turned it on me now!

It was the next day that the dog caught her attention.

Where it had come from no one knew. It had been hanging about the château for days, being cursed by the servants and set upon by the resident dogs. Its eagerness to please, its desperate search for affection struck a chord in Sabina. As she dismounted from her ride she caught sight of a groom aiming a particularly vicious kick at the luckless animal.

"Stop that!" she cried. "There's no need to treat the poor creature so!"

Whether the fellow understood her or not she did

not know, but he touched his hat to her and slunk away. At the sound of her voice the dog pricked up his ears and ran towards her, pushing his head importunately under her hand for a caress.

"You'll never be rid of him now, *dame*," said Cudenec, the head groom, in French. "Let me take him and have him drowned."

"Certainly not!" Sabina was appalled at the idea. "There's no need for that, he's not vicious."

"What's to be done with him, then, *dame?* He'll follow you closer than your own shadow now you've shown him kindness."

"Never mind, leave him to me. I'll think of something," said Sabina. She knew there was only one solution. The mute appeal in the dog's eyes was too desperate, too familiar; she knew what it was like to be the butt of everyone's disapproval.

"My stars, mistress! What have you got there?" exclaimed Alice as Sabina entered the bedchamber closely followed by her new acquisition.

"I would have thought it was obvious. It's a dog."

"Aye, mistress, but whose is it?"

"Mine."

Alice looked doubtful. "Does the Seigneur say you can keep it?"

"He doesn't know yet. I don't see why he should object. He has dogs of his own. He can hardly begrudge me just one."

"Aye, mistress, but what a one!" Alice regarded the animal warily.

Sabina began to share her misgivings; the creature was unprepossessing, not to say ugly, and clearly could not claim an ounce of pedigree.

"Well, I'm keeping him, all the same," she said obstinately.

"You've said that before, mistress."

This was true. Back home she had collected a long string of strays and misused animals to care for, only to have them taken from her by her wrathful parents. She could still hear their complaints: "You know not what sickness the filthy creature might carry. It cannot stay!"

The Seigneur was proud of his hunting dogs, they were of an old and distinguished strain. How would he react to the inclusion of this ungainly newcomer to his household? She decided not to put it to the test, at least, not immediately.

"I'll keep him hidden for a few days," she said.

"You do realise the beast is flea-ridden, don't you, mistress?"

A violent need to scratch was already demonstrating the fact to Sabina.

"We'll start by giving him a bath," she said.

This proved to be an arduous operation. But once the animal was clean and dry and had been given the largest meal he had ever experienced in his life, he showed a welcome inclination to sleep. A small closet under the stairs next to the bedchamber seemed the ideal place; it even had ventilation from a small, slit window. Sabina piled rushes on the floor, and watched as the dog examined his new domain, turned round several times then settled down contentedly.

"With luck you'll not stir till the morning," she said as she closed the door.

The Seigneur was late returning to Plou-Aven from a boundary dispute that night. He barely managed to reach the château before dark, and he was more than ready for bed.

It's certainly not a good moment to introduce the subject of a stray dog, even if I'd wanted to, decided Sabina, as she extinguished the candles before retiring herself.

The howls that suddenly woke her from sleep might well have come from souls in torment.

"Holy Mother, what's that?" demanded the Seigneur, sitting bolt upright.

For a moment Sabina was too sleep-befuddled to think of an answer. Then the howls increased in intensity. They had an unearthly quality that seemed to echo through the château, reaching every space and every corner.

"It sounds like the Devil himself!" The Seigneur leapt out of bed. Pulling on his bedrobe he lit one of the candles. "You stay here!" he ordered, as Sabina rose too.

"But Seigneur—" she protested. Now she was fully awake she remembered all too clearly what could be causing the row.

"Stay here!" he insisted. "I'm not having any demons of Satan inhabiting my home!"

Arming himself with his sword, he flung open the door.

Ignoring his orders, Sabina pulled on a robe, too, and followed him, to find the whole château was awake and in uproar.

"Where's it coming from?" asked a dishevelled Giles, who was hurrying up from the stairs wielding a crucifix. "At first I thought it was from the top of the east tower—now I'm not so sure."

"No, sire, it sounded closer to the guardroom."

The terror-stricken face of Zacharie Le Godet peered timidly from beneath Giles's arm.

At once a dozen voices set up a clamour, each insisting that the unearthly howl came from a different area of the château. No one took any notice of Sabina, who was trying to make herself heard.

"Everyone be silent!" bellowed the Seigneur. "Then, perhaps we'll be able to locate it."

A hush fell upon the people while the baleful howls continued unabated.

Sabina took her chance. "If you please, Seigneur…" she said. Stepping past him, she unfastened the closet. The howls ceased immediately and a bundle of newly washed fur launched itself at her in joyous greeting, sending her reeling against the wall.

A shocked hush fell upon the gathering. Then someone began to chuckle. Before long the infectious laughter spread. Apart from an embarrassed Sabina and the still indignant Giles only one other person remained straight faced—the Seigneur.

"I know this wretched creature!" he declared. "It's the one that's been hanging about the stables! What in the name of all the saints is it doing in there!"

"I put it there," said Sabina defiantly.

"You did? But why? Do you keep dogs in closets in England?"

"No, Seigneur; but I had nowhere else to keep him."

"Why should you want to keep him? The grooms and the stablemen have been trying to get rid of him this week or more!"

"Then they need trouble themselves no further. He is my dog now and I will see to him myself." Sabina clasped her arms about the dog's neck and glared at the Seigneur, defying him to forbid her to keep the animal.

Ronan Guennec stared back at her, his face grim.

"And presumably I was to be kept ignorant of this new addition to my household?"

"Not at all, sire. I merely hid him until…until…"

"Yes?"

"Until you were in an amenable mood."

A fit of coughing prevented the Seigneur from replying to this frank remark. And Giles asked uneasily, "Are you convinced it is an earthly hound? Those howls sounded like the beast of hell itself! My blood is still chilled within my veins!"

The Seigneur gave him a contemptuous look. "It's a simple enough explanation," he replied. He opened the closet door even wider and held his candle aloft above the level of the top shelf. The dim flame was insufficient to penetrate the full darkness, but it was adequate to show the closet had no ceiling.

"This is really a shaft going up behind the stairs," said the Seigneur. "It was put in to enable the walls and the staircase to be repaired with greater ease. In my father's time someone thought to use parts of it for storage until it was needed. The shelves are easily removed."

"So?" Giles still did not understand.

"When the dog howled his cries echoed right up through the shaft," said Sabina. "It was the echo which made him sound so fearsome!" She was irritated by her brother's stupidity.

"Oh…" Giles managed a wavering grin. "So it's not a hell-hound after all!"

"No, it is not!" The Seigneur's patience was wan-ing. "It is a miserable cur. And it is keeping me from my bed. Get you gone, the lot of you! And I'll have no one making excuses for being sluggardly in the morning, hell-hound or no hell-hound!"

Everyone went off to their quarters good-humouredly, with the exception of Giles.

"So this was one of your pranks, sister!" he said. "I'd have thought it time you outgrew such nonsense now that you are married."

Sabina was about to retort that he was in a bad mood simply because he was ashamed of being scared by a dog, but the Seigneur intervened.

"Ma dame," he said crossly. "You may be happy to stand here talking but I am very weary and would go to my bed. Bid your brother good night and let us have no more chatter."

With the dog leading the way they returned to the bedchamber.

"I'm not sharing my bed with that cur!" the Seigneur cried as the dog showed every sign of jumping on to the coverlet.

"No, sir, of course not." With difficulty Sabina hauled her new pet down. "There, you see, he's settling in the corner."

"See he stays there!" The Seigneur flung off his robe and got back into bed. "You had no need to hide him, you know. You are the Dame de Plou-Aven, not a serving-wench, I wish you would understand that—then, perhaps, I'd get fewer broken nights. If you want a dog you can have one without seeking my approval, only, have a decent one, I implore you! My wife had a tiny creature, all white curls, that was her darling. I can get you one from the same dam—or you may prefer an Italian greyhound, they make suitable pets for ladies.''

Sabina noticed his slip of the tongue and winced. He still regarded Marianne as his wife, not her!

"This dog pleases me well enough," she replied.

"If it's a larger dog you'd like you can have a pup from my young bitch; she'll be old enough to whelp soon."

"I would like to keep this dog, if I may." Sabina's voice was very decided.

"But it's madness! Just look at him! He hasn't finished growing yet. By the size of his paws he's going to be a handful! Besides which, he's one of the ugliest dogs I've ever seen. His ears are slung too low, and that great long tail is out of all proportion to the rest of him. I'll have one of the grooms despatch him in the morning, and get you something more suitable."

"He is suitable!" cried Sabina. "There is no cause to kill him just because he is ugly!"

"Then, if that's your choice, so be it!" The Seigneur slammed his head on the pillow and tugged the coverlet firmly over himself. For a moment there was silence, then he said, "Have you got a name for the brute?"

"He's such a fool I thought Jester might be appropriate."

"Hm. I could think of other names that would fit him better!" With a mumbled "Goodnight" the Seigneur settled down to sleep.

Sabina lay wakeful for a while, not certain whether he actually approved or disapproved of the dog. Then she became aware of the Seigneur laughing quietly to himself. She relaxed. All was well!

* * *

Next morning most of the inhabitants of the château were still chuckling at the night's adventures, and even Giles had got over his ill-humour. He had good reason to be cheerful—soon after first light a messenger had come from the coast saying that the wind was now favourable and the ship would set sail on the evening tide.

In spite of her many disagreements with her brother Sabina felt sad; yet another of her links with home would be broken. But her unhappiness was nothing compared to Alice's; when the women heard the news she broke down and sobbed uncontrollably.

"Oh, mistress! To be going home like Master Giles! It's what I long for!" she wept.

Sabina could not think how to comfort her. She knew that homesickness was not the real root of Alice's misery. The tiring-woman had a child whom she had had to leave in England.

"Your sister and her husband will see to the babe, won't they? He'll lack nothing." Sabina tried to console her.

"He'll lack his mother, isn't that enough? And if I do go back in a year or two he won't know me! He'll run and hide from me and think me a stranger! Me, who bore him, and who will never again hold him in my arms!"

Alice's grief tore at Sabina. She could not bear to see this woman, who had been her faithful servant since she was grown, suffer so.

"Get your things," she said impulsively. "You go back tonight with my brother."

"Mistress…!" Alice stared at her, surprised out of her misery. "Mistress, you don't mean it!"

"Yes, I do. Go pack your things. My brother won't wait if you aren't ready."

"But I can't... How will you manage...? Who will tend you?"

The woman was torn between her duty to her young mistress and her overwhelming desire to get back to her baby.

"This is a big place—there must be a capable tiring-woman in need of employment somewhere. Hurry now! The horses have already been called for."

"Oh, mistress...!" Alice was at a loss for words. A smile of pure happiness spread across her face, and she forgot herself enough to fling her arms about Sabina in a great hug before running off to collect her belongings.

Sabina and the Seigneur rode part of the journey with Giles to see him on his way.

"I shall have such a deal to relate to the family when I get home," he said, when the moment came for them to part company. He was full of high spirits. "They will all be eager to hear about your wedding, and how you fare now you are a great lady. How they'll laugh when I tell them about your dog and the scare it gave us," Giles chuckled, conveniently forgetting his ill-tempered reaction to the incident.

"You might make the point that some folks were scared more than others by the hell-hound of Plou-Aven," put in the Seigneur drily. "I'd not have your people think we were lily-livered here in Brittany. It might encourage them to come on more raids."

"You are pleased to jest, sire," laughed Giles, completely missing the barbs in Ronan Guennec's comments.

But Sabina saw them and had to suppress a smile.

"Have you any messages I can relay for you?" Giles asked her dutifully.

"Oh, please! Give my respects to our honoured mother and father, my blessings to your wife and little ones; if you should visit Blanche——" Sabina caught the Seigneur's expression and checked herself. "If I complete my list you'll miss not only this tide but the one after," she said, suddenly feeling a tightness in her throat. "Just tell everyone at Corbyn that I miss them and mention them constantly in my prayers."

"I will do that."

Her brother kissed her farewell, but his thoughts were already on his journey home and she doubted if her felicitations would reach a single person. She could not hold back her tears at his departure, and her eyes misted over long before the clatter of his horse's hoof had died away.

The Seigneur, however, continued to watch his unwelcome guest ride along the road.

"Do I see a woman riding with the servants?" he asked. "Surely your brother isn't taking one of our Breton wenches with him as a memento! It's just the sort of fool thing he would do."

Sabina managed a ghost of a smile as she dried her eyes on her sleeve. "You did see a woman, sire," she said. "But a Devon lass, not a Breton. I have let my tiring-woman go home."

"Why on earth did you do that? Has she displeased you?"

"Oh, no. She was grieving for her babe back in England. It would have taken a stony heart to have kept her here."

"I am beginning to realise that your heart is far from stony." The Seigneur regarded her steadily. "Though I fear your kindness often works against you. You take in a stray dog which is certain to be naught but a nuisance to you, and now you let your tiring-woman go."

"I'll find another woman easily enough. One of the servants will do."

"Do you realise you now have no one with whom to speak your own tongue? Let me send someone to fetch Alice back."

He spoke with such concern that Sabina almost allowed self-pity to overwhelm her. "No, I thank you, sire," she said, quelling the urge to shed more tears. "I told her she could leave. I'll not go back on my word."

"Then I'll have Le Godet go to Brest for you. He might be able to find an English tiring-woman there or, at least, one who speaks your language."

"You are very kind, sire, but I've no wish to have Le Godet sent galloping about the country. I care little about my appearance, so, as I say, one of the servants will do very well. Besides..." she straightened herself in the saddle and brushed away a last obstinate tear "...it will be good for me to speak naught but French. It will improve my command of the language."

The Seigneur continued his steady gaze; there was an expression in his eyes that Sabina could not interpret. Then he reached across and, taking her hand, gave it a sympathetic squeeze.

"It shall be as you want, *ma douce dame*," he said.

It was the first time he had ever called her "gentle

lady". In fact, it was the first time he had used any sort of endearment towards her. All the way back home the touch of his fingers lingered on hers as a pleasant memory.

"You'll need someone to help you out of your riding-clothes," observed the Seigneur when they had reached the château. "You'd best choose your body-servant now. Pick whoever takes your eye."

They were walking through the great hall and obediently Sabina looked around. At first sight none of the maids seemed suitable; then she saw one girl who looked different. She was neatly dressed and had an air about her which set her apart from the others.

"You, girl, come here," ordered Sabina.

The girl looked alarmed, and pressed against the large hanging on the wall as though she wished to hide herself in its heavy folds.

"Come here," repeated Sabina. "Don't look so worried. You've done nothing wrong."

In spite of her reassuring words the girl approached warily. As she came forward the Seigneur swore violently in Breton.

"Choose someone else," he said. "She's not suitable."

But Sabina, her attention focused on the girl, did not hear him. "You speak French?" she asked. "Good. Then I would have you to be my tiring-woman. Come with me to—"

"If you please, *dame,* I cannot," said the girl, her face white with anxiety.

"Your duties will not be arduous," Sabina tried to reassure her. But the girl shot an appealing glance towards the Seigneur, who glowered angrily.

"I am sorry, *ma dame,* truly I am. But—but I am

not free to come.'' The poor girl was obviously in distress.

''Cannot come? Not free? But who is your mistress if I am not?'' Sabina was beginning to lose her temper. ''I will have you as my woman, I say.''

''P-please, *ma dame*—'' The girl burst into tears.

''What *is* the matter with the wench?'' Sabina turned to the Seigneur, but his face had grown even more grim.

''Get you gone!'' he snapped at the weeping girl.

''I don't understand!'' Sabina looked after the fleeing girl in angry bewilderment. ''Why can't I have that wench?''

''Simply because you cannot,'' growled the Seigneur. ''Just pick someone else, and quickly.''

''But you said I could choose whomsoever I wanted,'' protested Sabina, her jaw beginning to jut obstinately.

''And so you can—all save that one.''

''But she's the one I want! She's the only one suitable!''

''By all the saints, *dame!* I say you cannot have her and that's the end of the matter!'' roared the Seigneur.

''Oh, so that's how you Bretons keep your word! I might have expected something of the sort. You say one thing and mean another!''

''Dame, you are provoking me! Choose a wench and be finished!'' said the Seigneur through clenched teeth.

''In that case, I might just as well pick the first one who can speak French, seeing that my wishes are to be disregarded without good cause!'' Sabina was in a high state of indignation. "You, girl! The one scrubbing the table! Do you speak French?"

The grubby serving-wench was so startled at being addressed she slopped water down the front of an already dirty gown.

"Me, *dame?*" she asked apprehensively, wiping her raw, wet hands on the only dry bit of her coarse apron.

"Yes, you! What is the matter with everyone today! The whole world has turned either perverse or stupid. Do you speak French?"

"A-a little, *ma dame.*"

"Then you will be my new tiring-woman."

"Me, *dame?*" repeated the girl, her hands nervously pushing back her greasy hair under a decidedly grubby cap.

"Who else, you dolt?"

"*Dame,* you go too far!" protested the Seigneur angrily.

"Oh, don't tell me there is some reason why I can't have this wench too?" retorted Sabina.

"No, of course not, but—"

"Then I choose her, and the matter is ended." She turned back to the serving-wench, who was still dumbfounded. "Go and get clean then attend me in my bedchamber. And be quick about it or I'll box your ears!"

Sabina stalked off without waiting to see what her husband's reaction was. She stamped up the stairs, an anxious and puzzled Jester at her heels, then plumped down on the bed in a disgruntled attitude.

She had thought that life here in Brittany might be tolerable, that she would have more freedom, that her husband would prove an easier taskmaster than her parents had been—but she was wrong. The Seigneur had seemed to offer liberty, only to take it away again. Under the strict regime of her parents she had had some choice in the matter of her body-servant. Well, now she had chosen a girl from the kitchens, one who knew more about scouring pots than dressing a lady's hair... Oh! What did it matter what she looked like, anyway! She had no interest in her own looks—and certainly no interest in trying to win approval in her husband's eyes. She might as well have a scullion to attend her as anyone else.

Frowning at the dismal prospect of life in general and her marriage in particular, Sabina settled down to await the arrival of her new servant.

The knock at the chamber door was hesitant.

"Come in," called Sabina. "And about time too!" she declared when the door finally opened. "I told you to get clean and you've been long enough about it to have scrubbed the whole..." Her voice died away in surprise.

She had been expecting the serving-wench to appear. Instead, the girl who stood before her, trying unsuccessfully to suppress a smile of nervous excitement, was a model of neatness and cleanliness. Clean and tidy she might have been, but the girl was a complete stranger.

"Who are you?" she demanded.

The smile faded from the girl's face. "I am Catell, *dame*," she said in heavily accented French, "Catell Le Braz."

"Well, Catell Le Braz, what do you want with me?"

"But you told me to come, *dame*. You said I was to attend you here and be your tiring-woman... Perhaps you didn't mean it... Your pardon, *dame*.'' The girl, her face pinched with disappointment, turned to go.

"No, wait!" commanded Sabina. "Are you telling me you are the wench who was scrubbing the tables?''

"Yes, *dame*.''

"I didn't recognise you...!" Sabina was astonished at the transformation.

"It was Seneschal Le Godet's doing." A hopeful look was beginning to return to the girl's dark eyes as she ran an appreciative hand over her spotless, starched apron. "He said that if I was to be the tiring-woman to the Dame de Plou-Aven the least I could do was to look the part, even if I had no skill. He had these clothes found for me, *and* he made me take a bath." The memory of the latter humiliation made the girl's cheeks redden with indignation.

"It was worth it. The change is quite extraordinary.''

"Thank you, *dame*.'' The girl paused then added shyly, "I'd no need to be clean before doing the dirty jobs.''

"I suppose not."

"*Pardon, ma dame*—but—but I am to stay?'' The question was asked with painful longing.

"Do you want to be my tiring-woman?''

"Oh, yes, *ma dame!*'' Catell's eyes were shining.

"Well, there is no one else I can call upon... And I suppose I can train you up... Very well, you are now my body-servant. Make a start by fetching me water for washing. You will find a linen towel and soap in the large chest.''

"Thank you, *ma dame*... Thank you...'' Catell's

thanks continued as she ran down the length of the
stone stairs.

Sabina soon found that her new maid was quick
to learn and eager. The dressing went far better than
might have been expected. The greatest problem was
Sabina's hair. Catell had to try several times before
it was arranged satisfactorily. At first, nervousness
made the girl silent as she concentrated on her tasks,
but as she grew in confidence her tongue loosened.
Sabina learned more about Plou-Aven after half an
hour in Catell's company than she had done in all
the time since she had set foot in Brittany. Sometimes she found the maid's French difficult to understand—but then, she observed to herself, it was
not the mother tongue of either of them, there was
room for improvement on both sides.

"How is it that you speak French?" she asked.

"It was my grandmother who taught me, *dame*.
She was a servant here at the château when Dame
Yolande, the Seigneur's mother, came here as a
bride."

"She was a tiring-woman?"

"Oh, no, *ma dame,* just a chamber servant. But
she was often in the company of the gentry and the
upper servants when they spoke French. What she
picked up of the language she passed on to me. 'You
must know some French to get on in the world,' she
would say, 'whether you like it or not'. She was
right, too, wasn't she, *ma dame?* It is thanks to her
I'm now your body-servant."

The maid put one more pin in Sabina's headdress
and asked anxiously, "Is that satisfactory, *ma
dame?*"

"Yes, that is splendid."

Someone with more vanity might have found much to fault in Catell's handiwork, but as Sabina prepared to go down to the great hall she felt pleased with her unusual tiring-woman. Having a Breton might prove to have unexpected advantages. One thing still nagged at her, however. Before she left the chamber she asked, "Catell, you seem to know everyone hereabouts. Tell me, who was the saucy wench who would not be my tiring-woman?"

At once the open frankness left the girl's eyes. "I'm sure I don't know anyone who would be impertinent enough to refuse you, *ma dame*," she replied.

Sabina was in half a mind to press the point, then she noticed Catell's reddened cheeks and decided against it. For the moment it was sufficient to know that her new servant did not tell lies easily.

"Very well," she said. "That will be all for now."

With a hastily bobbed curtsy the girl fled from the room.

In the great hall the food had already been served when Sabina entered. As she took her place at the high table beside the Seigneur he looked at her reprovingly.

"I was beginning to wonder if you were going to honour us with your presence at this meal, *dame*," he grumbled.

"If I have kept you waiting, sire, then I beg your pardon." Sabina neither felt nor sounded sorry.

"Having taken the trouble to provide hot food, it displeases me to have it go cold through other people's tardiness!"

"I have already apologised sire. But as you know,

I have a new servant, and new servants need to be given time."

"Particularly if they have to have the smell of the kitchens scrubbed off them first, eh?"

Sabina smiled at him sweetly. "If I'd been allowed the wench I wanted first of all I would not have been late for dinner."

"Don't keep harping on the subject," snapped the Seigneur. "I've no wish to hear it mentioned again, do you understand?"

"Just so long as you understand why it took me longer than usual to get dressed, sire." Sabina's sweet smile had become even more honey-like.

Ronan Guennec exclaimed, "You try my patience, *ma dame!* For pity's sake let us eat and talk about something else!"

Sabina decided she had baited him long enough, and shaking out her linen napkin applied herself to the meal set before her.

The food and wine did much to soften the Seigneur's temper.

"Your mare is behaving herself?" he asked conversationally.

"Yes, thank you. Whoever schooled her is to be complimented."

"I'm glad she still pleases you. And what of the saddle? Now that you have used it several times does it still suit you—?" He stopped and shifted his gaze to Sabina's head.

For some minutes Sabina had suspected that all was not well with her headdress. Even as she had begun to eat, it had started to feel insecure, and now her long braids were gradually breaking free from their confining net. The ends would have dropped into the bowl of soup in front of her if the Seigneur had not come to the rescue.

"Late as you were, I think you should have given that new servant of yours even more time," he observed as he flicked the offending plaits back over her shoulders.

Sabina looked at him warily, suspecting sarcasm. The incident reminded her uncomfortably of her state of disarray upon her arrival in Plou-Aven. Her husband must think her incapable of maintaining a tidy head.

"And risk displeasing the Seigneur even more?" she replied.

"In truth, now that your temper has cooled, admit that serving-wenches do not make good tiring-women. Let me send to Brest for someone more skilled."

He was being reasonable! Moreover, he was showing some concern for her welfare! Sabina was agreeably surprised. Even so, she was not sure she wanted to fall in with his wishes.

"Someone else might be more able, but would she please me as well?" she said.

"You actually like your little scullion?" the Seigneur was incredulous.

"Yes," she replied without hesitation. "She is very willing, and already better at her new tasks than I expected. I'm sure she will improve more. I'm convinced she's honest. Added to which, it would disappoint her terribly to be sent back to the kitchens now."

"You would put up with untidy hair sooner than disappoint a servant?" The Seigneur's incredulity increased.

"It won't be for long. She's quick to learn."

"I'm not sure I share your confidence in her."

Ronan Guennec said no more, but gave her a curious look, then continued eating.

Once again Sabina was unsure whether or not he was annoyed. He was a difficult man to fathom—except when he was in a temper—and she found such uncertainty hard to cope with. Giving an indignant sniff, she decided that she had better things to bother about than her husband's moods. If he was angry then he would have to get on with it by himself!

She took a sip of wine and allowed her gaze to wander over the other diners in the great hall. Le Godet was sitting close to the dais, as his rank demanded, ready to pounce at the slightest fault. Catell was there, too, obviously immensely proud to be sitting with the upper servants. One face was missing; she could see no sign of the impudent girl who had refused to be her tiring-woman.

Recollections of the incident still made her angry and with the anger there was perplexity. She could not work out who the girl was, or why she had refused one of the best positions of employment at the château. Nor had the Seigneur's illogical anger done anything to point to a solution. Even the honest little Catell was reluctant to discuss it, and this aggravated Sabina's curiosity more. It was a puzzle she was determined to solve. But, as time went by, she saw no sign of the mysterious girl, nor could she find out anything further about her. In the end she had to admit defeat.

She began to look for something else to occupy her time. Even to herself she was reluctant to admit that she was lonely. Back home she had never lacked companionship; here at Plou-Aven there was no one of her own rank to keep her company, and she found the enforced solitude alien.

She did consider visiting Dame Morgan, who had issued more than one warm invitation; the snag was that the Château de Saint Léon proved to be a good two hours' ride away. Of course there was always the Seigneur—he was someone she could talk to—if only he were there. She seemed to see less and less of him with each passing day. If anything underlined the fact that theirs was an arranged marriage it was the way he seemed unwilling to spend one minute more in her company than was necessary.

She knew she could not complain that her husband spent so much time on his people and his land, but when he was absent for three whole days with no explanation she felt justified in protesting. She greeted his eventual reappearance at supper one night with raised eyebrows.

"Sire! How good of you to honour us with your presence," she said.

Ronan Guennec chose to ignore her evident sarcasm.

"I presume all has been well in my absence?" he said.

"Yes—which is a good thing, for you did not tell me you were going or that you would be away so long."

"I said that I had business to attend to and not to look for me too soon."

"Too soon, certainly! You said naught of being away for three days and nights. How would I have contacted you if the château had been burnt to the ground or attacked by barbarians?"

"If either event had occurred, I would have heard soon enough." The Seigneur washed his hands in the bowl held by his manservant and dried them on a fresh linen towel. "My bailiff had word of where I'd gone."

"You thought to tell your bailiff and not your wife!"

"My bailiff needed to know, my wife did not!"

"I think you carry logic to extremes!" Sabina pushed her wine goblet away angrily.

The Seigneur gave a sigh. "*Ma dame,* if you are determined to have a quarrel can it please wait till I've eaten?"

"Quarrel? Who is determined to quarrel? I was merely making a sensible comment. You should be pleased to know the château was well tended in your absence."

"I was aware that the château was in good hands! Have I not told you, my bailiff knew where I was? Would you like me to send for the fellow so you can interrogate him?" He spoke in the exaggeratedly measured tones of a man whose patience was running out.

"It's a pity you didn't send him to me before, to give me some notion of where you were!"

"Are you trying to tell me you were anxious for me?" he asked scornfully.

"I thought it was usual for a wife to be interested in the whereabouts of her husband. I see I was mistaken."

Sabina had truly not meant to start a quarrel, but the loneliness of the last three days lent acid to her tongue.

"For most wives, that is true. I seem to remember

we agreed to live our separate lives. And that, *ma dame,* is exactly what I have been doing. I wish you to understand that the matter is closed. I will not have my supper spoiled. Nor will I have everyone in this hall sniggering because you and I are exchanging angry words. I am the Seigneur! I do not have to account to anyone, save God and the Duke of Brittany! I certainly do not have to account to you! Do you understand?''

''Yes, Seigneur.'' Sabina spoke through thin lips. Her anger had been swept away by another emotion curiously close to hurt. She had not expected him to fling the conditions of their marriage in her face quite so vehemently. His blunt reminder of the state of things between them was strangely wounding.

The rest of the meal continued in a strained silence, and Sabina, whose appetite had abruptly diminished, was thankful when it was at an end.

The tense atmosphere persisted until long after they had gone to bed. She lay still and wide awake, sensing that the Seigneur was finding sleep difficult too.

''Since it is so important to you I'll tell you where I was,'' he said at last, in the darkness.

''Important to me? You are mistaken, Seigneur. I have no interest in where you were.''

''I went to Brest… It's this eastern border dispute. It's proving more and more complicated. I thought I'd be finished soon. I didn't expect to be away for three days.''

''Three days! Three months! You are the Seigneur de Plou-Aven. You can be away for as long as you please.''

''Nevertheless, I should have sent you word… It's

been a long time since I've needed to consider anyone other than myself.''

In his own way he was admitting his thoughtlessness. Part of Sabina wanted to accept his apology—but she could not. Deep inside her was a vulnerable pride that would not risk such a reproof again.

''You have no need to consider anyone,'' she said. ''As you say, you are the Seigneur.''

Another frigid silence settled on the bedchamber.

It was broken again by the Seigneur.

''If you are lonely you can send to England for one of your sisters or some other female to join you here,'' he said.

''Lonely? Who said I was lonely?'' she demanded. ''I've no need of anyone else!''

And just in case he wished to pursue the subject she pretended to settle down to sleep. His unexpected perception had touched a raw spot. She did not want him to feel sorry for her. She did not want his kindness. Above all, she did not want him to know that if she did send home to England no one would come!

Chapter Four

In the days that followed, the Seigneur seemed to involve himself even more deeply in estate matters. However, he became punctilious about informing Sabina when he would be late or if he would be away from home. She noticed this new trait and considered it to be an improvement in their relationship.

Another change for the better was brought about by Catell. The girl was growing more skilful at her tasks, and if her dexterity at hairdressing was sometimes faulty, or she had not managed to iron the linen too well, then Sabina sensibly gave encouragement sooner than a scolding. Such minor inconveniences were well worth tolerating for the benefits which Catell brought with her, particularly the girl's ability to speak Breton. No longer did all of Sabina's requests to the servants have to go through Le Godet.

Her first experience of this independence was with the cook. Sabina's normally robust digestion was suffering from the aftermath of the marriage feasting. She longed for plain food but, no matter how often she asked the seneschal, the dishes always arrived at table richly cooked in butter or highly flavoured with spices. His excuses were always plausible but did nothing to ease her indigestion. A week of feeling liverish proved too much for her.

"Catell, come to the kitchen with me," she ordered.

"What have I done wrong, *ma dame?*" cried the girl in distress. "Whatever it is I promise never to do it again!"

"You haven't done anything wrong, you silly goose! I'm not sending you there for good. I must speak to the cook and you shall interpret for me."

"Oh, *ma dame!*" exclaimed Catell. "With pleasure!"

When they entered the kitchen, Alain, the head cook, came forward and bowed, with such anxiety on his face that Sabina wondered if visitors to his domain always boded ill for the poor fellow.

"I said I would return, did I not?" she said.

Her words, when repeated in Breton by Catell, did nothing to ease the cook's worried look.

"He says a visit from you, *ma dame,* is a great honour," reported the maid.

From his expression, he was gaining little pleasure at being so honoured. Sabina attempted to put the man at his ease.

"I wish to discuss menus," she said. "But first, I must know who sculpted the model of the ship from butter which decorated the table at my wedding feast?"

"It was his own unworthy effort, *ma dame,*" translated Catell.

"Unworthy! What nonsense! It was the work of a master craftsman. I regret we could not preserve it in some way."

As the cook heard her words translated a beam of pleased astonishment crossed his features. Sabina guessed that the poor fellow received precious few compliments.

"It was Seneschal Le Godet who chose the subject—such a vessel brought Dame Sabina to us," repeated Catell.

Such a stiffly formal, and insincere, compliment was typical of Le Godet. Sabina said, "Yes, and such a vessel takes you Bretons across to England when you think we are not looking, eh?"

A shocked hush fell upon the kitchen, until the assembled cooks and kitchen-maids saw that she was grinning. The laughter was slow to start, but once it had begun it was hard to stop.

"I have no wish to waste your time," Sabina said, when the chuckles eventually died down. "I have one immediate request to make. Would it be possible at meals to have one plain dish? A little boiled chicken, or a baked fish with no garnish? My English stomach is slow in growing accustomed to your rich Breton food."

"Nothing could be simpler, *ma dame*," answered Catell. "He is only desolate he did not know the *dame's* wishes before."

So much for Le Godet's excuse that the cook was stupid and uncooperative.

As they left the kitchen Catell was still chuckling. "They hardly recognised me, *ma dame!*" she exclaimed, unable to keep her delight to herself. "They hardly knew me now I'm clean and grown so grand!"

"I hope you aren't grown too grand to repair the hem on my blue Flemish gown," Sabina said.

"Indeed no, *dame*. Though how you came to rip it I've no idea. No doubt romping with that foolish dog!" There was faint reproof in the girl's voice.

"Whether you approve of it or not, I fear that same foolish dog needs exercise, and so do I," Sabina said with a grin. "Send down to the stables to have my mare saddled."

"Yes, *ma dame*." Bobbing a curtsy, Catell hurried off.

At supper that evening, Sabina noted with relief there was a dish of trout, done to perfection, but simply cooked. Le Godet noticed it, too, and would have sent it back to the kitchen if she had not intervened.

"What is the trouble, seneschal?" she asked.

Le Godet bowed low. "It is this fish, *ma dame*. I regret to say it is not fit to grace the high table. I will speak most severely to the cook."

"There is no need. I ordered that dish myself."

"You did, *ma dame*?" The seneschal could not hold back his surprise. "But was not the menu we discussed agreeable to you? My humble apologies for any—"

"I think we can ignore the humble apologies," Sabina cut in briskly. "Most of the menu was perfectly acceptable but my requests for plain food seem to have fallen upon stony ground."

"Indeed, *ma dame*. That imbecile of a cook—"

"Exactly! I decided that his imbecility had gone on long enough, so I went to see him this morning. We had a good and fruitful talk. You will now find that there will be no more problems about his understanding orders."

She fixed the seneschal with a hard stare so that he could not misinterpret her meaning. Le Godet's mouth tightened in annoyance. "It was good of *ma dame* to intervene, though *ma dame* should not have troubled…"

"It was no trouble," said Sabina pleasantly. "Where there is a lack of communication among my servants I am always happy to take action. You had best go to your supper now, Le Godet, before it gets cold."

"Thank you, *ma dame*."

"Is something wrong?" asked the Seigneur.

"Nothing is wrong—just a small confusion. I have seen to it, sire," she said.

"Good." He said no more, but reached across and helped himself to a portion of the trout, which he proceeded to eat with evident relish. Sabina was surprised; she knew her husband's tastes ran to highly spiced food. It was only later that she began to wonder if it was his way of showing his approval at her small victory over Le Godet.

That night, as they settled into bed, he said, "I noticed you ate quite sparingly at supper, and only of the plainest foods. Is anything amiss?"

"Nothing, sire. I'm suffering from a slight indisposition caused by too much feasting, that's all."

"You are sure? You do not think that perhaps…?"

"No, sire. I regret it is purely digestive. There is no other cause."

"Oh…!" He was silent for a while, then he said, "I fear it is distasteful to you, *ma dame,* but Plou-Aven still needs an heir."

"I understand, sire."

"Then, if you have no objections…?"

Sabina had plenty of objections, but she kept them to herself.

This time there was no pain. But afterwards, when his body had moved away from hers and he had fallen asleep, she was left with an even greater, more incomprehensible sadness than before. She lay wakeful, unable to stop herself from imagining how different things must have been for Marianne. She would have known tender words and soft caresses, a gentle arousal to passion, then, afterwards, she would have lain in Ronan's arms happy and contented. Everything would have been governed by love and mutual pleasure, not by the cold duty that she, Sabina, experienced. Moonlight was shining through the narrow window, touching the dark disorder of Ronan's hair and tracing the outline of his bare arm as it lay outside the coverlet. She had an extraordinary impulse to draw near to him, to nestle against the warmth of him with her arms wound about his body. Unaccountably she wondered what it would feel like to press her lips against the soft flesh at the back of his neck and to feel her cheek against his skin. To fall asleep like that, as Marianne must have done so often, suddenly seemed very desirable—and unobtainable. Instead, she moved further away from him until she lay on the edge of the bed, and there she stayed until sleep eventually claimed her.

Next day, Sabina was restless.

"Catell, do you ride?" she asked.

"Yes, *ma dame*, if the beast isn't too frisky."

"In that case, send for my mare to be got ready and a quiet mount for yourself. We are going round the parish."

"And how many grooms to accompany us, *ma dame?*"

"We'll be staying well within the parish bounds. Do you think we are likely to be attacked by the residents?"

"Just let them try! They'd have me to deal with!"

"Well, then, I think we can go by ourselves."

"I'll send down to the stables, *ma dame—Mon Dieu!* Won't everyone stare to see me riding along behind *ma dame.*'

"If they do I hope you will maintain your dignity and not fall off."

"Oh, *ma dame!*" Chuckling to herself Catell hurried away.

The pair of them set out with an ecstatic Jester in attendance. As usual, the local people treated Sabina with wary deference, but as their eyes travelled past the Dame de Plou-Aven to her companion expressions changed rapidly. The folk of the parish were quick to recognise Catell, plodding along on her mule, and they showed no reticence in challenging her. Sabina needed no command of Breton to get the gist of the good-natured banter that was flung at the maid. Catell took it all in good part, giving as good as she got, to judge by the laughter which greeted her replies. Gradually the inhabitants of Plou-Aven forgot their reserve and pressed forward, ignoring Sabina in their eagerness to talk to Catell.

"Tell me the names of some of these people," Sabina said eventually.

At the sound of her voice a suspicious silence fell upon the crowd. Catell gazed at them and clicked her tongue in annoyance. Then she harangued them in a stream of Breton.

"I'm just telling them that you are a good, kind lady, *ma dame*," she explained, "and that you are concerned for their welfare." Then, with her small nose in the air, she added, "They are but ignorant peasants, *ma dame*. They fear anything and anyone they don't know."

Sabina saw that being on horseback was no way to get to know the people. "I wish to dismount," she said. "Ask that fellow there to help me down." She pointed to a wiry-looking man who had been determined to be in the forefront of the crowd ever since they had stopped.

"Oh, *ma dame!*" Catell gave a giggle. "That's my father, Pol Le Braz!"

"And you didn't think to tell me? Well, make amends now. Ask him to give me a hand."

Pol Le Braz responded to the request eagerly enough. With a broad smile on his face he said something in Breton which his daughter was at first reluctant to translate.

"Tell me, I would know," demanded Sabina.

"My father said that since I am tiring-woman to the Dame de Plou-Aven he supposes he's not too proud to be groom," said an embarrassed Catell.

"He said that, did he? Well, Pol Le Braz, it's a good thing your daughter's not as saucy as you are!"

Sabina's words were greeted with laughter, and more than one person dug a chuckling Pol Le Braz in the ribs. The ice was broken, and if any vestige of reserve remained it was swept away by Jester setting off in pursuit of a plump hen. By the time the dog was restrained and the fowl returned to its grateful owner Sabina felt more at home in the parish than she had dared to hope. She walked along, her horse's reins over her arm, a tight grip on Jester's collar, talking to the people, finding out who they were. It was what she had loved doing back home at Corbyn, and now, thanks to Catell, she could do it here.

It took a long time for them to make their way round the *bourg* of Plou-Aven, the thriving village that was the "capital" of the parish, a crowd of chattering villagers following at a none too respectful distance.

"Where are we going now?" she asked Catell.

"You did say you wanted to see as much of Plou-Aven as possible, *ma dame,* and we are approaching the *lavoir,* where the women do their washing. Do you wish to see it?"

"Certainly! Lead on."

The *lavoir* was in the middle of the village, a fresh spring feeding the water into a stone-lined pool. Several women were energetically pounding their washing, but at the approach of Sabina and her unofficial retinue they rose uncertainly. Catell started speaking to them, but Sabina's attention was drawn to a girl who could not have been much older than herself. Already she had one child clinging to her skirts and another strapped to her back in a shawl. But it was not this which drew Sabina's notice; it was the way the girl's face was white and pinched with pain. Then she saw that her foot was wrapped in filthy rags and that the portion of skin visible above this rough bandage looked raw and angry.

"Ask what is wrong," Sabina instructed.

"She knocked a pot of boiling water over herself," Catell reported. "Her foot was badly scalded and refuses to heal."

Sabina winced. "No wonder the poor soul limps!"

she said. "Tell her to keep still while I look at it. I promise I won't hurt her."

In spite of the reassuring words it was obvious that the girl was hesitant. But Sabina gently eased the top of the rags, then winced again.

"How has she treated it?" she asked.

"Poured cold water over it and wrapped it up. That was all she knew how to do."

"There's little chance of it healing that way. She must have it properly attended to."

"But by whom, *ma dame?*"

"The priest, or the nearest religious house. Anywhere where someone has a knowledge of remedies."

"There is no one, *ma dame.*" Catell gave a shrug.

"What do you mean, no one? Surely there is some person in this part of Brittany with such knowledge?"

"There is the wise woman at Sainte Anne. But that is a lengthy walk with two good feet. Goodness knows how long it would take to limp along—and trailing a couple of babies besides! There is the Abbey at Brézel. The holy brothers are renowned for their skills in healing, but they are even further away."

"This is incredible! Have the people of Plou-Aven never had anyone to tend them?"

"Not for many a year, *ma dame.*"

The thought of the poor girl being in constant agony horrified Sabina. "Tell her to come to the château gatehouse tomorrow afternoon," she said. "I will dress her foot for her. Oh, and tell that woman over there to bring her little boy at the same time. I will make something to ease his cough."

"You know about such things, *ma dame?*" Catell asked in awe.

"A little, but enough to give some relief."

Catell's translation of Sabina's words was greeted by an excited buzz of chatter. And the mother of the small boy with the bad cough called out something.

"She said, 'We've been without a *dame* for far too long'," explained Catell proudly.

"I've only a little knowledge," Sabina warned.

"It's more than we had before, *ma dame.*"

"That's true enough, I suppose. However, if I am to make remedies we must first look for the right herbs. My tour of Plou-Aven will have to be completed another day. Come, let's mount up and begin our search at once."

"What must we look for first, *ma dame?*" asked Catell.

For a moment Sabina was at a loss. She only knew the English for the plants she wanted and she guessed her maid would only know the Breton names. Casting her gaze about her she noticed a small elder bush.

"To begin with, some of that," she said. "Do you know where it grows more profusely? I need blossom and bark as well as leaves, if that's possible."

"Indeed I do, *ma dame.*" The girl was delighted that their first quest should be so easy. "There's a fine thicket not more than ten minutes' ride away and I expect there'll be some blossom left."

In no time they had gathered all they needed, much to Sabina's relief, for elder had so many uses and she knew she could make a number of remedies from the one plant. Horehound, to ease coughs, proved more difficult, both to explain and find, until

Catell remembered seeing some in the herb garden at the château.

"I didn't know there was such a garden!" exclaimed Sabina.

"It's a pretty poor sort of place, *ma dame*. The herbs for the kitchen are well cultivated of course, but as for the rest, no one bothers about them very much."

"Then I suggest you take me there straight away. There are other plants I need that perhaps I will find…"

"Very good, *ma dame*. From here there is an easy shortcut to the château."

Catell took Sabina along a pleasant lane she had never travelled before. They encountered only a few isolated cottages—the land was a rough tangle of rocks, heather and gorse, not fit for much cultivation; Sabina was surprised when, as they drew closer to the château, they came upon a house set back from the lane. It was stone-built, like everything else at Plou-Aven, but far superior to the poor dwellings of the peasants. It was of a good size, with an upper storey, and bound within its wall was a well tended garden.

"I had no idea there was such a house close to the château," said Sabina. "Who lives there?"

"No one of any consequence, *ma dame*." Catell had begun to look uneasy.

"Of no consequence? That can't be! It's such a fine house! Just look at the garden! If I'm not mistaken there are stables and outbuildings behind. It must be inhabited by someone important."

"I assure you, *dame,* it is not. Can we go, please,

dame? We've a deal to do to make these remedies, I dare say.''

Sabina looked at her maid sternly, and saw that the girl's unease had grown. Instead of scolding her she said mischievously, "Perhaps I will call upon the occupants. It would be the proper thing to do.''

"It would not, *ma dame!*" Catell cried desperately. "Your pardon, it would not be the thing at all! Oh, why did I bring you this way! Why didn't I think!''

"Catell,'' said Sabina firmly. "Stop making this fuss and tell me who lives there. The way you are creating I shall begin to think we have a witch or an enchanter living within the shadow of the château.''

"Never that, *ma dame!*" The maid's dark eyes had grown round with horror. "If you are determined to know, *dame*, then I must tell you... The house is lived in by Louise de Lannion.''

The name meant nothing to Sabina. "So?'' she said.

"*Ma dame*... She's...she's no better than she ought to be.''

"You mean there is a woman of loose morals living right on my doorstep?'' laughed Sabina. "Is that what all the fuss is about? I dare say I'll survive without going into a swoon from the shock. I must say, sin pays very well in Plou-Aven. She certainly lives grandly.''

"Oh, *dame*, you are pleased to laugh.'' Catell's distress was as intense as ever. "Can I beg you— pray you—*ma dame*, don't let the Seigneur know it was I who told you? Else he'll have me whipped from here to Brest and back.''

Sabina was certain that he would do no such thing.

She had already noticed that, for all his explosive temper, he was unusually sparing when it came to thrashing his servants. She was about to point this out to her maid when she saw that the girl's face had gone white with anxiety.

"I see no reason why I should mention the house or its occupant to the Seigneur at all," she said.

"Oh, thank you, *ma dame*," Catell said with relief. And the colour began to creep back into her cheeks.

As they rode on towards the château Sabina wondered at her maid's agitation. She knew the girl was no prude; some of the gossip Catell had related was decidedly earthy at times. However, she had no time to ponder over inconsistencies in her maid's character.

The herb garden was tucked in a corner of the outer bailey and, true enough, the medicinal area was sadly neglected. All the same, Sabina was able to gather the herbs she required to serve her immediate wants. Making a mental note to have the garden reorganised, she strode towards the great hall, her arms full of greenery.

"There's more than enough work here for the pair of us," observed Catell, trotting at her heels. "It seems to me you need a good, reliable maid to help you."

"And you know of just a one?"

"Yes, *ma dame*. Marthe Trévez. She doesn't speak much French—but she's hard-working, with a lot of common sense."

"And would she be a relation of yours?"

"Yes, *ma dame*." Catell grinned unrepentantly.

"Though, even if Marthe wasn't my kinswoman I'd still recommend her."

"Very well, I shall try Marthe as my herbs-woman."

The first person Sabina encountered in the hall was Le Godet. Normally, she would have relished the look of shocked disapproval that flickered over his face at the sight of her dishevelled appearance, but on this occasion she had not the time.

"Seneschal! Just the man I want to see!" she said. "I need a room with a good fire and a stout table. I also need the services of Marthe Trévez."

An all too familiar stubborn expression replaced Le Godet's look of disapproval. "Indeed, *ma dame*, she is working in the stillroom at the moment. I regret—"

"Regret all you please but send Marthe to me directly!" Sabina cut in. "And when she comes she'd best have news that there is a room ready for me!"

"Very good, *dame*." The seneschal could hardly utter the words for indignation. Sabina, however, was far too occupied to bother about his bruised dignity.

Marthe Trévez presented herself with surprising promptness. She was older than her kinswoman and lacked her pert prettiness, but there was much sense and good humour in her face. Her expression lit up when it was explained what was expected of her; seemingly it was a job after her own heart. Her limited command of French was soon exhausted, but Sabina took to her at once, confident that the woman was a good choice.

She was less satisfied with the workroom Le Godet had provided—it was not a proper room, but a hut, dark and dirty, and it reeked most unpleasantly. True, it did have a fireplace, but that one amenity did nothing to recommend it.

"This won't do!" she said.

Catell and Marthe were evidently of the same opinion if their voluble conversation was anything to go by. "The impudence of that seneschal!" Catell's awe of Le Godet had long since vanished. "Fancy him expecting *ma dame* to work in here!"

"What is this place?" asked Sabina. "It smells repulsive!"

"It's where they boil down the fat to make the soap and the candles, and all nasty jobs like that. Ugh! How can anyone stay in here for long?"

"Not Marthe, that's certain!" The woman had disappeared.

"*Pardon, ma dame.* She thinks she knows of somewhere more suitable. She's gone to see about it."

"Thank goodness for that! We'll wait for her outside." Sabina gladly closed the door on the stench of rancid tallow.

They did not have to wait long. Marthe was soon back, her cheery face betraying her mission had been successful. She led them to a door at the back of the kitchen. When Sabina opened it she found herself in a storeroom. Alain, the head cook, was supervising the removal of baskets and sacks. At the sight of her he bowed enthusiastically.

"He says that if *ma dame* will be kind enough to take her ease for a few minutes he will soon have this place cleared," translated Catell. "Already he has a servant bringing fuel to light a fire. This used to be the old kitchen," she added, "but it proved too small."

"This is ideal." Sabina was delighted. "Tell Alain my thanks for his efforts."

Alain was more than happy to provide the utensils they needed, so the brewing of remedies began. Because of the language difficulties Sabina found it easier to demonstrate what she wanted, and before long she was totally absorbed in her work. When the pangs of hunger eventually aroused her it was long past suppertime.

"The Seigneur will have been kept waiting!" exclaimed Catell, horrified. "Perhaps if I run to your chamber and put out your clean linen now..."

"There is no time," said Sabina. "I must tidy myself as best I can."

"Oh, *ma dame!* I should have stirred myself sooner," Catell wailed, frantically trying to put Sabina's hair into some sort of order. "I should have had your fresh clothes ready..."

"You couldn't be up in my bedchamber and down here at the same time. I required you here... There, leave my head alone now. It will have to do. Go off to your food, the pair of you, before it's all gone."

The two maids hurried off. Sabina followed at a more sedate pace, though, in truth, she had to fight back the unseemly desire to hitch up her skirts and run too. She knew very well her husband would be furious with her for being late again.

It did not happen as she expected. There were no angry exchanges at the high table, for she met the Seigneur in the doorway.

"So you have deigned to come at last!" he greeted her, his voice cold and furious.

"Your pardon, Seigneur—" she began.

But he was in no mood for apologies. "It might

have been more courteous if you had informed me you would be late! Or even of your whereabouts! I've had servants searching for you this age! You made a great to-do about it when I was remiss, as I recall, yet you yourself show no consideration.''

"I *was* in the château," protested Sabina. "You talk as if I was wandering the countryside, when in fact I was only in—"

"I have no interest in your whereabouts, *ma dame*. If you wish to divert yourself by playing hide-and-seek then you may, but pray do not waste my valuable time and that of my servants in doing it. Above all, don't let good food go to waste while you amuse yourself."

The injustice of his comments inflamed Sabina's anger. "I was not amusing myself!" she declared. "And I was certainly not being idle. I was very busy."

"Yes? And at what? Not adorning yourself, that much is obvious!"

The scorn in his voice made her look down at herself. The early summer sun had already tanned her skin to a most unfashionable brown, the front of her gown was dirty, streaked with green from the plants she had been using, and her hands, despite some energetic scrubbing, were heavily stained.

"I knew I was late..." she explained. "The time went by so quickly... I thought it best not to delay any longer."

"Can I request that another time you delay long enough to make yourself clean?" His voice was heavy with sarcasm. "I would be grateful if you would remember to come to table as befits your station, and not like some peasant woman who has just cleaned out her pigsty!''

''It was the plants and herbs—their juices stain so!''

''Herbs! Pigs! It makes little difference! I'll not have my wife looking like a vagabond! Though, I suppose with a scullion as a tiring-woman I can expect no better.''

''It isn't Catell's fault!'' she cried, suddenly afraid he might make her dismiss the girl.

''I don't care whose fault it is. Surely it is not setting too high a standard to insist that my wife be on time for meals and be neat in her attire? Not that it matters tonight. I've no wish to dine here. My appetite is spoiled for sitting at my own table.''

''But where will you eat?'' asked Sabina as he stalked past her.

''Somewhere where the company is more agreeable,'' he called. ''Do not look for me to return tonight.''

She heard him send a servant to saddle his horse, and she watched as he strode towards the stables. Not once did he give her a backward glance, and she was left with a cold feeling of distress. His anger was unjustified, she knew, but his comments on her appearance... In her heart she was aware that every criticism was true—and the knowledge stung her.

The great hall door opened, letting out a flood of light and noise into the gathering dusk. ''Is that you, *ma dame?*'' came Catell's voice. ''When you didn't come to your supper I was concerned. I thought something was wrong.''

''Wrong? What could possibly be wrong?'' Sabina answered with an irritability born of hurt feelings. So the Seigneur was displeased with her conduct and appearance? She cared nothing for that! In fact, she was happy at his displeasure. Tossing back her head and jutting out her chin, she strode towards the open door and Catell.

Her defiance was short-lived. Although she sat proudly alone at the high table, glaring fiercely about her, inside she felt her anger crumble. One question gnawed at her: where had the Seigneur gone? Gaming? Wenching? Had he drinking companions somewhere? The uncertainty was enough to drive away her appetite. She toyed with the food, changed her mind several times as to what she would have, and in the end ate almost nothing.

She was certain that Catell would know where Ronan had gone, but it would not be seemly to question the girl. All the same, when she retired to her bedchamber it took an extraordinary amount of self-control to prevent herself from trying to prise the information from her tiring-woman. In the end she contented herself with asking, "What was Dame Marianne like?"

"Dame Marianne?" Catell paused, a comb in her hand. "Oh, she was a lovely lady, God rest her soul! Little, and so fragile—you'd think a breeze would blow her away like a piece of thistledown."

Sabina regarded herself in the mirror. She was little, too, just like Marianne. But there, all resemblance ended; no one had ever referred to her as fragile. Her slight frame, small-boned as a bird's, was, nevertheless, strong and tireless; it was ceaseless energy which drove her, not a slight breeze.

"And her colouring?" she asked.

"She had the palest, most beautiful hair I've ever

seen, *ma dame*. Silvery-gold it was—and did it shine! As for her complexion, that was pink and white like apple blossom. But the most striking thing about her was her eyes. Would you believe, dame? They were violet! As true in colour as the violet flower itself.''

"How extraordinary," said Sabina without enthusiasm.

Surreptitiously she glanced again in the mirror at her suntanned cheeks, her hazel eyes, at the unremarkable brown hair. What she saw depressed her. She was so ordinary-looking! No, less than that—she was undeniably plain!

That night the big curtained bed felt very empty without the Seigneur. How vast and cold it seemed lying there alone. It was incredible she should have become so accustomed to the warmth of his presence in such a short time. She tried not to think of where he might be at the moment. Such ponderings provoked only annoyance, indignation, and another painful emotion she could not begin to identify.

He will be back eventually, she told herself. When he grows bored with whatever company he's in he'll come back. It was too much to hope that when he did come he would be filled with remorse for the harsh things he had said to her. Nevertheless, she lay for a long time anticipating the creak of the heavy oak door which would herald his arrival. No creak came, however, and in time she fell asleep.

When she awoke, soon after dawn, it was to find herself still alone in the huge bed. The Seigneur had not returned.

"Why have you got out my old grey homespun?" Sabina demanded of Catell. "It's not fit to wear. I'll have my blue Flemish instead. And my best red leather shoes, not the scuffed brown ones.''

Not for the world would she have admitted she was dressing with extra care that morning. She told herself that the Seigneur's stinging words on her appearance had had no effect. But it was a neat and tidy Sabina who later went downstairs.

The château had an oddly unoccupied air about it, despite the numerous servants milling about; she was certain it had nothing to do with Ronan's absence.

The morning proved to be a long one. Her daily interview with Le Godet began even more frigidly than usual, the seneschal still very much on his dignity. It seemed an excellent opportunity to make clear to the little man that she meant to have a voice in her own home, but that she had no intention of usurping his authority. To her surprise the combination of firmness and reassurance worked and the seneschal's parting courtesies—"Yes, *ma dame.* Thank you, *ma dame!*"—held hopeful promise of co-operation.

The day continued interminably. When it was past noon she summoned Catell and Marthe to attend her, with the necessary ointments, bandages, and syrups, and set off for the gatehouse. The sight which met their eyes stopped all three of them in their tracks, for a crowd of people had gathered outside the château entrance.

"*Le Bon Dieu* be praised! You've come, *ma dame!*" The gatekeeper greeted her with intense relief. "I don't know what is going on—they all say they are waiting for you! And a real nuisance they have been, too, blocking up the gateway—no one can get in or out!"

"I only told one woman to come and another to bring her child," protested Sabina.

A peasant, who was pressed against the gate along with two small children, overheard her and cried out something. At once a score of voices set up a clamour.

"What is she saying? What are they all saying?" demanded Sabina above the row.

"She says her boys have got terrible coughs too, if *ma dame* has any syrup to spare." Catell had to shout to make herself heard. "And all the rest are telling you about their ailments as well. Word certainly spread quickly."

"Too quickly for the number of remedies we prepared. Never mind, we'll do what we can…" Sabina had been sizing up the situation. "Catell, tell these people I will see everyone, though I do not have enough medicines for all at the moment. Gatekeeper, I'll have to take over your room for now—never fear, I'll make other arrangements for the future."

During the next few hours Sabina worked harder than she had ever done in her life, with Catell translating and Marthe helping to dress wounds, administer medicinal draughts and apply ointments. The small supply of concoctions she had prepared was soon exhausted, but, true to her word, she saw everyone. She listened to all their ailments, and where she was confident she knew of a remedy she told the sufferers to come back in a couple of days. Far from being disappointed, they accepted the delay cheerily enough.

"Is this the last?" asked Sabina wearily.

"Yes, just Jeanne, the miller's wife. She's got a nasty ulcer on her leg," said Catell.

"Tell her I'll wash and bind it now, and I'll make some salve to ease it but it won't be ready for a few days."

The woman grinned at the news. As Sabina treated her leg she kept up a steady steam of rapid chatter in Breton.

"She says how grateful everyone is that *ma dame* has come," explained Catell. "Now the women have someone they can bring their troubles to."

"I've only been married two months myself. I'm not qualified to give advice," protested Sabina in alarm.

"Don't agitate yourself, *ma dame,* Catell consoled her. "The women only want someone to talk to, really. Your pardon, but I don't think they'd take your advice anyway, no matter how sensible it was. All you need to do is listen."

"It seems to me the sooner I learn Breton the better—though I think I already know the Breton names for just about every ailment under the sun!" Sabina eased her aching back. "Now let me see...what was it? Skin complaints, ulcers, coughs..." She ticked off on her fingers the various illness for which she had to make remedies.

"That's an awful lot of work, *ma dame,*" said Catell.

"It is!" Sabina was suddenly daunted by the prospect. "But we've done enough for today. I must go and get clean. I dare say you two are weary also."

She brushed a strand of hair from her perspiring forehead, conscious that her attempt to be the trim and seemly Dame de Plou-Aven had not lasted long. The day had grown warm, and being confined in the hot gatehouse with a succession of unwashed bodies had done nothing to maintain her earlier neatness. She was afraid it would take a lot of effort to get her blue gown presentable again. Just as she was contemplating the damage done to her appearance an uncomfortably familiar voice demanded, "By the Mass! What has been going on here!"

The Seigneur was home!

Sabina groaned. Another half-hour and she would have been tidy!

"What sort of welcome is this?" he demanded. "The gatekeeper meets me halfway down the hill to complain that he has been turned out of his home and the place is in chaos!"

"The man's a fool! He was only dispossessed temporarily, as well he knows," Sabina said.

"I wish to know why he was dispossessed at all."

"Sire," said Sabina wearily, "I am tired. Every bone in my body aches. Can we talk later?"

"And why are you in such a state, eh? What foolishness have you been up to to get in such a mess?"

"No foolishness... Oh, if you had only come home a little later you would not have seen me so! I did try to be a fitting Dame de Plou-Aven, truly I did!" Her determination to remain cool dissolved in a sudden need to explain.

"Your efforts have apparently been wasted if this is the result," said Ronan coldly.

She swallowed hard, fighting back an unexpected urge to burst into tears. Reluctant to betray her weakness to him, she pushed past her husband and would have hurried away if a hesitant voice had not called out, *"Ma dame—ma dame!"* She turned to confront a young man.

"What can I do for you?" she asked.

By way of reply he smiled shyly, held out a rush-basket to her, and said something in Breton.

"I'm sorry, I cannot understand you," she said.

The young man spoke again, thrusting the basket towards her, clearly wanting her to take it.

"He says it is a gift to you in gratitude." The Seigneur came forward. "Why should he be grateful to you?"

"Since I do not know the fellow I cannot say," replied Sabina.

The Seigneur turned to the young man and began speaking to him in Breton. The young man answered with animation and enthusiasm, the smile on his face growing broader. When he had finished the Seigneur said quietly, "Aren't you going to see what he has brought you?"

Sabina opened the basket and saw half a dozen plump freshwater crayfish laid out on fronds of green bracken.

"Hm, a delicacy indeed," said the Seigneur. "This fellow is Bertrand Le Bec. He says these are an inadequate thank you for tending to his wife's scalded foot. His wife, it seems, has been in agony ever since the accident, but now *ma dame* has seen to it already she feels easier. He is very grateful."

"Oh...!" said Sabina, realising at last that here was the husband of her first patient. "He had no need to bring me a gift, but I thank him. And tell him to make sure his wife comes back to me in two days' time."

"He assures me he will," the Seigneur translated, as the young man bowed and left them. "He told me other things," he continued. "That you have been at pains to get to know the local people and talk to them, that you spent long hours yesterday preparing medicines for them... He told me a great deal I should have known but did not.''

Sabina was at a loss, not knowing what to say. ''They had no one,'' she said at last. ''I didn't expect so many... I suppose they had nowhere else to go.''

''You did this, yet you said nothing when I grumbled at you for being late and untidy.''

''I was *very* late and *extremely* untidy,'' she said honestly. ''And you were not to know what I had been doing, sire.'' She was surprised at her own mild tone.

''I should have known!'' cried the Seigneur. ''But I didn't! How is it that when dealing with you I always seem to finish in the wrong? No matter how justified I believe myself to be, it always turns out that my anger was hasty, or unreasonable, or incorrect... Frequently all three! Inevitably I end up being full of remorse. Why is that? Can you tell me?''

''No, Seigneur,'' said Sabina. ''I have that effect on many people. I think, perhaps, it is why I am so frequently in trouble.''

The Seigneur stared open-mouthed at her frank reply, then he gave a snort that might have been suppressed laughter.

''I think you may be right,'' he said. ''It has troubled me for a long time that my people were so poorly served. I never thought you would be skilled in such things.''

''Did you think I was quite without talents!'' She was stung by the surprise in his voice.

''Of course not. Don't be so quick to bite back. I'm only trying to say how glad I am my people now have someone to turn to in such matters.''

"I have only a little skill," she said eventually. "I hope you don't expect too much of me."

"Whatever you do will be of benefit to the peasants—that is the important thing." There was a silence and he dug his thumbs into his belt, a gesture of his when he was feeling awkward. Then he said, "I expect you wish to go and refresh yourself. I'll not keep you longer."

Not sure whether or not this was his way of pointing out that she was looking dishevelled she thrust out her grubby hands and replied decidedly, "I'd every intention of washing before entering your company again. I'm very well aware that my appearance is not fitting for the Dame de Plou-Aven!"

He winced at this reminder of his earlier reproof. "You've been busy. I would not expect you to look any different under the circumstances."

The mildness of his reply confounded her. Perhaps he had not intended a reprimand. The uncertainty annoyed her. Surely after all these weeks of being married to the man she ought to be able to know when he was angry and when he was not? Before she could make some tart response he said, "I've a fancy for music tonight. I'll send for the harp-player. It is your favourite instrument, so don't be late."

His words had the crisp urgency of command about them. She answered cautiously, "As the Seigneur pleases." Surprised that he should have taken note of any of her preferences, she realised that he might be trying to please her. "I would like to hear the harp very much indeed, Seigneur. Its music always gives me pleasure."

His only response was to grunt and nod his head.

Clearly the Seigneur de Plou-Aven was finding it difficult to show his approval of his wife's activities.

As the evening wore on, good wine and fine music smoothed away any awkwardness and the conversation flowed. When Sabina questioned him about one of the local families Ronan launched into a series of stories, most of them hilariously funny, about the happenings at Plou-Aven. He proved very knowledgeable about his people; even Catell would have been hard-pressed to equal him. As she laughed at his tales Sabina noted that her husband could be an extremely agreeable companion when he chose. But then, she had to admit she had had remarkably few long conversations with him. All too often the discourse between them was short and heated. She began to wish that more evenings could be as delightful as this. Perhaps if she made the effort…if she could curb her sharp tongue… The prospect was such an agreeable one that she resolved to try.

That night, in his sleep, Ronan flung his arm across her in an easy embrace. She made no attempt to push him away, but lay there comfortable and warm. Only in the moments before drowsiness claimed her did she remember he had not told her where he had spent the night. But by then she was so relaxed and content that such matters seemed unimportant. He had called in the harp-player for her delight; she was willing to accept that as his way of apologising.

Chapter Five

Next morning Sabina was surprised to see the Seigneur dressed for a journey. She refused to give in to her curiosity and ask where he was going. She assumed an air of indifference, remarking, "I wish you Godspeed, Seigneur," as he was preparing to mount his horse.

Ronan fidgeted with the bay's bridle. "I will be away for a few hours only," he said.

Sabina appreciated he was making an effort to inform her of his intentions for the day, but her satisfaction was swept away when he continued, "I've to go to Trémazan—"

"Trémazan? I've heard of that place! When our coast was plundered!" she declared. "You aren't planning another raid on Devon, are you?"

"Ships set sail from Trémazan for destinations other than the English coast, you know!" he answered curtly. "Nor do I spend all my waking hours devising methods of harrying your people!" Then immediately he sounded almost apologetic as he explained, "This is an innocent commercial venture to Spain."

"Your pardon..." Sabina was contrite. "There, I fully resolved to guard my tongue, and what happens? The sun is scarcely up and already I've spoken harshly to you, and without provocation, for a change!"

At this final remark the Seigneur's mouth almost twitched into a smile—almost, but not quite.

"Your tongue has had a lifetime of being sharp. Perchance it needs a little more practice at speaking sweetly," he said. "You can give it free rein tomorrow. We'll go riding. It's time we were seen in the parish together, we've not been since our wedding guests departed."

He spurred on his horse, not waiting to see if this arrangement was convenient or even agreeable.

But Sabina was not capable of objecting; she had been rendered speechless by his suggesting such a thing.

"Not more herbs, *ma dame!*" protested Catell, as they in turn set out for another plant-hunting expedition.

"I fear so. We used up a prodigious amount yesterday, far more than I'd anticipated. Still, when you have taught me the local names for what I need it's a job we can hand over to the children of the parish. I'm sure they will be glad enough to earn an extra *denier* or two to swell the family purse."

"How did you come to learn so much, *ma dame?*"

"I keep telling you, my knowledge is meagre. My mother taught me a few cures for everyday maladies. The rest I learned from the village priest. I fear he was not adept at saving souls, he was too impatient with sinners to persevere, but when it came to ailments, whether in Christians or animals, there was not his equal for miles.''

"We could do with a priest like him, here,'' Catell remarked. ''Père Martin, bless him, is too holy for a place the likes of Plou-Aven! The good father would be better off teaching in a seminary. He's not quite of our world. I'll swear he doesn't know what we're on about half the time at confession!''

"In that case, it would be better if you led the sort of life where you had little to confess.''

"Yes, *ma dame*,'' replied the maid primly, though her eyes twinkled with mischief. ''Now, what are we looking for this time?''

In spite of Catell's mock grumbles it was pleasant wandering about the countryside searching for the different herbs. They had gone on foot, with Jester for company; bright sunshine was warm on their backs as they stopped to gather leaves and flowers here or dug roots there. A rough stretch of moorland proved to be a most rewarding area, luring them on and on until Sabina, straightening up to ease her back, realised that they were out of sight of any habitation.

"Perhaps we'd better go back now, *ma dame*,' said Catell uneasily. ''We've come a bit far.''

"We'll go on just a little. I'm sure that's a patch of comfrey I can see over there—those tall plants by the clump of hawthorns.''

"Oh, *ma dame*, must we?''

"They are just over yonder. It will only take a few minutes to reach them... There's no need to look so nervous. There's nothing out here can harm us.''

"I'm not so sure, *ma dame*. These lonely places,

they have their spirits guarding them. They might be angry if we intrude.''

Sabina was growing used to her servant's superstitious fears. She found the solitude very agreeable, but she knew the girl's anxiety, though groundless, was keenly felt.

"No hobgoblins or elves have shown their displeasure so far,'' she said cheerfully. ''I don't suppose they'll object if we take a few more steps. You can stay here if you like. It would be foolish to miss the chance of some comfrey when we are so close.''

"Don't leave me, *dame*, I pray! I'll come too!''

Sabina made towards her goal with Catell pressing uncomfortably close to her heels. Soon she found herself plunging through waist-high bracken.

It was then that the man jumped suddenly from the thicket, uttering odd noises. One look at his wild, unkempt appearance, and they both fled.

Sabina had not run far when she discovered that her dog was not with her.

"Jester! Here boy!'' she called.

"Oh, *ma dame,* come away!'' pleaded Catell. "The dog will be all right. Let's go before the fellow does us harm.''

"But the man's just standing there, making no attempt to follow us.''

"He doesn't need to, *ma dame!* He's possessed by demons! And who's to know that they can't reach us from there!''

"You know him?''

"Yes, *ma dame.* He's Daft Yannick. He lives out here on the moors most of the summer, like a wild animal. He's quite mad. Oh, please, can we go?''

Sabina was intrigued. Jester was a good judge of

character and he was now inviting this madman to play. The man, seeing her eyes on him, took a step forward and began waving one hand in the air. Not a normal wave as in a greeting, but a strange sinuous sideways movement.

"Whatever is he doing?"

"Magic! He's putting a spell on us! Don't go any closer!" the maid implored as curiosity drove Sabina to move nearer. "Can't you see, he's already cast a spell on the dog? He's bewitched."

Jester was certainly behaving like a mad thing, chasing about, but Sabina suspected the cause was overexcitement rather than witchcraft. Then, in a frantic attempt to involve someone in his game, the dog hurled himself at the man. Caught unawares, Daft Yannick staggered back beneath the animal's weight and fell with a sickening thud.

"Now's our chance!" cried Catell. "We can run away, *dame!*"

Sabina was too concerned to leave. "The man hasn't got up. Do you think he's all right?" she wondered.

"What does it matter? It will stop him from following us."

"But he might be hurt. Jester is no lightweight. And the poor fellow went down with a terrible bang... Perhaps I'd better go and see."

Ignoring her maid's anguished protests Sabina moved forward cautiously.

Yannick was on his knees among the bracken and heather when she approached. He was breathing deeply, as though he had been winded, and at the same time he was trying to fend off the wet caresses of Jester. At first he did not seem to notice her. Not until she hauled the dog off him did he know she was there. When he did, he scrambled away from her in terror, giving grunts like a frightened animal.

"It's all right. I'll not harm you," said Sabina. "I've only come to see if you're hurt."

Yannick said nothing. He stayed behind in a tangle of brambles, regarding her with scared, wary eyes.

"There's nothing to fear," said Sabina softly. "Catell, tell him so in Breton."

The maid had summoned up her courage and joined her mistress. "It will not do any good, *dame,*' she said. "He can't speak. He just gives those grunts."

In an attempt to calm his fears Sabina sank to her knees and regarded him through the stalks of blackberry and fern. The eyes that looked back at her were frightened still, and suspicious. She had never looked into the eyes of a madman and she had not expected them to look so intelligent.

"Has he always been mad?" she asked.

"Ever since I can remember, *ma dame.* Though, they say he was normal enough as a small child. Then he caught a bad fever and afterwards was given to madness and fierce tempers. That was when he become possessed."

Sabina continued to regard Daft Yannick. There was no way she could judge his age, for his hair was long and matted and his skin was encrusted with dirt.

"And he lives out here, you say?"

"Yes, when the weather is warm. Now that his mother is dead he finds himself some hole or other about Plou-Aven the rest of the time."

"It doesn't sound much of an existence for a Christian." Sabina's heart was stirred by the plight of the poor creature in front of her, and she stretched out a hand towards him.

"Don't touch him, for pity's sake, *ma dame!*" cried Catell, running off a short distance in fright.

Immediately she did so Yannick arose swiftly to his knees, shaking his head and grunting, while again he began the same strange movement with his hand. Catell screamed and ran further. He shook his head again, and looked at Sabina. There was no mistaking the expression in his eyes, it was pleading and imploring.

"He's trying to tell us something!" exclaimed Sabina in astonishment. "He can't speak, yet he has something to tell us. That waving of his hand, he means something by it—but what? A fish? A stream?" In her enthusiasm she moved closer to him, waving her hand in imitation of his. This time he did not draw back, but watched with tense excitement.

"I know!" Sabina exclaimed. "It's a snake. Am I right?" Then, in case he did not understand, she hissed like a serpent.

He made no response to either her words or the sound.

"I'm sure I'm right!" cried Sabina. "I'll try something else."

Seizing a twig she drew the outline of a snake on a small patch of bare earth. The response from Yannick was astounding; he nodded violently, grinning all over his face; then in his delight he leapt to his feet and jumped up and down, setting Jester barking.

"Can you doubt he's mad, *dame?*" cried Catell.

"Of course he's not mad! I think the poor fellow is deaf. Look, see what he's doing now!"

As if to prove his sanity, Yannick dropped to his

knees beside the drawing and with a filthy fingernail drew a zigzag down the back of the snake. Then with a sweep of his arm he indicated the bank of thick bracken.

"A viper!" exclaimed Sabina. "The man's been trying to warn us that there are vipers about." To affirm that she was right she pointed once more to the drawing then to the stretch of bracken.

Yannick nodded, suddenly still, as though the burst of activity had exhausted him... As Sabina watched tears began to trickle down his cheeks, leaving streaks in the grime.

"Holy Mother! If that doesn't beat everything!" whispered Catell.

"The poor soul! The poor soul!" Sabina said. "To be shunned throughout his life as being mad when all the time he is as sane as you or I..." Then she had an idea. "The food we brought, is there any left?"

"Some, *ma dame*." Catell rummaged in the roomy leather pocket hanging from her belt.

"Give it to him."

Gingerly the maid handed the food to Yannick. And he wolfed it down.

"*Ma dame*, it grows late. We must go now," said Catell.

"Yes, you are right. I wonder if he'll follow us?"

"Sure to, *dame*, now that you've fed him."

Yannick did go with them, though Sabina was convinced that being understood at long last was a greater attraction to him than the food. He walked ahead of them beating the earth with a stick to frighten off the vipers while they continued gathering herbs on the way back to the château. He showed great interest in what they were doing and in the plants they had already collected. Only when they reached the road to the château did he begin to hang back.

"We must take him with us," said Sabina. "There's no reason for him to live like a wild creature now." But though she held out her hand to him and pointed out the château he shook his head.

"He doesn't understand," said Catell.

"I'm sure he does. He's lived wild for so long he has a fear of being within walls. No doubt he has got little cause to love his fellow men, either. Well, if he won't come the least we can do is to make sure he doesn't starve. I'll have food sent out to him every day."

It was surprisingly easy to explain to Yannick through signs what she intended to do. He stood motionless for a while, as though he could hardly credit his good luck, then as they moved off once more he kept pace with them at a distance.

They did not see him go. They looked around to wave farewell and he had disappeared. Catell shivered, not absolutely convinced that there was not a hint of the Black Arts about him somewhere.

When they reached the château, Sabina turned her attention to making her remedies. The more she considered them, the more she realised that her knowledge and her equipment were inadequate.

"Catell, Marthe," she said, "I need help and advice about making some of the draughts and the potions. Can either of you suggest someone to whom I can turn for assistance?"

"The wise woman at Sainte Anne is the nearest, *dame*," said Catell. "But though she is knowledge-

able she can be cantankerous when she's a mind... I
think the abbey at Brézel is your best hope.''

"It is some distance away, I hear," said Sabina.
"And I've not got time for travelling at the moment.
I will have to send a letter. Would Père Martin be
capable of writing it for me, do you think?"

"Yes, *ma dame,*" replied Catell. "I think he'd be
delighted to undertake the task; his talents get little
use here in Plou-Aven."

At that moment there was a knock at the door and
it was pushed open. Sabina looked up, expecting to
see one of the servants bringing water or fuel. Instead
she saw the Seigneur.

"Ah, so this is your witches' kitchen," he said.
"My business was completed early so I thought to
come and see what you are about."

Surprised that he should have sought them out,
Sabina said, "As you can see, Seigneur, we're brewing and boiling; your description is not far wrong."

Ronan gazed about him. "What is this place? I
was never here before."

"I don't suppose you were," she replied. "This
was once the old kitchen. It was being used as a store
when I commandeered it."

"Is it adequate for your needs? Are you in want
of aught?" he asked, watching with interest as she
strained some liquid through a linen cloth.

"The room lacks shelves. Apart from that it is
ideal."

"Tell Le Godet what you require and he will have
the carpenters attend to it immediately. What else?"

"What else, sir?"

"Yes. I can tell from your voice there is more."

"There is, Seigneur…if you will permit it. I want to send a letter to the Abbot of Brézel."

"To Abbé Tanguey? Whatever for? Having disrupted life in an English convent, are you now considering creating chaos in a Breton monastery?"

"I am not! I am considering ways of making a still, and I must have advice."

"A still! You are a lover of strong drink, *dame?*"

"You are refusing to be serious," she said. "The still is for brewing my remedies. I am sorely restricted without one. I think I know the general description but it is important to understand exactly what one is doing. Faulty stills can be dangerous. At home, one of Father Joseph's exploded, sending a jar of tansy liniment hurtling through the window. The shock put his hens off laying for a full week— You are laughing at me, Seigneur!"

"How can I help it after such an absurd description? A grown man throwing hens through windows! No wonder the unfortunate fowls refused to lay!"

"It was not the hens which went through the window, it was the liniment! You misunderstand me on purpose!"

All too often the seriousness of Ronan's expression made him seem older than his years. Seeing him so amused, she could well imagine how he must have been before sorrow and responsibilities weighed him down. For once the look of pained sadness had gone from his eyes. He made some remark to Catell and Marthe in Breton which sent both maids into shrieks of laughter. It occurred to Sabina, not for the first time, that her husband was a comely man. He did not have the angelic good looks of Giles but there was a strength and compactness about his well-muscled body which was attractive. If only his expression could be merry more often…his dark eyes sparkling with amusement…

He turned his attention back to her. "And is a still your only requirement?" he asked.

"No, I need to know where to get more herb plants, varieties which don't grow wild. I intend to restock the herb garden, if you will permit it."

"You know you have no need of my permission, but you have my approval. What else?"

"Knowledge! I am only just beginning to appreciate how little I know."

"And how do you propose to send your request for help to Brézel?"

"I thought, perhaps, Père Martin could write a letter for me, and then a servant could take it."

"If it is a long list, don't you think it better if you write yourself?"

"If I were in England I would." Sabina's reply was swift; she did not want him to think her lazy or uneducated. Then honesty overcame her. "I am not confident of my spelling in French," she said.

"I have a better idea. Consult Père Martin about your needs, make sure he understands, and write a detailed list. Then we'll send the good father himself, so that he can explain things more clearly."

"He'll have to be away for some days. Will he like that?"

"Like it?" The Seigneur sounded puzzled. "We'll arrange it in a way which doesn't interfere with his religious duties. There can be no other objection."

"I only meant—"

"I know well enough what you meant." His face almost relaxed into a smile once more. "You are afraid a man of his years will not relish such a long ride. You need have no fears. I assure you Père Martin will be only too delighted to abandon his wayward flock for a short spell and spend some time among men of letters.''

"In that case, I think it is a splendid idea."

"I would hope, as a dutiful wife, you think all my ideas are splendid."

For a moment she thought she sensed another reproof, then she glanced at him and saw he was teasing. More than that, the expression on his face was approving.

Ronan headed for the door. "I've disturbed your work for long enough," he said. "I'll go and leave you in peace. I shall see you at table, *ma dame*."

As he left, Sabina caught sight of Catell and Marthe; they were both watching his departure with fond, wistful eyes. The two servants were both more than a little in love with him. Sabina was surprised—then she was surprised at her own reaction. Having acknowledged that he was well-favoured, it was only to be expected that female eyes would look upon him with admiration. Why was it so unexpected, then, that other women should love him? For some reason this problem occupied her for quite a while. The conclusion, when she reached it, was painfully simple; she associated Ronan and love with one person only—Marianne. Their story had been so tragic and his grief was still so heartfelt, it seemed impossible he might ever love someone else. His heart was destined to lie in the grave with her for the rest of his life.

The day changed abruptly. The sun did not seem to shine so brightly; her work did not absorb her so completely. She put the onset of such unexpected low spirits down to fatigue.

As the Seigneur had predicted, Père Martin was delighted with his assignment. "*Ma dame,* such an honour! Such a pleasure!" he puffed when he was shown into the solar, out of breath from his walk up the steep path to the château.

"Are you sure it won't overtax your strength?" asked Sabina, concerned at his breathless state.

"*Ma dame,* some exercise is what I need. And you've no idea what pleasure it will give me. It is so long since I was able to discuss the scriptures or theology with men of my own kind." The chaplain's face was bright with happy anticipation.

"I understand very well, *mon père.* It is a long time since I have spoken my mother tongue."

"Ah, yes, *ma dame,* I had forgotten. *Ma pauvre dame!*"

"I thank you for your sympathy, *mon père,* though I'm sure there are worthier causes. Now, shall we begin my list? I fear it will be prodigious."

Next morning Sabina was up betimes to see Père Martin off on his way to Brézel.

"You are certainly well protected," she said, looking at the sizeable retinue accompanying him.

"Oh, such precautions are not for my old bones," the chaplain smiled. "They are for what I carry." He patted his saddle-bag and leaned forward confidentially. "The Seigneur has been very generous. On his behalf I am taking a large donation to the abbey coffers. You see how determined he is that you shall have what you want. It is proof of his regard for you as a wife. I praise the blessed Virgin that you came to give the Seigneur comfort. He deserves the happiness and companionship of such a wife as you, *ma dame.*''

''Thank you, *mon père,*'' Sabina smiled at the chaplain's high praise. She would have liked to have believed it; she was all too well aware that the gentle father saw everything through a rosy haze.

It was at this point that Ronan arrived. ''The servants have been given their orders and are ready for the journey, *mon père,*'' he said. ''You'd best be starting if you wish to reach Brézel by nightfall. Give the Abbé Tanguey my sincerest respects. I wish you Godspeed.''

The procession rode through the gateway. Sabina and Ronan watched it take the dusty road to Brézel. When it was out of sight Ronan said, ''Now, *dame,* it is time for us to mount up.''

''Mount up, Seigneur?''

''We are to ride out together, had you forgotten?''

''I had not forgotten. I wasn't sure you meant it.''

''Why should I say something I didn't mean?'' He looked surprised. Then when she made no answer he continued, ''I hope you do not intend to disappoint me.''

''I have no intention of doing anything so silly,'' replied Sabina. ''You know I love to ride.''

''Good. Then I'll send for the horses.''

They rode out in silence, holding their mounts to a sedate trot. Sabina grew impatient at their slow progress. It was a glorious day; the sun burned down on them from a sky which seemed more vast than that which covered Corbyn, and everywhere skylarks were propelling themselves heavenwards in an upsurge of song. Every instinct in her wanted to urge

her mare forward in a wild, gloriously free gallop.
But the Seigneur kept his bay tightly reined, so she,
perforce, had to match her pace with his.

Not until they reached *la lande,* the open moorland
on the outer fringes of the parish, did the trot gradually quicken to a canter. As they gained speed the
Seigneur glanced down at her and seemed surprised
to find that she was quite happy to keep up with him.
Gradually the stride of his horse lengthened, covering
the ground more swiftly. Heartened, Sabina followed
suit, feeling the gorse-scented wind blowing in her
face and pulling at her headdress. From time to time
the Seigneur glanced in her direction, as though he
were testing her. She grinned back at him, finally
letting the mare have her head. The little palomino
was no match for the huge bay, of course, and Ronan
soon surged past. But it did not matter. To Sabina
the joy of the gallop was all important. She followed
after him, her long skirts whipping in the wind, her
mare's hoofs casting up divots of springy turf behind
her.

At last the Seigneur reined his mount to a halt and
waited for her, his face flushed, his eyes bright with
enjoyment.

Taking an appreciative gulp of air, she cried,
"That was splendid!"

"You did well," he said. "You like to gallop?"

"Of course! What finer activity is there?" she answered.

"For a man, none. But I didn't think ladies were
of a like mind."

"Obviously you haven't ridden out with many
ladies, Seigneur," she smiled.

"Not at such a pace," he admitted. "Marianne preferred to travel in a litter."

Sabina wondered how anyone could prefer such a jolting mode of transport to riding on horseback. She commented, "I find horses more comfortable. Litters make me feel sick."

"I've only ridden in one once," he said. "When I broke my ankle as a lad. I'm inclined to agree with you."

While Sabina was digesting the amazing fact that she had something in common with her husband, he continued, "Now, if you have recovered I suggest we move before the horses get cold."

They set off again, at a more leisurely amble, the horses breasting their way through the high bracken.

"Cudenec says that your riding has improved greatly," Ronan remarked, "and I can see he is right."

Sabina had not realised he took so much interest in her activities. "Who would not improve on such an animal?" she replied, giving an affectionate tug at the mare's pale mane. "She's a lovely creature… You are a good judge of horseflesh, sire."

He made no answer, but looked pleased.

Another silence settled on them, though this time it had an affable quality about it. Their route gradually curved, taking them back in the direction of Plou-Aven. Sabina was sorry the ride would soon be over, she was enjoying herself very much.

They were passing through a copse, heading towards the road, when a sudden commotion behind them made the horses start and dance in alarm.

"What's happening?" asked Ronan, fighting to hold his spirited bay.

Sabina was too busy trying to control her mare to answer. When she had got the creature calmed she turned in the saddle. What she saw horrified her. The grooms were in pursuit of a wild, unkempt figure that darted through the trees. The quarry was swift and agile, twisting and turning, never once letting go of the rough bundle he carried under his arm.

"Holy Mother, it's the madman!" exclaimed Ronan.

Sabina urged her horse forward. "He's not mad! He's deaf!" she cried. "Let him alone! Don't you dare touch him, I say!"

The grooms were lashing out at the unfortunate man with their whips. Startled by her unexpected shouts, they stayed their hands and look round in astonishment. Yannick took his chance and dashed towards her.

Ronan pushed forward on his bay. "Don't worry, I'll get rid of the wretch!"

But Sabina put out a hand and took his rein. "He's quite harmless. Please don't hurt him," she begged.

"He leapt out on you! He deserves a thrashing, mad though he is!" declared the Seigneur. "Come here at once!" he bellowed at Yannick, who was now cowering in the thick undergrowth.

"He can't hear you! He's deaf! I assure you, he means no harm."

Ignoring Ronan's warning cry, Sabina slipped from the saddle and approached Yannick. Straight away he retreated nervously into his prickly refuge. "Come," she said to him, gesturing with her hand. "Come."

At first he made no move, then, as she persisted, he began to creep towards her. Suddenly he darted forward, dropped the bundle he was holding at her feet, then dashed back into the thicket again.

The bundle proved to be a rough bag, coarsely woven from rushes. Opening it, Sabina gave a cry of delight.

"Plants!" she exclaimed. "All the kinds Catell and I were collecting yesterday! He must have noted every single type. You see, he's not mad, sire!" She went on to relate the events of the previous day.

She turned back to Yannick, who was waiting nervously for her reaction, a wary eye on the grooms. "Good," she said, beaming and nodding her head.

A slow smile spread across his face and he nodded too.

"*Mon Dieu!* If that doesn't beat everything!" the Seigneur exclaimed. "Everyone thought he was mad, including me! He certainly acted like a lunatic!"

"Wouldn't you act like a lunatic if you couldn't hear what was being said to you and you couldn't make yourself understood?" demanded Sabina. "No wonder the poor fellow flew into rages! People have done nothing but chase him off and thrash him every time he appears. The miracle is that he has remained sane at all!"

Ronan shook his head in amazement. "And what do you propose to do with him?" he asked. "Take him on as a servant or keep him in a closet as you did with that dog of yours?"

"I don't think he'd take to life in a closet after living free on the moors," smiled Sabina. "Nevertheless, he could be employed as my herb gatherer, couldn't he?"

"I spoke only in jest. I didn't intend you to take me seriously," protested the Seigneur. Then he gave a sigh. "Very well, if you want him to come back to the château then I suppose he must come..."

"That is kind of you, sire. However, I'm not sure he would wish it."

She was right. Yannick shook his head and backed away at the idea of accompanying them. He was much more enthusiastic when she indicated that more food would be left for him.

"Now you've pleased him, he's grinning all over his face," observed Ronan. "What message were you giving him?"

"Only that food will be put out for him—if the Seigneur will permit?"

"Go right ahead..." The Seigneur sounded resigned. "Already I seem to have given my home over to be a refuge for the unfortunates of the parish; my doorway is crammed with the sick and injured; a flea-ridden dog frequently occupies my bed; kitchen wenches are elevated to body-servants... Why should I object to feeding a lunatic or two?"

Sabina hesitated, trying to determine which she should believe, his disgruntled words or her instinct that he did not really disapprove. "It is not a lunatic I plan to feed, Seigneur. Just a man who cannot hear or speak," she said eventually.

"Oh, feed who you will!"

The Seigneur turned his horse and rode off as if impatient with the subject, leaving Sabina to wish yet again that she understood her husband better.

The crowd of people waiting to see her was larger than before. Despite the able assistance of Catell and Marthe she still had more patients than she could cope with.

"This cannot continue," said the Seigneur, after she had worked continuously for hours at a stretch. "What will be the benefit if you make yourself ill through overwork?"

"I can cope," Sabina assured him. "Although I am small I am surprisingly strong. I do not tire easily."

"You do not need to get tired at all," he pointed out. "Not with the place full of servants eating their heads off and doing precious little else. You must have more women to help you, and a man for the heavy work."

"Thank you, Seigneur." She was gratified by his concern. "Things will improve in time, I expect."

"Will they? I hear that folks are coming in from far distances, not just from the parish. No, you must restrict the times when you will see the sick. The plant gathering and the brewing must decrease also."

"They will, now I've got Yannick to search for the herbs... I seem to be acquiring a deal of servants! Are you sure they can be spared from other duties?"

"Of course they can be spared if I say so!" Ronan's eyebrows rose haughtily. "Would you like me to give the orders to Le Godet?"

"There is no need to trouble yourself, I thank you. I will inform him," she replied.

So Ronan approved of her ministering to the peasants. His approval lightened her day considerably, enough to make her forget her sore muscles and weary limbs.

Life at Plou-Aven was becoming remarkably pleasant—Sabina had to acknowledge that her husband could be surprisingly agreeable. In time, she felt, she might get to like him very much indeed...

Then she shrugged off the thought as ridiculous. Their marriage was a matter of business, likes and dislikes did not enter into it. To dwell on such things was nothing but folly.

Late one afternoon a flurry of activity at the gatehouse announced the return of Père Martin, tired, covered with dust from the road, but triumphant.

"*Ma dame,* the Abbé and the good brothers, they showed me much kindness!" he declared when Sabina hurried forward to greet him. "They were most interested in your work and engaged me to assure you that they will pray constantly for the blessings of *le Bon Dieu* upon you—"

"*Mon père,* it can all wait, at least until you have dismounted," she laughed. "Come, refresh yourself, then you can tell me your news."

Stiffly, Père Martin climbed down from his mount. "I fear my anatomy and that of the horse are no longer compatible, *ma dame,*" he winced. "To stretch my legs will be luxury indeed."

"Surely you have brought more things that I requested?" she said, noticing the extra pack-animals being led into the inner bailey.

"The brothers have been most generous, *ma dame.*"

"That is wonderful! Come, tell me everything." She was so intrigued by the bundles the chaplain had brought from the abbey she was hard put to it not to question him immediately.

"Did the brothers send me instructions for making the still?"

"Better than that—they sent you a complete still, one they no longer need."

"Oh!" Sabina was struck dumb. This was more than she had anticipated.

"I have full instructions on how to assemble it. I only hope it has survived the rigours of the journey." He began pulling notes from his pocket. "Frère Laurent, the herbalist, has answered your queries most fully. He has also sent you plants and cuttings he hopes you will find useful, and begs you do not hesitate to call upon his help should you need it."

"Oh…!" said Sabina again, totally overwhelmed. "The Abbé and the good brothers have been very generous indeed!"

"Ah, *ma dame,* but the Seigneur was exceedingly generous to the abbey," said the chaplain with a rare hint of worldliness. "The Abbé Tanguey said, 'Such generosity shows how high in affection and esteem the Seigneur de Plou-Aven must hold his new bride'. Those were his very words, *ma dame.* And he said that *le Bon Dieu* must surely smile upon such a union."

"The Abbé Tanguey said that?" Sabina felt the colour rise in her cheeks. Could it be that her husband held her in high esteem? Had she managed to earn just a little of the fondness he had showered on Marianne? It was a prospect she had never dared contemplate. She suddenly felt warm and happy inside. There had not been much affection in her life, and she had never thought to find any here in Brittany.

In a sudden upsurge of high spirits, Sabina felt the need for activity after the chaplain had left. She would go riding!

Setting off at a brisk pace, she sang to herself in time with the quickening rhythm of the mare's hoof.

Her future appeared bright with hope. There seemed a real chance of happiness here for her with Ronan, and the prospect made her heart grow even lighter. The countryside had never seemed more beautiful, the birds had never sung sweeter, her mare had never moved with greater ease. She galloped on and on. Only when the palomino's stride began to falter did she consider curtailing the joy of the ride. As she reined her mount to a halt she turned to discover that Cudenec and Jester were puffing away far behind her.

An exhausted, panting Jester reached her first, followed by an equally fatigued groom.

"I'm relieved to find you, *ma dame,*" he puffed, pulling at the neck of his tunic. "I'm growing too long in the tooth for such capers as these."

"Your pardon, Cudenec. I should not have put you to such exertion," said Sabina.

"Bless you, *dame,* you have no need to apologise to me! I may be getting on in years, but I can still remember the thrill of being young and full of energy!"

"We'll go home at a more sedate pace," Sabina promised.

As the small party plodded homewards Jester soon recovered his energy. When an isolated collection of buildings caught his eye he made straight for them in his constant quest for hens to chase. Fortunately Sabina caught sight of his multicoloured body squeezing through a gate. Knowing all too well what mayhem he could cause, she urged her mare forward and dismounted. Cudenec shouted in protest, but she was too intent on capturing Jester to notice.

Following the dog through the gate she found herself in a pleasant garden. Deprived of his favourite sport because of a lack of hens, Jester was making himself agreeable to the sole occupant, a young serving-maid, who had been spreading washing on the bushes to dry.

"Catch hold of his collar, if you please," she called, hurrying up. Then as the girl did as she was bid she added, "Thank goodness! I was afraid I'd never…!" Sabina's voice tailed away. "Surely, I know you…? You are the wench who refused to be my tiring-woman!"

"Yes, *ma dame*. Your pardon, *ma dame*." The girl stared down fixedly at the top of Jester's head, embarrassment staining her cheeks bright pink.

Sabina had all but forgotten the incident, but now, noting the maid's discomfort, her indignation and her curiosity were aroused once more.

"You caused me much anger and inconvenience by refusing to enter my service, do you know that?" she said sharply.

The girl's head hung even lower.

"What explanation have you? Was it the fact that I am a foreigner, an Englishwoman?"

"Oh, no, *dame!*" The girl looked up, her face registering genuine surprise.

"Then, why?"

"I cannot say, *ma dame*."

"Cannot or will not? You are truly the most perverse wench I've ever encountered! Just give me a reason!"

But the girl only hung her head once more and refused to meet Sabina's gaze.

"What is your name?" she asked more gently. "I suppose you can tell me that much?"

"I am called Agnès, *ma dame*."

"I promise you, Agnès, there is nothing for you to fear. I am well satisfied with the tiring-woman I found in your place. However, I am still much puzzled by your refusal and would like an explanation."

"I told you, *ma dame*. I already have a situation."

"Then, if you already had a situation, what were you doing at the château? Obviously you weren't working there!"

"Please don't question me, *ma dame*. I implore you!" There was genuine distress in the girl's voice.

Sabina was reluctant to increase her anxiety by pressing her any further, no matter how insistent her curiosity was. All the same, it was very frustrating, and she heaved a sigh of regret.

"No matter," she said. "We will let it rest there. Thank you for catching my dog."

Then Sabina noticed the stables abutting the yard, and beyond them stood a house. "What is this place?" she asked.

There was an almost imperceptible pause before Agnès replied, "It is Ty Lannion, *dame*."

"The house of Lannion?" she repeated. The name had a familiar ring to it. It took Sabina a moment to remember... So this was the house which had caused Catell such embarrassment. What was the name of the mysterious woman who occupied it...? Louise de Lannion, that was it! "No better than she ought to be" was how Catell had described her... So Agnès was her maidservant!

Sabina looked about her with fresh interest. Coming upon the house from the rear, she had not recognised it. Regarding the stoutly built stables and the well kept garden, she chuckled to herself—sin certainly did pay very well—though she wondered how the de Lannion woman managed to find enough affluent customers in Plou-Aven to maintain such a prosperous-looking household. No wonder Agnès had not wanted to change situations. But why she had been up at the château that day was more than Sabina could fathom...

The truth hit her like a physical blow. She wondered at her stupidity. How could she have been so blind, so obtuse? It was all so blatantly obvious! Louise de Lannion had no need of a succession of clients. She was the mistress of the most important man in the district—the Seigneur de Plou-Aven! Sabina rocked on her heels. The reasons for her husband's anger, Catell's embarrassment, even Agnès's distress, all became painfully clear.

Beside her the maidservant began to sob. Over at the open gate Cudenec stood holding the horses. The old groom, normally so frank and outspoken, would not meet her gaze. There could be no doubt about it—Ronan had a mistress living almost within the shadow of the château!

She should have guessed it, of course. For any man to keep a leman was quite usual. For a virile, comely man like the Seigneur to do so was almost expected. Why, then, had the discovery come as such a shattering blow?

Cudenec approached her, "*Ma dame,* you've had a wearying day. We'd best be getting back, eh?" The sympathy in his eyes stung her. Did everyone know about her husband's woman? she wondered. Was she the only one kept in humiliating ignorance?

Aloud she said, "You are right. We'll go."

Giving a curt nod to Agnès, she strode out.

On the ride back to the château she kept her back poker-straight, her face impassive… Why should she care if Ronan had a mistress? It meant that he would be less likely to bother her! The pain inside her was only anger. To keep his mistress so near the château in which he kept his wife! That was what angered her. She wished she had never wed him—but, at least, she had the consolation of knowing that she had not done so willingly. Reluctant she had been as a bride, and reluctant she would stay as a wife!

Sabina, who prided herself on her boundless energy, was astonished at how exhausting the last few hours had been. Every muscle in her body protested, her limbs felt leaden. Her hopes for a warmer relationship with Ronan were dashed, but she refused to accept that this had anything to do with her physical state.

"I'm tired," she told an anxious Catell. "Too tired to eat."

"But what of your supper? Shall I bring you something?"

"I've no appetite. Sleep is what I need, not food."

Sabina heard Catell muttering to herself. "This is not like *ma dame*. She's sickening for something, I'm sure of it!"

The Seigneur put another interpretation on Sabina's indisposition. Upon hearing that she would not be dining in the great hall with him, he had come up to the bedchamber to see how she fared.

"Perhaps there is some other natural explanation for your extreme fatigue?" he suggested.

It took Sabina a moment or two to realise what he meant.

"Important as producing an heir is to you," she

snapped, "I wish you would stop making it the cause of every trifling ailment I suffer! I'm tired! Nothing more! And I can assure you that I am not carrying your child!" Then she added vehemently, "Thank goodness!"

The Seigneur flinched at the force of her words, and his face took on cold, dour lines. "You have made your views on the subject painfully clear, *ma dame*," he said icily. "I regret that I have distressed you by referring to it."

"Distressed? Who is distressed?" she demanded. "I am bored at the way you keep on harping on the subject!"

"I am sorry if the idea bores you. I must remind you that the production of an heir is a vital part of our marriage contract. I repeat this in case you have forgotten, or did not fully understand and have some notion of not fulfilling your part of our bargain. If you are harbouring such an idea I bid you forget it at once!" Ronan's fury had been mounting. Then, abruptly, he took control of himself. Speaking more calmly but with no less animosity, he said, "However, you are indisposed, and since I have no wish to be a further trial to you I will go. You need not worry that I will bother you with unwelcome attentions tonight. I won't even be sharing your bed!"

He left the chamber, every line of his figure registering displeasure. To Sabina's ears even his footsteps sounded angry as they hurried down the stone stairs.

She wished fervently she had managed to curb her tongue. She could not think why she had said such things. They were not true. She longed for a babe of her own, to hold in her arms and love. Why, then, had she spoken as if a child were the last thing she desired? Sabina cursed herself for her stupidity. She felt an overwhelming desire to apologise, but it was too late. Ronan had already gone and she knew where he would be spending the night. He had made it painfully clear he had no use for her, save as the producer of an heir for Plou-Aven. That knowledge provoked such a profound misery that she cried herself to sleep.

Chapter Six

It was a more self-controlled Sabina who summoned Catell early next morning.

"Come, come," she called briskly. "I've got a great deal to do. As soon as I've eaten I want Seneschal Le Godet to attend me about ordering the household for the day. Then I'll go riding. And after that I must busy myself in the herb-room."

She avoided her maid's questioning look at such feverish activity. In the cold, early hours she had come to a conclusion—if her husband had no need of her, then what need had she of him? She had her horse and dog to lavish affection upon, there was the château to run and the people of the parish to care for. She had more than enough to occupy her.

Sabina set about her daily tasks with a vigour which soon had the servants flagging in her wake. And her day continued at the same furious pace, with only one interruption. As she was crossing the inner bailey the Seigneur arrived home.

"You have recovered from your indisposition?" he asked.

"Indisposition? Oh, that! Yes. I was simply tired." Sabina kept her voice breezily causal.

She noted with satisfaction that he looked pale and there were dark shadows under his eyes. What more can he expect, she thought, sharing the bed of that de Lannion woman all night?

"You are looking peaky, Seigneur. Perhaps you had a sleepless night," she said, with a false sweetness. "Shall I fetch you a draught of my yeast tonic?"

"I have no need of a tonic."

"Then how about a glass of wine fortified with herbs? It's good for restoring the strength!"

"Assuredly, I have no wish for your wine, either!" Ronan spoke with growing irritation.

"Then, perhaps, you're just constipated. I've a remedy for that—"

"By all that's holy, dame! I'm not constipated nor do I want any of your foul potions," roared the Seigneur. Then he realised that a clutch of grinning servants were standing within earshot, and he gave a loud groan of exasperation.

"In that case, if you want nothing of me, may I beg leave to go?" she asked. "I've a busy day ahead of me." With head erect and eyes wide with innocence, she bobbed a curtsy to the Seigneur and left.

Her sense of triumph did not last long. Once out of sight of Ronan she was beset by gloom. She fought to focus her thoughts on her remedies, on the people, on anything other than the relentless misery nagging away at her. With relief, she turned to setting up the new still. The concentration required to erect and operate it ensured she had no opportunity to think of anything else.

"Have you managed to light up your still?" asked Ronan when they met in the great hall later that day.

"I have, sire."

"And it goes well?"

"Of course!"

"I thought it must be so. There were no loud bangs or exploding hens hurtling through the heavens."

"Of course not! The instructions sent by the good brothers were very explicit. It works beautifully. There was no damage from the journey and…"

She saw that his face had grown cold once more. Too late she realised he had been handing out an olive branch.

"Seigneur!" she said urgently, aware of a sudden longing to bridge the growing rift between them.

"Ma dame?" His voice had grown icily impersonal.

She knew there would be no reaching out to him now. "I've sent a draught of medicine to your manservant with instructions to see that you take it," she said with asperity. "It's a purge. It should do you good. Among other things it sweetens the temper!" She stamped away from him, not waiting to see his reaction to her words.

From then on Sabina's life became curiously empty although she was so busy. She only seemed to meet Ronan at table and in bed—and frequently not even then. They were frigidly polite to one another, putting on a façade for the benefit of the servants, all of whom knew exactly how things stood between them. Sometimes she could not help remembering the few affectionate moments there had been between them. With the memories came a regret that those times were unlikely to return.

In sharp contrast, the other part of her life, the caring for the sick of the parish was going extremely well. Her reputation was growing throughout the countryside, drawing more and more people to trudge up the steep path to the château gate in search of relief from their ailments. Her command of the Breton language was improving, too. Her ear was quick and, hearing it spoken regularly, she found that she was becoming reasonably fluent. Remembering Le Godet's remarks on the subject, she wondered if her new accomplishment was quite proper.

But one day Marthe remarked, "You're getting to sound just like Dame Yolande, the Seigneur's mother, the way you deal with folk, *ma dame*. She'd stand no nonsense, yet still send folks away smiling."

"I wish I'd met her. Tell me, did Seneschal Le Godet interpret into Breton for her?"

"The seneschal? Bless you, no, *ma dame!* She could speak for herself."

"You mean she spoke Breton?"

"Certainly she did. They say her Breton was a deal better than her French. But having little French myself I couldn't judge."

"I did not realise ladies spoke Breton."

Marthe chuckled. "You've been listening to Seneshal Le Godet, *dame*. He thinks Brittany is a God-forsaken land—and everything connected with it. He can't help it—he comes from Paris!"

"So there is nothing against me learning Breton?"

"I thought you were doing that already, *dame*. You're coming along fine in the tongue."

"I do well enough. But you see no reason why I should not learn Breton properly?"

"None I know of, *ma dame*. The person to ask would be the Seigneur."

"Hm..." Sabina's mind was already busy with a new plan. She would take proper instruction in the language from Père Martin, but without informing the Seigneur first, lest she prove to have no real aptitude. If she were going to fail she would do it discreetly, and not expose herself to his scorn.

At once she knew she was being unfair. Ronan Guennec was too generous a man to deride anyone else's efforts, even hers. Nevertheless, she would keep her new studies to herself. The problem would be how to explain to Père Martin why she wanted such discretion. At her hesitant request the chaplain smiled with understanding. Unfortunately he jumped to the wrong conclusion.

"It will be an honour to share such a secret with you, *ma dame*," he beamed. "And if you will permit me to say so, I think it is a wonderful thing you are doing. It is a gesture after the Seigneur's own heart. He cares for his native land very deeply—of course, you know that, else you would not be going to such trouble."

"But I'm not—" Sabina began to protest, then she stopped. For the life of her she could not give a convincing reason for her determination to learn Breton. Surprisingly, the thought uppermost in her mind was that Marianne had not spoken the language at all.

Père Martin proved to be a born teacher, and was soon delighted with her progress. Keeping their lessons secret turned out to be no problem. Her conversations with the Seigneur were few these days, and he certainly never expressed any interest in her activities. Nor did Sabina concern herself with what he did with his time—or so she tried to convince herself. She never again rode anywhere in the vicinity of Ty Lannion—but that was pure coincidence.

Riding through the countryside was proving to be her chief pleasure and relaxation. Usually her dog ran alongside, his company adding to her enjoyment. Being the mistress of Jester had certain disadvantages, however, chief of which was his passion for chasing fowls.

On one riding expedition, Sabina set out clad in a fresh gown of green linen, her headdress crisply starched, her shoes immaculate—proof of Catell's growing skills. Unfortunately, before long, Jester spied a tempting fowl and set off after it, emitting excited barks. The barks soon changed to anguished yelps as the quarry turned and made a stand. The bird Jester was pursuing proved to be a battle-hardened gander, the lord protector of a gaggle of plump geese. The gander had no qualms about teaching this noisy intruder a sharp lesson. The ensuing fight was violent enough to rouse the entire parish.

Alarm that, for once, her pet was coming off worst, Sabina swiftly dismounted and entered the fray, ignoring the horrified protests of her grooms. By the time she emerged, dragging a battered and pitiful Jester, she was sadly dishevelled; her clean gown was streaked with blood, fur, and feathers, her shoes caked with mud and much else less mentionable.

"*Ma dame,* I'm so sorry! Your poor dog, *ma dame!*" The distraught owner of the bird was beside himself with anxiety lest her wrath should come down on him because his gander had attacked her dog.

Sabina looked at Jester, who was whimpering and pawing his rapidly swelling nose. Sending one of the watching children to soak her kerchief in a nearby well, she applied the wet cloth to the dog's injured snout.

"There is no real damage—except to his pride," she said in Breton. "For a long time I have tried to stop my dog chasing fowls. I think your gander has done me a service."

She delved into her purse and gave the delighted man a *sou*. Then she remounted her mare. Quite a crowd had gathered, drawn by the noise and the excitement; it took time for a path to be cleared for her. While she waited she noticed that a woman, also mounted on horseback, was regarding her with unconcealed interest. She was handsome, with dark almond-shaped eyes, and the hair visible beneath her veil was black. Sitting erect in the saddle, the full curves of her voluptuous figure showed to advantage beneath the rich silk of her gown.

Sabina wondered who the woman could be. For a moment they stared at each other across the heads of the peasants. Then the contemptuous way those almond eyes raked over her and the slight, derisive lift to the scarlet lips told her. This had to be Louise de Lannion! It could be no one else! Beneath that insolent gaze she suddenly became very conscious of her own dishevelled appearance, and automatically dabbed at a dark stain on her skirt. Immediately she grew angry, first that she had appeared at such a disadvantage before her husband's mistress, then at herself for caring about it.

Using every remaining vestige of dignity she urged her horse forward, acknowledging the smiles and waves of the people and ignoring the dark-haired beauty who still smiled scornfully in her direction.

There was no point in continuing the ride any further, so Sabina turned homewards. Those dark eyes haunted her every step of the way. But by the time she reached the château doubts had begun to creep into her mind—perhaps the unknown woman was not Louise de Lannion after all. She might merely have been a stranger passing through. The only way to find out for certain was to question the servants. At her first tentative enquiry Cudenec answered so forcefully, "Woman, *ma dame?* I can't say as I saw any woman!" that she disbelieved him on the spot.

Her questioning of the young undergroom was more subtle. "Jean," she remarked, "do you often encounter the de Lannion woman on the Brest road as we did today?"

Jean was less worldly-wise than Cudenec. He answered, "Sometimes, *dame*. I think she has kinsfolk in that direction."

Now she knew for certain! She took stock of the situation: Ronan's mistress was dark and beautiful—his first wife had been pale and beautiful—and she, his second wife, was... She decided it really did not matter what she was. The Seigneur had a living mistress whose bed he frequently occupied and a dead wife whose memory he adored. He did not need anyone else. Certainly not her!

The days were growing hotter and Sabina began to seek out cooler, more shaded places in which to spend the hot noonday hours. On the ramparts, she eventually found the perfect refuge, a small niche in the curtain-wall shaded by one of the turrets and high enough to catch the least breeze. This seclusion was just what she wanted, and she settled down. Behind her the château drowned in the hot sunshine, the stillness broken only by the screams of swallows as they dipped and swooped over the reedy moat. In front of her the countryside of Plou-Aven stretched out into a haze of heat. Taking up the exercises set for her by Père Martin, she began to study them.

The sound of someone singing broke through her thoughts. It was a familiar tune, a catchy little air, and soon she was humming it softly under her breath as she studied. Then she sat up, the Breton grammar forgotten. She knew that tune! It was one she had heard often at home. Who could be singing an English song here? Immediately she looked around for the singer.

"Hello…!" she called, in English. "Who is there…?"

The singing stopped.

"Hello…!" a man's voice answered. "Hello, mistress, we're up here!"

Shielding her eyes against the glare of sky she peered upwards to the top of the tower and saw four faces looking down at her.

"Who are you? And what are you doing up there?" she asked.

"We're taking the air, mistress," called one.

But a second man chided him, "This is no time for your jests, Ned… We're four Englishmen, mistress, held prisoner here."

"Held prisoner? But why—? How long—? Have you just arrived?"

"Just arrived, mistress? Nay!" the one called Ned replied bitterly. "We've been here over two and a half years. I can give you the exact number of years, months, weeks and days. I've had little else to do but calculate the passing time."

Sabina was appalled. "You've been here all this time and I didn't know! Oh, the raid on Saint-Mathieu! You were part of that?"

"You've got it first time, mistress," replied Ned. "Four of us locked up like linnets in a cage. There were five of us, but one has flown. You couldn't expect the gentry to stay here like us common herd. No, he went back to England with never a thought for us—though it was his foolishness which got us into this mess. But what does he care?"

"Guard your tongue, Ned!" admonished the second man. "Don't you know who you are talking to?"

Ned leaned over to scrutinise Sabina's upturned face. "You don't look like him, but I suppose you must be sister to that fool, Giles Corbyn, our beloved commander," he said.

This impertinence penetrated Sabina's bewilderment.

"I am Sabina Guennec, the Dame de Plou-Aven," she said haughtily. "And Giles Corbyn is indeed my brother."

Ned was not at all subdued by her tone. "I should have known. We heard that the Seigneur, God rot him, had wed a Devon lass. Well, you've got your brother's share of spirit by the sound of you."

"I apologise for my friend here, my lady," said the other man, who sounded older. "He means no disrespect."

"Yes, I do," replied Ned. "Where Giles Corbyn is concerned—but not you, lady. I like a wench with a bit of spark. If I've been saucy to you then I apologise."

Sabina was marshalling her thoughts with difficulty.

"My husband has kept you locked up all this time and never said a word to me about it," she said. "I wonder why?"

"Who can tell what goes on in the mind of a plaguey Breton?" answered Ned. "Now you've found out about us, though, maybe you'll see your way to helping us. We're good Devon lads, after all. We're of the same soil."

"Oh, yes!" cried Sabina without hesitation. "I will."

"I suppose we'd best introduce ourselves. I'm Edward Prettyjohn, otherwise Ned. Old sobersides here is Dick Hannaford. The lad is Jack Bowden, and the long-shanks on the end is Christopher Perrett."

"Known as Coughing Kit for obvious reasons, my lady." The fourth man spoke for the first time. As if determined to earn his nickname he burst into a paroxysm of coughing.

"There, now you know us all—" began Ned, when he was interrupted by the boy, Jack, saying something Sabina could not hear. After a moment he leaned back over the parapet and whispered urgently, "The guards are coming. Hide yourself. If they learn we've had contact with you they might not let us up here again."

Sabina responded automatically, pressing herself flat against the wall of the turret, praying that the overhang of the battlements would shield her from the view of anyone looking down. She heard voices, scuffling feet, then the dull thud of a trapdoor closing. Afterwards there was silence, but she did not move. She found she was shivering even though the wall against which she pressed had been warmed by the sun.

Englishmen here at Plou-Aven! And Ronan was keeping them locked up like wild animals! How could he be so cruel and unfeeling? And why had she not known of their presence sooner? Angry and distressed, Sabina wondered how she could bear to go on living with a man who was capable of behaving so.

She stayed in her secluded corner of the ramparts for a long time. She could hardly take in this newest discovery; she could almost have believed she had fallen asleep and dreamed it. But no, it was certainly not a dream!

Her first thought was to rush to the Seigneur and confront him with his inhumanity—her second thought counselled caution. Her interference at this stage might cause more harm than good. The decision, though wise, was not easy to maintain. Of one thing Sabina was certain, she had to talk to the Englishmen again. Not sure where they were being held, she decided to go back to the ramparts at the same time next day.

When she climbed up to the corner beside the tower for a second time it was so quiet that at first she was convinced no one was there. But at her call four heads appeared over the battlements.

"There, didn't I say she would come?" exclaimed Ned.

"Of course I came! I don't go back on my word!" Sabina was quite indignant.

"Put your claws in, lass!" he grinned. He turned to the others and said, "She's a regular little spitfire, isn't she?"

"And you're an impudent knave!" she retorted.

"So I am!" Ned was unrepentant.

"Take no notice, my lady. His tongue is ever a source of mischief," said Dick.

"How do you fare?" Sabina asked.

"Well enough, I thank you," Dick replied.

"You're easily satisfied, friend," Ned snapped. "What's well enough about being deprived of our liberty?"

"I don't like it any more than you do. But you must concede the Seigneur treats us well."

"Where are you lodged?" asked Sabina.

"Lodged! I like that! We're imprisoned in a stinking hole," declared Ned.

"We're in a chamber at the base of this tower," countered Dick. "It's dry and airy, and we're allowed a good fire in winter. The conditions here are better than we ever experienced aboard ship, and that's a fact!"

"The only difference is we were on board ship of our own free will—you can't say that of our stay here!"

"Is there nothing I can get you?" asked Sabina.

"Yes, there is, my lady." Kit spoke up. "A mug of real Devon cider, and the lass who serves in the pastrycook's on Plymouth Barbican—the plump dark one, mind, not the skinny one. I want something worth putting my arm around."

"Now there, see what your jesting has done!" admonished Dick, for Kit had begun to cough and it was some time before the spasm subsided.

"You need to take something for that. I'll send some syrup to you," said Sabina.

"Best not—my lady—thanks all the same—" Kit replied breathlessly. "It might cause trouble—for you and for us—"

"The lad's right," agreed Dick. "Better leave things as they are for the time being, my lady."

"But surely I can do something for you!" she exclaimed.

"Aye, let us hear your voice and see your friendly face whenever we can. That's the best help you can give us." Ned grinned down at her. He was blunt and outspoken to the point of impertinence, but she could not help liking him.

"Is there no hope of your going home?" she asked.

"There was talk of an exchange, back in the early days. But we've heard no more about it," said Dick.

"Surely, my brother…"

"Oh, him!" Ned's tone told exactly what he thought of Giles. "He's a deal better getting people into a scrape than getting them out."

"What happened? Did you have bad luck?" asked Sabina, though she suspected she knew the true reply.

"We fell in with Giles Corbyn. How much more bad luck did we need?" grumbled Ned.

For once Dick did not try to contradict his friend. "Your brother's plan sounded well enough, my lady. We were to anchor to the north of Saint-Mathieu's Point, and cut across the land to take the folks of Brest from the rear by surprise. We were told it was open moorland most of the way, with nothing to hinder us."

"Aye, can you imagine such stupidity?" broke in Ned. "Nothing but a few castles, fully manned and armed! Your precious brother neglected to discover the true lie of the land. We walked straight into the arms of your husband!"

"A good thing we did," said Dick. "Most of our band fell into the hands of the Breton peasants and some were killed."

"I knew nothing of this!" Sabina declared, appalled and ashamed at her brother's lack of forethought.

"Don't sound so downcast." Ned's voice was cheerful again. "It's not your fault. You didn't choose that gangling fool as your brother."

"Indeed—" she began. But another fit of coughing from Kit cut across her words. "I wish you'd let me help that poor fellow," she cried. "I could send him a draught of something to give him ease."

"Best not, my lady," said Dick, his face full of anxiety.

Even Kit, too out of breath to speak, waved a protesting hand.

It was time for her to leave. "I'll be back tomorrow," she promised.

"See you do, else I'll be disappointed!" exclaimed Ned.

To her relief no one had missed her during the last hour. Of the Seigneur there was no sign.

"He's down at the stables tending to his deerhound bitch, *ma dame,*" Catell grinned. "You'd think a dog had never had pups before! Most of the women in the parish give birth with half the fuss. You've never seen anything like it!''

"Nor am I likely to—I haven't time to go down to the stables and watch the spectacle," smiled Sabina, considering Ronan's preoccupation with his deerhound to be a blessing if she was to help the prisoners.

It was Kit she was worried about. Her ears told her he was far beyond the simpler remedies, so she spent the afternoon preparing a stronger concoction of lungwort in case it should be needed. The occasion came more quickly than she had anticipated. Next day when she reached the ramparts only two heads responded to her call.

"Where are Kit and Dick?" she asked.

"Down below," Ned informed her, his voice grave. "Young Kit's been laid low with fever. He's been coughing all night and not got any rest. Dick's staying with him."

"And you wouldn't let me help! Well, this non-sense has gone far enough. I'm going to the Seigneur at once and make him let me care for Kit properly!" So saying, she ran down the stairs.

Striding towards the chamber used by Ronan for estate matters, she flung open the door.

Ronan looked up at her from a desk strewn with documents. The day was hot and his hair lay in damp dark strands across his forehead. He looked tired and his eyes held their old bleak expression once more. Sabina made up her mind not to let his air of melancholy weaken her resolve.

"Good day, *dame*," he said. "And of what atrocity do you intend to accuse me today?"

She was taken aback by his greeting. "How did

you know I was about to accuse you of anything?'' she asked.

"Every time you have looked at me these last few days your expression has been so full of disgust and censure I would have been blind not to notice.''

Sabina had not realised how much her face had betrayed her emotions. "I never meant—'' she began in a rush of remorse. "I don't think so badly of you...'' Then she recollected herself. "Oh, yes, I do!'' she declared.

"Have you a specific accusation or is this merely a general annihilation of my character?'' The Seigneur sounded bored.

"You are keeping four Englishmen incarcerated in one of your dungeons. Is that specific enough for you?''

"It will do. Inaccurate, but certainly specific!''

"It is accurate! I've spoke to the men myself!''

"Oh, and where were these fellow countrymen of yours?''

"Why, up on the battlements of the north tower.''

"Hm... Our builder must have been a man of original ideas, constructing dungeons on the tops of towers! I can't understand why the fashion never caught on.''

"It may please you to make a jest of it, but I am serious. You are holding those men against their will in a most inhumane manner, and I would know why.''

"Holding men against their will is a far cry from being inhumane. By your own admission you are aware that they are allowed into the fresh air. They are well housed and they are given good food. What do they lack?''

"Their liberty!"

"You think I should let them roam about Plou-Aven?"

"I think you should send them home to England."

"But they came here of their own free will. I do not remember inviting them."

"You know why they came!" cried Sabina angrily.

"And I know why they will remain! Until four of my men imprisoned in Plymouth are returned to Brittany. Good, honest men who, at the last report I had, were being kept in appalling conditions. No basking in the sun for them, no comfortable quarters, no three meals a day! When those men set foot on Breton soil again then I'll return your Devon men, but not one minute before!"

"You still have men in Plymouth? I didn't know… But why have you not made any exchange— you've had long enough. What is the problem?"

"The problem, *ma dame,* lies in the Englishmen I entrusted with the arrangements… A greater pair of selfish numbskulls I have never come across!"

"But if it means those poor men being released, then I'm sure my father would help, if you will only write to him…" Sabina's words faded as she caught the Seigneur's expression. "You have applied to him, sire?"

"Innumerable times. Ever since the four Englishmen and your brother fell into my hands. With my every demand for a ransom! It is my regret that my contacts in Devon are restricted entirely to the Corbyn family."

"You can be assured there is a good reason for the delay!" Sabina blazed.

"If you can think of one I'd be glad to hear it. I set out my wishes clearly and concisely more than once. You knew nothing of this?"

She shook her head. She well remembered the arrival of the ransom demanded for Giles and the uproar it caused, and the letters which followed, but she had no recollection of any mention of other prisoners.

"You appealed to Giles also?" she asked.

"Yes." The Seigneur sounded sour. "Knowing him as I do, I had little hope of a response. I was not disappointed."

It was no use; there was no way of avoiding the truth; her father and brother had completely ignored the plight of their own men and proved themselves quite indifferent to their fate.

With annoyance Sabina acknowledged that her family's indifference had shown Ronan in a very favourable light.

"You once claimed that whenever you felt justifiably angry somehow I always made you feel full of remorse. Now you're doing exactly the same thing to me," she protested.

"I'm tempted to say that it demonstrates how well-matched we are, but I fancy such an observation would be unwelcome to both of us!"

"Why did you never tell me about your prisoners?" she demanded, switching to the attack.

"You ask me that?" Ronan's dark eyebrows rose in surprise. "It's not an easy topic to raise in polite conversation: 'Good morrow, *dame.* I hope you slept well. By the by, I have four Englishmen locked in the north tower'. I can honestly say a convenient opportunity to enlighten you never presented itself. I'm only astonished you took so long to discover them yourself.''

"Now that I have discovered those poor souls I am not going to leave them to rot," she declared. "I will spend all my energies to make you send them home."

"Not without the return of my men in exchange!"

"Is that your final word...? Then be prepared! I'll make your life a misery until you change your mind!"

"You do that already! And very skilled you are at it!"

Sabina jumped to her feet and made for the door.

"Where are you going, *dame?*" he bellowed.

"To see the prisoners."

"No, you are not! I refuse to give you permission!"

"I don't need permission. You tell me so often enough!"

"And I am telling you now that you are not to go near those men! I forbid it!"

They had been yelling at the tops of their voices, their quarrel reaching the ears of just about every occupant of the château. Now, Sabina suddenly lowered her tone. "One of the prisoners is sick with lung fever, and no one is going to stop me tending to him."

She left the room closing the door behind her.

At once it was flung open.

"*Dame!*" roared the Seigneur, his voice setting the dogs barking and sending the château pigeons whirling skyward. "You are not to go alone! You must have a chaperon, do you hear? Take Père Martin and Catell!"

Surprised at his acquiescence, Sabina replied obediently, "Of course, sire."

The guards led her into a sizeable room, stone-walled but far from being a miserable dungeon. Ned stepped forward to greet her. She was not prepared for his great height, nor for the burnished red cast to his sandy hair.

"We knew you were coming," he grinned. "What an upheaval! We've never got ourselves tidy so fast in our lives. Look! Clean fingernails and no dirt behind our ears!" He first held out a hand, then presented an ear for inspection.

"There's room for improvement round the back of your neck," she told him with mock severity.

"Some say the only improvement to my neck would be a rope with a noose," he grinned.

"It can be arranged," she replied.

"That's telling him, my lady," chuckled Dick. He was shorter than Ned, with greying hair. His kindly face grew serious. "It's good of you to come. I confess I'm sorely troubled about Kit."

They moved to where the young man lay on a narrow truckle-bed. Sabina knelt beside him, listening to the harsh rasp of his breathing, her fingers already smoothing back the damp hair on his brow. She was pleased to note how clean and comfortable his bed was, with a thick, straw mattress and plenty of covers. There was even a fire burning in the hearth.

"Lit at the Seigneur's orders," Dick informed her, noticing the direction of her gaze. "Directly he heard how sick Kit was."

Sabina said nothing. Some of the harsher words

she had spoken to her husband recently she now wished unsaid.

"I've something here to ease the congestion of his lungs and bring down the fever," she said softly.

Pouring a strong draught into a beaker, she held it to his lips.

"With luck he should find his chest easier soon," she informed the others. "Give him another dose when the bell goes for Vespers, and another when it grows dark. Apart from that, he needs plenty to drink and be kept warm. I'll come back this evening. If he grows worse send for me at once."

"You aren't leaving us already, are you?" asked Ned, as she gestured to Catell to gather up the basket.

"I came to tend Kit, and, that accomplished, I must leave." Sabina was rather taken aback by the frank admiration of his gaze.

"Aye, don't be so forward, Ned, lad," said Dick reprovingly. "The lady has better things to do than talk to us."

"What better things than conversing in her native tongue for once? And not having to bother with all this French nonsense? What sort of language is that, I ask you?" Ned grinned, still unabashed.

"It is the language of my adopted country." Sabina tried to sound reproving too, but it was a hard task.

"That's no reason why you can't give your tongue a holiday. Or perhaps you're afraid you might speak too freely and tales will get back to certain quarters." Ned looked significantly towards Père Martin who was sitting in a corner, quietly dozing.

"The good father neither speaks nor understands English, nor does Catell." Sabina spoke haughtily.

"Besides, if I have aught on my mind I say it openly and frankly to my husband!"

"I'll wager you do!" cried Ned in delight.

"There is no setting you down, is there?" observed Sabina.

"Not at all, my pretty," agreed Ned, his eyes sparkling. "And you wouldn't like it if there were! Don't deny it! You enjoy a battle of words—English words!"

She was about to protest, bu then she held back. It was good to hear the familiar Devon accent again, and to speak it. She gave a wry smile. "Very well, I won't deny it. You're a persuasive man, Ned Prettyjohn, with an eye for other people's weaknesses. Take care; such a talent could get you hanged."

"You're not the first to give such a warning," Ned smiled. "But you aren't leaving are you? I haven't frightened you away?" for Sabina was making for the door.

"You'd need to be a bigger man to frighten me," she grinned. "Nevertheless, I *do* have other duties to attend to."

"You'll be back soon, though, won't you?" said Ned.

"Of course I'll be back..." Sabina paused significantly "...to see how Kit fares!"

Chapter Seven

Sabina left the prisoners, conscious that she had an uncomfortable duty to perform. She sought out the Seigneur.

"I have been to see the English prisoners, sire," she said. "No doubt Père Martin has already informed you of the fact."

"I do not question the chaplain about you!" Ronan snapped. "Nor do I intend to!"

"You would find out precious little if you did. There is naught to report. But I have not come to quarrel. I have come to beg your pardon."

"This is a novelty! What have you done?"

"I have been unfair and misjudged you."

"Now that is *not* a novelty!"

"Do you want to hear my apology or not?" demanded Sabina.

"Apologise away…" He waved a casual hand.

"I accused you of keeping those men in appalling conditions, and I find it is not so. You have been most Christian in your treatment of them, particularly Kit Perrett, the one who is sick… I humbly beg your pardon."

"I am relieved that you no longer consider me a barbarian." He seemed pleased at her apology.

"It is only fair to take back my unjust words."

"And I thank you for it."

They faced each other across the table, neither knowing what to say next.

Ronan broke the silence. "And how did you find the sick man?"

"Very feverish and grievously ill, though I did what I could."

"Is there aught else he needs?"

"Only to return home."

Ronan's mouth tightened. "Ah, I see where this is leading. To yet another appeal for the release of your fellow countrymen. I wondered what was amiss when I heard amiable words from your lips. Well, I fear your efforts are wasted, *ma dame*. The men stay!"

"Such a thought never entered my mind. I wanted only to make amends for words that were rashly spoken. But since you mention the subject I will make a plea for their release."

"No."

"You dismiss me so curtly? You refuse to send them home? I don't understand you. You are determined to keep them prisoner, yet you treat them well. They are better lodged than they would be at home!"

"You should be able to read my character by now, *ma dame*. I intend to get my own men returned from Plymouth. Until then the Englishmen remain here!"

"I understand now!" Sabina gave a contemptuous sniff. "What I took to be Christian concern was merely prudence. You tend your prisoners well because you want to keep them alive. There would be no exchanging a live Breton for a dead Englishman, would there? I should have realised!''

''Put what interpretation you please on my actions,'' said the Seigneur. ''And now, if you have no other matter to bring to my attention…?''

Sabina strode away from her husband fuming with anger, at the same time regretful. Her attempt at an apology had been genuine, yet she and Ronan had finished up quarrelling again. How, she was not quite sure… Yes, she was! Her uncertainty disappeared as the reason for the quarrel suddenly became apparent: it was because she was married to a heartless, pigheaded, obstinate brute of a man, that was why! The only way to avoid falling out with such a monster was to keep out of his way!

It was a good resolution; for a time Sabina managed to achieve it with remarkable success; during the day he was often absent. Pleased as she was, she found the reason mystifying. It was Catell who provided the solution.

''There goes the Seigneur again,'' she observed, looking through the solar window. ''Did you ever see a man so anxious?''

''Why, where is he going?'' asked Sabina.

''To the stables, *ma dame*. It's that bitch of his; she's overdue.''

''Overdue?'' Sabina's brow wrinkled in perplexity. ''Oh, the puppies! Hasn't Juno whelped yet?''

''Not the last I heard. Still, it's her first litter. Though if these pups don't arrive soon the Seigneur will go into a decline, you mark my words!'' Catell chuckled to herself, her head bent over the seam she was sewing.

Sabina threaded her needle, trying not to feel relieved. The uncomfortable thought that perhaps he had been spending his time at Ty Lannion had troubled her like a bothersome itch. Instead, he had been in the stables fussing over a pregnant hound. She began to hum to herself as she stitched.

Her song was interrupted by the door crashing open. The Seigneur entered, his face white with fury. *"Dame—! Dame—!"* he spluttered. He was too angry to utter any comprehensible words. Seizing an alarmed Sabina by the wrist, he set off down the stairs, pulling her after him.

"Have you gone mad? What has befallen you?" she demanded.

An equally alarmed Catell followed at a discreet distance, pausing only to seize the iron poker from the hearth lest she should be forced to defend her mistress from the madness which had suddenly beset the Seigneur.

Jester went, too, determined to take part in this new game.

Across the inner bailey went the strange procession, down the stone steps and thence to the stables.

"There!" exclaimed Ronan in a voice which shook with emotion. "There! Look!" Taking Sabina by the shoulders he hustled her forward to a far corner. She did look. Behind her Catell took an anxious peep, choked back a snigger and beat a hasty retreat.

Nestled in the straw was Juno, the Seigneur's well-bred deerhound, his pride and joy. Contentedly she licked at her litter of new-born pups, six of them, as strong and healthy as anyone could wish. Sabina drew in a deep breath, but not being able to think of anything to say she let it out again. The puppies, immature as they were and still damp from their birth, bore the unmistakable stamp of their father. They did not seem to have inherited a single trait from their gentle, aristocratic mother. It was not just the harlequin multi-colouring of their meagre coats—the ears were set low on each small skull, and their tails, scant and bedraggled, were disproportionately long for their bodies.

Jester pushed forward to regard his new family with bemused satisfaction. He allowed his own over-long tail a few self-congratulatory sweeps, then celebrated fatherhood by scratching at an importunate flea.

"Oh…" said Sabina.

"You might well say 'Oh', *dame!* You might *well* say 'Oh'! How did it happen, I say? That's what I want to know!" The Seigneur was recovering his power of speech with increasing fluency.

"You want me to explain to you how to get a bitch in whelp? A man of your years!" asked Sabina, feigning astonishment as the only defence she could think of.

"I know how bitches get into whelp! So does that flea-ridden, scurvy cur of yours! To his misfortune and that of his ill-bred brood! He's got to go! They've all got to go! Cudence will drown them, every one! No—better still—I'll do it myself! It will give me great satisfaction!"

"You'll do no such thing!" cried Sabina, thrusting herself between her husband and the dogs. "I won't let you!"

"I've suffered that mangy beast of yours long enough. He's been naught but trouble since you took him on!"

Ronan made to dodge round and grasp Jester's collar but Sabina was too quick for him. "You'll not touch him!" she declared, pushing away his outstretched arm. "Nor will you harm those puppies. They've done you no hurt!"

"No hurt?" Ronan was almost beside himself with fury. "They've only made me a laughing-stock. The Plou-Aven strain of hounds was once the source of much admiration in the land; now it will be the butt of jokes in every *auberge* and wine-shop from here to Brest!"

"Oh, so it's your pride that's dented!" she cried, scornfully dismissing such a minor consideration. "What reason is that to slaughter innocent beasts?"

"I know you think naught of Plou-Aven, *dame,* but it means a deal to me. I'll destroy anyone or anything bringing dishonour to its name."

"Dishonour!" yelled Sabina. "We're talking about dogs, not your flesh and blood!"

"Dogs! Kinsfolk! I don't care who or what! I'll not be the target of cheap jibes and sneers!"

"Your family honour must be a fragile thing, sire, if it can be so easily ruined."

"At least, I do *have* a family honour, *dame.* I agree, it must be a hard notion for you to understand, being reared alongside that fool of a brother of yours."

"My brother may be stupid but he has enough sense not to fear humiliation because the wrong dog got at his bitch. That is the nub of the matter, isn't it? That's what is gnawing at you like a rat in a wainscot!"

"What is?" asked the Seigneur, suddenly bewildered.

"Why, the fact that your dog, your beloved

Apollo, didn't measure up. He was too slow. He was beaten by a better dog.''

"A better dog? Your miserable, scabby cur?"

"Of course he is! And Juno clearly thinks so. She certainly preferred him to that hair-covered thing of yours. She's a creature of sense."

"Ha! You think you've got Juno on your side now!" The Seigneur's voice was heavy with sarcasm. "Pray, would you be good enough to explain how your misbegotten wretch, who was spawned goodness knows where by goodness knows what, can be better than my Apollo, who can trace his ancestry back through twelve generations to a hound in the kennels of Duke Arthur himself?"

"Easily!" Sabina was triumphant. "He's more spirited, for one thing. He wooed and won Juno while Apollo was still wondering what to do. And more discerning—for Juno is undoubtedly the best, most handsome bitch in the whole château. And virile—did you ever see healthier pups? And ingenious—Juno is much taller than he, it can't have been easy for him to—Seigneur, stop laughing at me! Seigneur, you are not to laugh!"

Ronan had given a sudden convulsive splutter which turned into full-blown, deep-throated laughter, his head thrown back, his dark eyes bright with merriment. Something about the way in which he stood there infuriated her. "Stop it! Stop it! It's no laughing matter!" she protested, overcome by an uncontrollable fury. His laugher did not abate so she began pummelling at his chest, until he was forced to grasp her arms and hold her hard against him to save himself from further punishment.

"Sire…!" She began to object to such unexpected

contact, but she was prevented from saying more, for he tightened his hold, his arms encompassing her completely. Even as she became conscious of his heart beating against her breast he bent his head and claimed her mouth with his. It was no formal kiss, nor was it the customary cold gesture with which he usually saluted her. This embrace was hard and demanding, filled with the raw energy of a man's passionate needs. Helpless and pinioned as she was, Sabina could neither struggle nor protest. Nor did she wish to! How many long weeks had it been since she had felt his body craving against hers—four, five? She could not remember. Until that moment she had not been aware of how much she had missed him. The pressure of his form against hers brought an immediate and startling response. She could not help herself; her answer to his urgency was one of hunger. Her mouth sought his lips, tasting the sweetness of him, revelling in the fragrance of his sun-warmed flesh. Her fingers, crushed as they were against his chest, entwined themselves in the soft wool of his tunic in her efforts to draw him even closer and be a part of him.

He released her with shattering abruptness, pushing her away until he held her at arm's length. For a long moment he gazed at her, his face white and set. Deliberately he took a slow, deep breath, as if he were making a conscious effort to control his emotions. Then, just as slowly and deliberately, he loosed his grip on her.

"Your pardon, *dame*. How else could I stop you from hitting me?" he said. There was no laughter in his voice now, only a restrained chill. Without another word he walked out of the stable.

The pressure of his fingers lingered on her arms. Her mouth felt hot and bruised from the intensity of his kisses. But he had meant nothing by them! They had been an extension of their quarrel, nothing more! Yet the wrenching pain that ripped its way through her told a very different story. Her reaction to him had been an instinctive appeal for love—and it had been rejected.

Sabina wrapped her arms about herself protectively to hold in her hurt; she would not give way to the anguish that seemed to have taken over her whole being. Then she saw the dogs, Jester, Juno, and the puppies curled up together in the straw, an indistinguishable mass of furry bodies. They were sleeping soundly. Their instincts had told them that the Seigneur was no threat to them and never had been. She cursed herself for not realising it too. The quarrel and its emotional aftermath had been unnecessary!

Ronan referred to the incident only once. "The pups can remain, *ma dame*," he had said. "And that brute of yours. But if he gets at my bitch again I'll despatch him with my own hands."

And that was all. No mention of what had happened afterwards. It was as if he had never held her in his arms and never kissed her. But he wanted me, I know he did, she told herself... She gave a bitter laugh. No, he didn't want her—he just wanted a woman—any woman!

"Then why didn't he go to that trollop of his instead of troubling me so?" she cried aloud. But she knew it was the last thing she really wanted to happen.

Sabina's visits to the north tower now became a daily event. She told herself her concern was purely for Kit, who continued to make steady progress. Only in her franker moments did she admit she was beginning to regard the north tower as a refuge. All four men inevitably greeted her warmly, and she found it so pleasant to sit with them talking in English and exchanging recollections of home. Also, there was Ned. She had never met anyone like him before. He was bursting with ideas, often revolutionary, always controversial, but never dull. His talk appealed to her lively mind.

The Seigneur made no mention of her regular visits to his prisoners, but Catell was less reticent.

"You've no need to go there so often, *ma dame*," she protested one day.

Sabina eyed her haughtily. "You have some objection?"

"I'd not be so impertinent, *ma dame!* It's only that you are driving yourself too hard. What with the folk of the parish, and the Englishmen, as well as the household to attend to, you are growing quite pale and wan. When did you last get out in the fresh air for any time? Your poor mare must think you've deserted her. You'll help no one by making yourself ill."

Sabina's reproof died on her lips. Catell was right, it had been some time since she had had any leisure. The notion of going riding was suddenly very attractive.

"Very well, as soon as we have called on the prisoners I will go," she said. "And since you make such a thing of it you can join in the exercise too."

Only when she was in the saddle did Sabina acknowledge how much she had missed her regular rides. She revelled in the baking sunshine, causing

Catell to grumble disapprovingly lest she got her face suntanned. Much as Sabina enjoyed the heat, even she grew too warm eventually and longed for some shade. They found it in an oak wood, where a spring reputed to have been found by the magician, Merlin, bubbled into a natural granite basin. They were not the only people to slake their thirsts there.

"Oh, it's only Yannick!" said Catell with relief. "For a moment I thought it was Merlin himself."

"If it had been Merlin I'd have asked him to turn this lot into something a bit stronger," muttered Cudenec, taking a draught of the springwater.

"I'm pleased to see Yannick, anyway," smiled Sabina.

Yannick was showing the benefits of regular food. Although he was neither cleaner nor tidier, he had put on weight and looked much less gaunt.

As they resumed their ride he began to run alongside at Sabina's stirrup. The track wound through gnarled oak trees and great granite boulders clad in thick velvety moss. In no hurry, the little group made their way leisurely, enjoying the green shade.

Suddenly Yannick put out a dirty hand and grasped the mare's bridle, bringing the party to an abrupt halt.

"What is the matter?" asked Sabina.

"Most likely starting at his own shadow..." grumbled Cudenec.

"No, someone's coming," broke in the sharp-eared Catell. "I can hear horses' hoofs."

"By the holy saints, you're right!" said Cudenec. "Best let me move ahead of you, *dame*. There's no knowing who's abroad these days."

Hardly had he begun to edge his way forward than

the party of oncoming travellers came into view. It consisted of only one lady attended by some half a dozen servants. Sabina's sigh of relief was superseded almost immediately by a snort of annoyance. Louise de Lannion was the last individual she wished to encounter!

Recognition was mutual!

Louise de Lannion rode forward until their two horses were almost nose to nose.

"I think I have the honour of addressing the Dame de Plou-Aven, have I not?" she said.

"You have," replied Sabina coldly.

"I thought I was right. The splendour of your entourage is a byword in the land." Her insolent dark eyes swept over Sabina's companions, coming to rest mockingly on Yannick's dirty, dishevelled figure.

Curving her lips into a smile she was far from feeling Sabina said, "I think you jest. As you see, I prefer to choose my attendants for their character and loyalty sooner than their appearance. After all, any hoyden can trick her people out in fancy livery and call herself a lady, can't she?" Slowly and deliberately she let her gaze linger over the uniform blue and red garments of the other woman's servants. From somewhere behind her she heard Cudenec smother a snigger.

Louise de Lannion's eyes narrowed. "Pray allow me to introduce myself, *dame*," she said. "I am Louise de Lannion, a close neighbour of yours."

"Why you should think I wish to be introduced to you I can't imagine," Sabina said evenly. "Perhaps you will be kind enough to stand aside."

The bright colour faded from Louise's face and

Sabina noted with much satisfaction that the other woman was older than she had seemed at first glance.

"You speak our language well, *dame*. Everyone was so surprised when the Seigneur went among the English to choose a bride." She made it sound as though Sabina had come from a midden.

"I do not know why they should be," Sabina said. "If there was no one of gentle birth in Plou-Aven then, of course, he needed to look further abroad."

"Our surprise was because he married again. It must be very difficult for you, being the second wife in a situation like that!"

Sabina suppressed her mounting fury. "You're wasting your sympathy, *demoiselle*, you truly are. Surely a man who has had one happy marriage is much more likely to be a good husband a second time. He has proven how fit he is for wedded life. Not all men are, you know. Some are quite content with hunting and hawking with their drinking friends. And for their carnal needs—well, there is never a shortage of strumpets, is there?"

Louise's eyes glittered with anger. "No one can wonder at the Seigneur going across the channel for a bride of such beauty as you, *ma dame*. Just fancy, all the gossips claimed the Seigneur had been fobbed off with a plain, drab little thing."

Sabina was surprised at the cheeriness in her own laugh. "Anyone who believes the Seigneur could be so easily fooled must have a very low opinion of him. I hold him in much greater esteem than that."

"The whole countryside has heard the story."

"I had not heard it, for one. I'm surprised at you listening to such tattlers. They do nothing but spread mischief. Why, do you know what those gossipmongers say about you? That you are a shabby whore who will lie with any man for the price of a glass of wine. Did you ever hear the like?''

Still smiling Sabina leaned forward and snapped her fingers under the nose of the other woman's horse. The startled beast bucked with alarm, forcing Louise to have to struggle with both her animal and her fury. Taking advantage of the confusion, Sabina urged her horse forward swiftly, causing the blue- and red-clad servants to leap out of the way.

After she had galloped on a while she stopped and turned to see if anyone was following her. All she saw were Cudenec and Catell coming after her at a leisurely pace, both their faces crimson with laughter.

''I wouldn't have missed that for a king's ransom,'' wheezed the groom, gasping for breath.

''I'm glad to hear it, for no one is going to give you a fortune anyway,'' snapped Sabina.

Now that the conflict was over she was beginning to feel shaky. She should not have allowed herself to cross swords with her husband's mistress. Where was her dignity, her pride? She had handled the situation badly.

''Understand me, the pair of you,'' she addressed her servants. ''If you breathe a word of this to a soul I'll have you locked up so long you will never see the light of day again, do you understand?''

''Yes, *ma dame*,'' they answered in unison. Then they both went off into fits of laughter again.

Sabina felt uneasy in case Ronan heard of the encounter, for she sensed he would not be pleased. She was right. He was furious.

''What's this I hear of you, *dame?*'' he demanded the next day. ''The story's all over the countryside.''

"To which story do you refer, Seigneur?" she asked, although she knew perfectly well.

"Is there more than one? Have you been making a habit of brawling in public, dragging my good name down with your behaviour?"

"Poor Seigneur! First it was your cherished deerhound bitch, now it is your wife! The reputation of *la famille Guennec* is certainly suffering."

"Don't make a jest of it! This is serious!"

"I'm not jesting!" cried Sabina. "I'm trying not to quarrel. I'm tired of the constant arguing and bickering that goes on between us. Why can we never talk calmly and reasonably about anything?"

"If you expect me to be calm and reasonable about your behaviour then you expect too much. I allow you considerable licence and this is my reward!"

"Licence? Me? When it was your mistress who was the cause of all the trouble?"

They glowered at one another.

"I notice you do not deny that the de Lannion woman is your mistress," Sabina said more quietly.

"There is no need for me to admit or deny any such thing," said Ronan haughtily. "The fact of the matter is that you, the Dame de Plou-Aven, behaved in an outrageous manner."

"And what did you expect me to do? Sit there meekly and let your trollop heap scorn on me? I suggest you teach her better manners before you begin criticising my behaviour."

"Louise de Lannion's manners are immaterial, your conduct is not! You are my wife, while she is— is unimportant."

"Ha!" snorted Sabina.

"Is that all you propose to say on the matter?"

"No. I am truly sorry. I'm not proud of what happened, but what else could I do? She confronted me."

"I understand you behaved like a fishwife."

"Well, that proves who spread the story, doesn't it? She came off worst and now seeks to play the poor injured maiden. Maiden, my foot! Not only are her morals straight from the gutter, she lacks sense too. And she's not as young as she pretends. You make such a fuss about your family name yet you associate with a silly, ageing whore! You should have more sense!"

"I'll not be spoken to in such a way!" shouted the Seigneur. "Guard your tongue, *dame!* I know what you're about! Playing your usual game—trying to put me in the wrong when the fault is with you! I won't have it, do you hear?"

"Yes, and so does half the parish! I have apologised. I shall do my best never to behave in such a fashion again."

"I have had experience of your best. It's not good enough!"

"You expect too much... No wife would allow herself to be insulted by her husband's mistress. I am entitled to pride and self-respect too, you know."

"Nonsense!"

"Sire, what if I took a lover?"

"What!" Ronan forgot his temper in a yelp of astonishment.

"Why should you be so incredulous?" asked Sabina indignantly. "Plainer women than me have had their paramours!"

"If you say so... Very well, carry on with our argument. It grows more amusing by the minute."

"I ask only for an honest answer. What would you do if I took a lover?"

"I'd kill him."

"Why?"

"Because I'd not allow anyone to besmirch my honour, nor cause me to be an object of ridicule. No man would do that and live!"

"Yet my honour and pride count for nothing. Why should you be ridiculed simply because your wife lies with another man?"

"I'll answer your question if only to gain respite from your clacking tongue—do you imagine I would tolerate having my manhood doubted? That I would let the world think I gave my wife so little satisfaction that she had to turn to someone else?"

"My point exactly! The whole parish knows you have a mistress. Do you imagine I enjoy having the humiliation of knowing everyone thinks it's because I can neither satisfy nor pleasure you?"

"But it is true! You cannot!"

At Ronan's words a silence fell between them—a sudden, profound silence.

At last Sabina found her voice. "I know I do not please you, sire," she said, speaking very quietly and evenly. "I ask only for you to be discreet so as not to shame me before the world, and not to ask for a greater forbearance from me than I am able to give."

Without waiting for a reply she walked from the room, a restrained dignity in every line of her slight, erect figure. She did not see the stricken look of remorse on Ronan's face. Her only wish was to get away from the world to a place where she could be alone with her misery.

"*Ma dame,* where are you going?" asked a puzzled Catell, as Sabina left the château on foot. Then she saw the expression on her mistress's face and asked no more questions.

Sabina was unaware of the maid's presence at a discreet distance. She walked away from the château and Ronan, her feet taking her instinctively towards the woods and a refuge in which to weep out her unhappiness undisturbed. She had never expected mere words to hurt so, just as she had never expected Ronan's harsh rejection of her to be so devastating. The anguish she was feeling forced her to face the painful truth. She did want to please him, yet she never would, and no amount of tears would change things.

The gathering dusk made Catell uneasy. While the sun had shone she waited for her mistress without complaint, but she had no wish to face the nameless terrors of the woods at night.

"*Dame,* let's be getting back, eh?" she asked.

Sabina did not seem to hear her.

"You don't want to be caught here after dark, *ma dame,*" she persisted.

There was real fear in her voice, so Sabina said, "You do not have to remain. Go back to the château."

"Without you, *dame?* Oh, no, I'll stay." Despite her terror the maid was determined not to desert her.

Sabina rubbed her sleeve across her wet eyes and stood up. She knew when she was beaten. She would not prolong the torment of her loyal little servant.

"We will go back," she said.

There was no sign of Ronan at the château. Sabina was glad. She felt that there was nothing left for them to say to each other—at least, nothing which would give her comfort.

Later, he came into the bedchamber while she was there.

"Good evening, *dame*. Have you been out taking the air?" he asked, with a forced cheerfulness.

"I have, sire," she replied.

There followed one of the awkward silences which seemed to punctuate their conversations so frequently.

"What I have to say will not wait—I promise I'll be brief." Ronan spoke hesitantly, as if choosing each word with care. "Earlier—when we quarrelled—I spoke to you roughly. Far more roughly than you deserved."

Sabina concentrated hard upon undoing her long dark braids. "You spoke the truth. There is no more to be said," she replied, not meeting his eyes.

"Your pardon, but there is—on my part at least. I spoke in anger and when I'm angry I often say things I do not mean. Surely you know that by now!"

"It's a fault we both share." Sabina kept her head turned away from him.

"As soon as I said those words I regretted them—the moment I saw the hurt in your eyes. I am sorry to have caused you distress. Pray do not think I am dissatisfied with you as a wife. You play your part as the Dame de Plou-Aven well—nay, exceptionally well for someone so young. You are still a mere girl; I tend to forget that... The people have grown to respect and love you to a remarkable degree. Usually they are reserved and suspicious with newcomers, yet they have taken you to their hearts within a few short months. They had been sorely neglected before you came...I blame myself...''

"You had no one to help you, sire. You could not do everything alone.''

"That is not true. I had a w——'' He stopped abruptly. "More in your favour is the way in which you control the household.''

"Most of that is Le Godet's doing.''

"It is Le Godet of whom I speak. Oh, he is efficient and an excellent seneschal, but I am well aware of his overbearing manner.''

"I confess I had difficulty with him at first, but all is well now.''

"Now that he knows he's not the only one who can speak Breton, eh? Don't look so astonished. Père Martin is well pleased with you.''

Sabina swung round on her stool to face him, her hairbrush still in her hand. "I had not thought the chaplain to be so untrustworthy,'' she retorted.

"Don't be too hard on the good father. His only thought in betraying your secret was to praise you and please me. And it did please me exceedingly. Marianne never thought to learn Breton...nor ever would have, had she lived. As a consequence she was ever complaining about Le Godet. I think she was afraid of him. Yet you have never shown such signs.''

Sabina was surprised. It was the first time he had ever uttered the least word of criticism of Marianne.

"I do not frighten easily, sire,'' she said.

"No, you don't, else I fear you would find my stupid rages alarming.''

"But you aren't at all frightening," said Sabina before she could stop herself. "In fact…"

"In fact, what?"

"In fact, I believe your rages are to hide just how unterrifying you really are," she retorted with something of her customary spirit.

"I suspected that was the case." A brief grin flickered across his face, then faded. "It makes me all the more ashamed that since I could not frighten you I used my anger to hurt you instead."

"It wasn't done deliberately."

"Maybe not, but it remains a despicable thing to have done. Sabina, I beg your forgiveness."

He had used her Christian name! Not since their wedding ceremony had she heard it from his lips! He had spoken soft words to her, too, praising her efforts, her skills, her persistence. Yet not once had he mentioned love…

He moved towards her, taking her arms and raising her to her feet. Fearing her love was marked too blatantly on her face, she backed away.

"No, do not try to escape me." Very gently he pulled her nearer until she was held against his chest.

She had no defence against him. Her thin linen smock was no protection against his closeness. She went to him, soft and yielding, her arms encircling him as though she would never let him go, her face upturned to his.

"I'm sorry. I'm truly sorry," he kept on whispering, his lips punctuating his words with soft kisses.

"Hush, hush, it doesn't matter," she kept replying, treasuring his every caress.

The misery and emptiness of the last few weeks were blotted out by the intoxication of his nearness.

Her heartbeat quickened as she grew aware of every swell and sinew of his well-muscled body pressing against hers. His fingers traced their way along the gentle curves of her figure, lingering at the rise of her breasts, the hollow of her narrow waist, the tapering length of her slender thighs. Her limbs trembled. Every part of her responded to the sensual delight of his growing fervour. Soon, they sought the soft seclusion of the bed, their naked bodies entwined with desperate need. There was no holding back for her now. Her passion took control—and her love. Her instinctive urge was to give him pleasure, to give him love, to give him herself! To every spasm of his desire she gave an answer that was eager, sensual, filled with an urgent longing, until finally the fusion of their bodies reached one great and unrestrained eruption of passionate emotion.

Now, the bedchamber was quiet... In the warm darkness Sabina gently disentangled herself from Ronan's tumbled limbs. Pulling the cool linen sheet about his shoulders, she lay down next to him. Outside the crickets chirruped, and in the distance a dog howled, a melancholy sound which found an echo in her heart. Ronan slept on contentedly, but there was no such oblivion for Sabina. She lay there trying to eradicate the words from her mind, without success. They were fixed there as though branded with a red-hot iron. Ronan's words! Uttered unconsciously in the explosive heat of his climax.

"Marianne! Oh, Marianne!"

Ronan's behaviour towards her during the next few days was full of consideration. Sabina did not even try to discern any hint of love or affection in

his conduct. He was a kind man. He knew he had
hurt her with his angry, thoughtless words and he
wished to make amends. Of his final and most dam-
aging utterance, he was unaware. For herself she
could think of nothing that would ever assuage the
pain of those words from her head or from her heart.
For the moment, at any rate, he was pleased with
her. It was better than nothing.

Each night she lay in his arms, accepting his need
for her, yet she could no longer summon any wild
passionate response. A chill knot of sadness made
her hold back. For her the walls of the bedchamber
still rang with that urgent cry, "Marianne! Oh, Marianne!"

It had been a day or two since Sabina had visited
the north tower so as soon as her morning duties
were finished she went there, Catell and Père Martin,
as ever, at her heels.

"There, I thought you'd abandoned us!" cried
Ned.

"Never that," she replied, touched by the warmth
of the welcome afforded her by the four men. "Now,
Kit, how do you feel today?"

"Fit and full of vigour," he said forcefully. Then
a bout of coughing interrupted him. "Well, nearly fit
and nearly full of vigour," he amended with a grin.

"And how do the rest of you fare?" she asked.

"We grow very dispirited, my lady," said Dick.
"We miss our homes and families. Above all, we
fear we'll be here to the end of our days!"

It was unusual to hear the mild-mannered Dick
speak so vehemently. His words stung Sabina with

guilt; it was largely her family's fault that these men were in such a predicament.

"I will try my hardest to get you freed," she promised. "I will send a letter to my father begging him to make greater efforts on your behalf."

"And if such a plea fails?" Ned's tone told exactly what little faith he had in the outcome.

"Then I'll think of something else. Never fear. I'll get you out of here somehow."

"In that case you'd best send the letter at once," said Ned. "Before the autumn gales begin. Let's have some news promptly before our wits desert us."

"I have promised I will help you, haven't I? And I will do just that! I will write immediately!"

As she left the tower Sabina knew she carried the hopes of the prisoners with her. It was a weighty burden, but she made up her mind not to let them down.

In the end, two letters were written. Ronan was so much in favour of yet another plea he wrote one himself.

"A messenger will be despatched first thing in the morning. With luck and a favourable wind he'll be in England within days," said Ronan as he accepted her letter.

"Please God we get a reply soon!" said Sabina, smoothing her skirt with hands that were decidedly inky. Looking down she saw smudges of black had transferred themselves to the pale cloth. "Oh dear! I'd best go and face Catell's wrath at once," she said ruefully. "I wonder if she can get the marks out."

"I'll do my best, *dame*," was her maid's reply, "but don't blame me if it leaves a stain."

"Save your scolding for later. Get me dressed in

whatever comes to hand, so I do not keep the Seigneur waiting for his supper.''

"There's only this, *ma dame*." Catell took out the pale pink velvet in which Sabina had been married.

"Then it must do!" Sabina allowed the soft fabric to be pulled over her head. As Catell laced it she gave a sigh. "It's fine enough, yet I fancy it does little to improve my looks."

"It doesn't, *ma dame*," said her maid bluntly. "Your pardon for saying so but the colour is wrong for you, and it doesn't fit."

"Catell! Have done!" said Sabina impatiently. "You can do what you like with this gown tomorrow, but now I am in a hurry!"

"That will have to do then, *dame*." Catell sniffed disapprovingly and stood back. "It needs a fair bit off the waist and the neck could be lower…"

Sabina could hear her as she hurried down the stairs. She allowed herself a secret smile. Catell could amuse herself all she liked with the neckline. However, she would have to leave the waistline alone for a while, for if her suspicions were right, and her hopes were fulfilled, she was pregnant at last!

Chapter Eight

Sabina told no one of her hopes. The absence of her monthly courses might be a cruel trick of nature, and if so her disappointment would be bitter enough without having to disappoint Ronan too. Yet as each day passed she grew more and more confident, even though she suffered none of the indispositions she had anticipated: no nausea, no sickness, no languor. In fact, she had never felt better or happier in her life, and her joy was reflected in her looks.

"I declare, you are growing really bonny these days, *ma dame*," stated Catell, as she helped her mistress to dress.

Sabina glanced at her questioningly, uncertain whether her tiring-woman suspected or not. But the maid attributed her glowing cheeks and shining eyes to another cause. "There, wasn't I right when I said you needed to get out into the fresh air more," she said with satisfaction. "It's done you the world of good."

"Indeed you were! I shall heed your advice much more in the future," replied Sabina smiling.

A spring babe! What better time could there be to

give birth, with the long kindly summer days to follow in which the child could grow strong and beautiful? For Ronan she wanted a boy, an heir to Plou-Aven, but for herself she did not mind. All she longed for was to fold her arms round a baby of her own, to lavish her love upon it and... But it was too early for such thoughts. She brought herself back to reality, aware that Catell was addressing her again.

"What did you say?" she asked.

"I said there's another rip in this blue gown of yours, *dame*. I'll be mending on top of my own mending soon." The girl held up the skirt which had been cobbled together again by her none-too-expert stitches.

"It will do," said Sabina impatiently.

"It will have to, you've few enough others, *ma dame*."

"I'll get more presently, when I have the time."

"And when will that be, pray?" Catell laced up the blue gown. "You've been promising yourself a new one for an age."

"What a bothersome creature you are! Stop nagging me."

"Nagging, is it, *ma dame?* When not five minutes ago you promised to take my advice more often?" The maid was indignant. "I only want to save you from the Seigneur's wrath. I'm sure he has no wish to see you looking shabby!"

Sabina had no defence against this argument. "Very well, next time the merchant comes I'll purchase some cloth."

Catell picked the pink velvet gown out of the chest and gave it a derisory shake. "Give me leave to alter this one, *ma dame*. It does nothing to enhance your looks.''

''Oh, do what you please with it. I do not care. Only, finish getting me dressed before the morning's quite over!''

''Do you mean that, *dame?*''

''Yes! Oh, yes!'' cried Sabina in exasperation. ''Now have done and finish my hair!''

Sabina had decided to spend the morning in the herb room. She was busy purifying a salve when Catell came rushing in.

''It's a messenger from England, *dame!*'' she cried. ''He's brought letters.''

Barely waiting to discard her apron, Sabina hurried to the solar and flung open the door. Ronan was reading when she burst in.

''Well, what news? Is the exchange arranged?''

The Seigneur looked at her, his face dark with anger. Sabina thought his fury was because of her unseemly entrance, but as soon as he spoke she knew it was because of the letter he held. ''There is no news!'' he scowled. ''Just platitudes and excuses. 'I fear I could get no one to listen to your case'. By Saint Jehan, it's his case too! Or has he forgot? If that brother of yours were half a man he would have made someone listen! Here, read it for yourself.''

He thrust the letter into her hand, and Sabina gazed at it, sick at heart. It was a vague, unsatisfactory missive full of phrases such as: ''I have done my unworthy best'' and ''Alas, the moment was not convenient'', but its message was clear enough—there was to be no exchange of prisoners.

''Oh, those poor men!'' whispered Sabina. ''They will be bitterly disappointed. They've set such store by…'' She could not finish the sentence, her heart was so heavy.

"And what of my Breton lads, eh? How do you think they feel?" Ronan was striding about the room in his anger. "Those two kinsmen of yours! Do you think they really made any effort? If they did it was a pretty lack-lustre try. But then, they are a pretty lack-lustre pair. Heaven only knows where you got your spirit from!"

Sabina was so distressed she barely noticed that he was speaking well of her. "What's to be done now?" she asked.

"Goodness knows!" Ronan ran his fingers through his hair. "I suppose I must write more pleas to the Mayor of Plymouth, and to the governor. Though with no one to present my petition I might as well throw my letters straight into the sea and have done with it!"

"Is there naught I can do?" asked Sabina.

"Yes, there is. You can let your countrymen in the north tower know they must continue to be unwilling guests at Plou-Aven. It will come better from you. If you want the truth of it, I have not the stomach to face them."

"I will do it, sire, but with a heavy heart." Sabina continued to scrutinise the letter.

"No matter how many times you read it, the meaning does not improve," observed the Seigneur, watching her.

"I just thought—I wondered if— Oh, it doesn't matter." She handed back the letter, unwilling to confess how hungry she was for word from home. But Giles had included no family news, merely the most formal of greetings.

"I understand, it is only natural for you to feel homesick. A few words written to you alone would not have taken much effort," remarked the Seigneur.

"But those words were not written, so there's an end to it. However, be assured, if there was trouble at Corbyn, or my family needed money, we would hear soon enough. Perhaps we had best be grateful for the silence."

Ronan began to laugh. "I think I must agree with you. At least, no one could ever accuse you of wallowing in self-pity. Nevertheless, I shall send word that the messenger is not to continue his journey until he has spoken to you. He might know something of your home and family."

The messenger proved to be a second disappointment. He was an amiable man and honoured to talk with the Dame de Plou-Aven, but he was just a paid courier, and an Exeter man at that. He could tell her nothing about Corbyn. Sabina gave a sigh, and wished him Godspeed on the rest of his journey. Then she set herself to tackle the most unpleasant task of the day—telling the four Englishmen that they were not to be released.

Ned took the news violently, sending the table crashing against the wall with one angry blow. All the time he swore and blasphemed, cursing the fates, the Seigneur, and everyone with the name of Corbyn. Finally he calmed down a little and begged her pardon.

"I should not have uttered such profanities in your presence, lass. I'm sorry, I truly am," he said contritely. "But to learn that we must stay here until we rot, and all because of someone's bungling…it was more than I could stand."

"Think naught of it. I can sympathise with your anger," replied Sabina. In truth, she found his fiery outburst much easier to bear than the reactions of the other three.

They remained silent, their faces pinched and white. She wished that they would yell and curse too, she could stand that. It was their mute misery which distressed her so terribly.

Dick spoke first, his voice soft. "Your pardon, my lady, but you are convinced your father and brother went to the right people, folk of influence? I know we are four poor men with no rich relations or patrons to speak up for us, yet I find it hard to believe that no gentleman back in England will set in motion a straight exchange—four Bretons for four Englishmen."

"We had one patron, Giles Corbyn, and look where that got us," muttered Ned.

Dick silenced him with a stern look and continued, "As I say, we have no grand connections. But my brother is bailiff to Master Gilbert at Greenway, and he's a man who would not let Devon lads rot for the want of a timely intervention. Or there's Master Yogge and Master Hawkins of Plymouth, they are both reputed to be just men. Did your brother approach either of them?"

"I think not."

"Then, my lady, in God's name who did he go to?"

"Men whose names I cannot recall, certainly not names I recognise. But then we lived very quietly at Corbyn. I am acquainted with very few families." Sabina felt obliged to protect her brother with a half-truth, for she did know some of the men mentioned, minor officials, go-betweens, men of self-importance but no standing. There was not one reliable character among the lot of them.

"My lady, would it be permitted for us to see the letter? I can read well enough," said Dick.

"Certainly not," she retorted. Then added more gently, "It contains private family business also."

Another lie. Every line of that letter showed what little effort had been made on their behalf. It would add naught to their comfort to learn that the man who had got them into their predicament had barely bothered to lift a finger to help them.

The gloom and despair in their faces hurt Sabina. "Could you not write a letter to your brother, the one who has the ear of Master Gilbert?" she suggested to Dick.

"Would that be possible?" Hope brightened his face. "But, my lady, the cost..."

"That need not concern you. In fact, I will speak to the Seigneur about it at once. Maybe he will write also. It can do no harm."

"How will we send it? And when?" demanded Ned.

"The messenger who brought this was *en route* for Paris. He has promised to call here on his return journey in two or three weeks' time, if all goes well."

"Which it won't!" Ned was sunk in gloom again. "Messengers never arrive when they are expected. We'll not see him inside a month, and by then we'll have autumn well upon us. Delays! Delays and more delays. This winter will still see us here in Plou-Aven!"

He glanced at Kit, and Sabina guessed what he

was thinking. Would young Kit survive another winter of imprisonment, no matter how favourable the conditions? Guilt tracked her again. What if the lad died here, far from his home? And all because of the Corbyns?

"No," she said decidedly. "You will get home and soon. I give you my word on it! I will begin by talking to the Seigneur about those letters. Even though the messenger is not due back for a while it will do no harm to have it all carefully thought out and written."

"Now we'll see some action!" declared Ned.

Sabina felt a qualm of self-doubt. It was a feeling she quickly brushed aside. She *had* to succeed. She had given these men her word.

"Not more letters!" groaned the Seigneur, when she put this new proposal to him. "Will they do any good? Do you know this Master Gilbert?"

"Only by reputation. He is spoken of as a sound man and a good Christian."

"Then I suppose it is worth a try."

"So Dick may write?"

"Yes, you may tell him so."

"And you, Seigneur. You will write also?"

"I may as well. I have made so many applications that one more will do no harm. Your Englishmen can have writing materials as soon as they wish. As for me, I have had enough of being indoors. I have a fancy for the open air. Will you accompany me, *dame?*"

"Gladly, Seigneur." Sabina smiled with pleasure.

"Good. I will send for our horses to be saddled."

"Riding? Oh no! I cannot... I don't think... I have

work to finish that I had forgotten, Seigneur. Perhaps you had best go alone.''

''What is this? I thought you enjoyed riding!''

''I do.''

''Then why the reluctance? Come, whatever duties you have can be finished later. It's a lovely day. Let's not waste it.''

''The thought is tempting, sire. All the same, I must decline.''

''You would not come riding with me the other day, as I recall. What's amiss? Does your mare no longer please you. Has she grown vicious or obstinate?''

''Certainly not. She's as sweet-tempered and biddable as ever.''

''Then why will you not come riding with me? If it is not your mare and it is not your health—I've never seen you looking so well—then the cause must be me. What have I done to displease you this time? Tell me, so that I can beg your pardon and have done!'' Ronan was growing irritable.

''You have done nothing, truly you have not, sire!''

''Then come with me!''

Sabina was sorely tempted, not only by the prospect of riding, but also because Ronan so obviously wanted her company. ''Oh, don't urge me, sire!'' she cried. ''I cannot come.''

''If that's your last word then so be it!'' With a dismissive shrug the Seigneur made for the door. Once there, however, he paused. ''...You cannot come, you say...? Why not...?''

''Because...because...'' Sabina floundered for some reasonable excuse.

Ronan strode back into the room. His face remained set, but the anger had gone out of him.

"There is one likely reason," he said. "If you are with child, why not say so! Do you not think I should be told?"

Sabina gave a sigh. "It's too soon," she said. "I might be mistaken."

"And you did not think it fitting that I should share your uncertainty?"

"Don't be angry," she pleaded. "I know how much you want an heir. I thought to spare you disappointment. Clearly I was wrong; that is no novelty to me, though. I have great difficulty in getting anything right it seems so... Oh, plague it!" Her exclamation was because, quite unexpectedly, tears had begun to course down her cheeks. She made to scrub at them hastily with her sleeve, but Ronan intervened.

"I beg you not to distress yourself," he said softly, taking out a linen kerchief and dabbing gently at her eyes. "I have heard that some women, when they are carrying a child, weep frequently with little cause. It could be that your tears are a sign of your condition."

Sabina took the kerchief from him and blew her nose hard. "I hate crying!" she said fiercely. "I feel such a fool and my face goes an unbecoming red!"

"Yes, it does," agreed Ronan. "I'm glad you are not one of those women who normally weep at everything."

She blew her nose again and regarded him cautiously. She had expected him to shout for joy, or at the very least smile. Instead, he remained oddly impassive.

"You give no indication that you are glad, Seigneur," she said. "About the possibility of a child, I mean."

"I am waiting," he replied.

"Until there is no doubt?" She wondered at his being able to control his emotions so finely.

"No. Until I know how you feel."

"I am very well indeed, thank you," she said surprised.

"You misunderstand me. It is not your health I meant, important though it is." He was regarding her steadily with anxiety in his dark eyes.

"If not my health, then— You think I do not want the child, is that it?" she cried in astonishment. "That I might be unhappy at the prospect? Not want my own child? What sort of woman do you think I am? Some unnatural monster?"

"I know you are no such thing. I just wondered— feared that you would be less joyous to bear *my* child."

"You remember too many of those angry things I said in the early days when I first arrived," she said. "I was unhappy then, aye, and frightened too, for I did not know what sort of man I was bound to. Those days are gone, and with them my fears and my unhappiness. You are my husband, and I am most glad to have a child, for you and for Plou-Aven."

There, she had gone as close as she dared to expressing her feelings for him.

His response was to give a sigh of relief. "I am thankful the prospect is not distasteful to you," he said. "And of course I am glad that we are to have a babe—I am convinced it is a certainty." He smiled down at her, his hands gently caressing her arms. "Such news, eh? Such wonderful news!"

"I would still prefer to wait a little before we spread the tidings abroad," she said, conscious of relief herself.

"It shall be as you wish." His smile was growing, spreading across his suntanned features. "Everything shall be as you wish, *ma chère Sabina,* and anything you want."

"I want nothing, only for the child to be born safe and well."

"Amen to that, and for your safe delivery also." His face became grave, his mounting excitement disappeared.

Sabina remembered Marianne: his first wife had died in childbed. No wonder his reaction to this babe had been strained.

"I am small, but I am strong. And I am seldom ill," she said reassuringly.

"Yes, praise be!" He lifted her hand to his lips and kissed it.

He was pleased! Suddenly all was right with her world, and her heart felt as light as a soaring lark. She made to touch his cheek but at that moment he threw back his head and said jovially, "If you do not ride and will not be carried, do you still walk?"

"Indeed I do, sire, and take great pleasure in it."

"Then let's walk together for a while before it grows dusk."

He held out his hand, and she stretched out hers to him, expecting him to take it in a formal grasp of fingers. Instead, he slid her arm through his, drawing her near so that they walked close together. They left the château and took the meandering track which skirted the moat, and every step was a pleasure to her. On the way back Ronan looked at the steep path up to the gatehouse, and his dark brows drew together in a frown.

"What a stupid fool I am!" he exclaimed. "Rest you here while I find someone to go up to the château."

"What for?" she asked in surprise.

"Why, to have a litter sent down for you, so you do not fatigue yourself climbing up the hill."

"I'm not in the least fatigued, I promise you. I would prefer to walk."

"Are you sure? It's quite a slope."

"I am absolutely certain. I am not sickly, you know."

"Very well, I'll not thwart you. I understand it is bad to cross women in your condition."

"Hopeful condition," she corrected gently.

With each passing day Sabina's uncertainty about the child diminished, until she felt safe to acknowledge at last that she was definitely pregnant. The prospect of an heir seemed to lighten the whole atmosphere of Plou-Aven, making everything joyous and festive. Or was it only the joy in her own heart? The news soon percolated down to the parish, and the time she set aside to minister to the sick had to be extended because there was not a woman in Plou-Aven who did not come to offer felicitations and good advice. Ronan treated her as though she were fragile and delicate; she found it touching that he could show her such consideration and pay her such marked attention. Sometimes she smiled now when she remembered how at first she had thought him brusque and cold-hearted. Cold-hearted! The man was all gentleness, though he fought so hard to conceal it!

Autumn was upon them now, casting a mellow richness over the land. It was a busy time harvesting the crops. The fields of grain had long since been gathered in, but there was fruit to be picked from the orchards, and grapes from the few vineyards that nestled in favoured spots. They only produced a thin, sour wine, which in Sabina's opinion was inferior to the local cider. Nevertheless, the cider-press and the wine-press were kept busy; the brewhouse gushed clouds of pungent steam, betraying it, too, was being used to the full. With Le Godet ever at her heels Sabina supervised the salting down of meat, and regarded with growing satisfaction the lines of preserves, conserves and cordials on the storeroom shelves.

She was so occupied she had little time to spare for the prisoners. It took the arrival of pack-animals from the coast to jolt her memory back to their plight. Hearing the noise and hubbub from the inner bailey, she thought that the messenger for England had come at last. When she went to investigate she found only that the saltfish for the winter had been delivered.

"Never mind. We've our letter ready and waiting for when he comes," Dick assured her after she had commiserated with them.

"If he comes," growled Ned gloomily. Of the four men he was beginning to show the strain of long imprisonment the most; he was losing weight, and falling prey to long fits of black depression. Sabina regarded him anxiously, aware that in the short time she had known him he had grown more tense and pale.

"The messenger will come," she said confidently. "He has to pass close by on his route to Roscoff and the coast. He's been promised shelter with us."

"He'll not miss the chance of a good supper and a night's rest here, not if he's any sense," remarked Kit who, although still haunted by his cough, had not lost his cheerful optimism.

But Ned refused to be encouraged. "I'll believe it when I see him!" he scowled.

Sabina left the north tower with a sore conscience at having neglected the four men of late. She resolved that if the unthinkable happened and the messenger failed to arrive she would plead with Ronan to send one of their own people. He was in such an amenable mood these days that she was certain he would agree.

Fatigued after her long, busy day, Sabina was glad to call for Catell and go to bed. She was so tired she expected to fall asleep immediately, instead she only managed to doze fitfully. The discomfort of her weary body did not decrease. Her back ached more and more, making her restless, until fingers of pain began to stab across her abdomen.

"Is aught amiss?" asked Ronan.

A sudden warm stickiness about her thighs and another spasm of pain forced Sabina to stifle a groan.

"You had best rouse Catell, and quickly," she whispered. "I fear I am miscarrying."

It was a long night of anguish. Catell and Marthe stayed by her every minute, gently rubbing her stomach with rose oil to give her ease, and offering what comfort they could.

"Here, *ma dame,* let me put this amulet on your wrist," urged Catell. "There's nothing like jasper to ease the ills of childbed. The Seigneur sent down to rouse Père Martin some time since. They say he's got so many candles burning for you the chapel is a blaze of light. All the doors of the château are shut, we've seen to that, and every rope and string in the place is being knotted to ward off this evil. Things will go well, *ma pauvre dame!* They will soon go well!"

Catell's optimism was misplaced. With each sharp paroxysm Sabina knew she was losing her child. Every instinct in her fought to hold it back, to retain the life within her. But her body would not obey.

"It's too soon!" she cried out. "The poor babe has no chance of life! No chance to draw breath!"

Her servants bathed her face and tried to ease her discomfort, but surreptitiously they crossed themselves and uttered silent prayers. They knew, as Sabina did, that events must take their course.

By morning it was all over. Sabina lay back on her pillows exhausted, her head spinning with weakness. She was too numb with grief to do anything but lie motionless. The child she would have loved so much—all her hopes—had gone; a bloodstained bundle of rags hustled away by a sobbing Marthe. Half-conscious, she was only vaguely aware of Ronan beside the bed. His hand held hers. His lips pressed against her brow. The dampness of his tears fell on her cheek as he bent his head, but Sabina was too desolate to respond.

She must have slept, for when she opened her eyes the afternoon sun was bright through the narrow window. Ronan was still beside her, the pallor of his face emphasised by the dark shadow of his unshaven chin, his body slumped with fatigue. Sabina looked into his eyes, red-rimmed with sorrow and weariness, and in her befuddled state thought she saw only reproach. She had lost his child!

"I'm sorry," she said, then again and again, "I'm sorry! I'm sorry!" Until the tears came.

Ronan's arms came about her quickly. "Hush…" he said softly. "Do not fret. Only get well again. That's all I ask."

But Sabina could not be comforted. She wept, until the Seigneur became alarmed and ordered Catell to fetch a draught of something to calm her.

She fell asleep at last, but even then there was no rest for her. She tossed and turned, crying out as fearsome images invaded her feverish brain; at one minute trying to push away the bedcovers from her burning body, and the next shivering with cold. Shadowy faces haunted her. She could recognise Ronan, Catell, and Marthe; others were strangers or only fleetingly familiar. It was a nightmare that went on and on.

Consciousness came slowly to her. She lifted heavy lids to see the morning sun shining against the rough, stone wall. But which morning? How long had she lain thus? Gingerly she turned her head to see a woman sitting by the bed sewing. She was no servant, she was too richly clad. Moreover, her plump, good-natured face stirred something in Sabina's memory.

"*Ma dame.*" She tried to speak but the words came out as a croak from her parched throat.

Straight away the woman dropped her needlework and placed a hand on Sabina's forehead. "It is cool, the beloved saints be praised!'' she said. ''You are back with us again! The fever has broken!'' Taking a beaker she spooned a little liquid between Sabina's lips, cool, refreshing, and very welcome.

''Thank you, *ma dame*,'' Sabina whispered. She knew that motherly face, that gentle smile... Then she remembered. The kindly matron who had stood proxy for her mother at the wedding. ''Dame Morgan... Dame de Saint-Léon.''

''You recollect me?'' Dame Morgan beamed in delight. ''I did not expect you to.''

''But... What are...'' The sentence tailed away wearily.

''What am I doing here?'' The *dame* spooned more liquid into Sabina's willing mouth. ''Your husband summoned me—nay, begged me to come. You have been so ill, and he was desperately worried about you. But that is enough chatter. See if you can sleep some more. I will send to your Seigneur. He will be so relieved, poor man.''

Sabina wanted to stay awake long enough to see Ronan again, she wanted to beg his forgiveness for something, she had done him a hurt which hurt her too, a great sorrow...but she could not remember what...if only her eyelids were not growing heavier and heavier...

Ronan *was* relieved to note her improvement, so much was evident when she woke to find him by her bedside once more.

''Have you been there long, sire?'' she asked.

''A few minutes only. I have been taking pleasure from watching you sleep so peacefully.''

''I've been ill, have I not?''

''Very ill. I—we all feared for your life.'' A

shadow crossed his face. "Two whole days and nights you lay in a desperate fever, two days and nights I would not wish to live through again."

"So ill!" Sabina was vaguely surprised. She was not accustomed to being ill, it was alien to her, unreal. "But why should I have been... Oh, I remember! The baby!" Recollection washed over her in a tide of loss and pain. "*Mon Seigneur*, what was wrong that I could not carry the child to full time?"

"Hush, hush..." Ronan gently soothed her mounting distress.

"Why did it happen? What did I do wrong? Perhaps I should have stopped riding sooner. Or maybe I was over-confident, boasting how I was never ill. Could this be God smiting my pride?"

"You must not blame yourself, the fault was not with you. Who is to know why these things happen? They remain a tragic mystery." Ronan was quick with his comfort, but the questions gnawed at Sabina.

The Seigneur visited her frequently, staying to talk or just rest quietly beside her while she dozed. She was heartened by his presence, yet every time she looked at his face her heart ached. He had wanted a child so much, as much as she had. He hid his disappointment well, with never a word of regret or reproof—his forebearance only added to her misery.

Dame Morgan saw Ronan's concern in a much warmer light. "Such devotion I have never seen," she said one day when she was keeping Sabina company. "You have no idea how delighted I am. I never thought he would feel so about a woman ever again."

"Don't be misled. He is a good man. No doubt he thought his second wife was going the way of his first. The poor soul has ever had ill-luck in the marriage market,'' observed Sabina bitterly.

"Such a thing to say!" exclaimed the *dame* reprovingly. "I know devotion when I see it! And do not compare yourself with Marianne. You are completely different."

"Not so very different. Neither of us have given Plou-Aven an heir!"

"Poor Marianne did not, of course. But as for you…there is plenty of time! Oh, I know things have gone ill for you on this occasion, but there will be others. You are young and strong. Goodness, look at you now! Sitting up in bed already and growing restless with inactivity. That is a sound constitution you have got! Plou-Aven will have an heir in good time, just you see!"

"I hope you are right." Sabina let her eyes grow misty. Tears were never far away these days.

Dame Morgan bent her head over her embroidery. "I am glad Ronan married you," she said.

"He still mourns Marianne, though."

"Of course he does! What else would you expect? We both know he is a man of deep feelings, and Marianne was the love of his youth."

"Do you not mean the love of his life?"

"No, I do not!" The *dame* stitched away briskly. "I know that their marriage excited much comment, they were so much in love. It was a delight to see them together. But I sometimes wonder what would have happened if Marianne had lived. Would Plou-Aven have been quite the Eden everyone expected?"

"Is there any reason why it should not?"

"Yes…Marianne herself. She was a delightful, charming child, and that was the problem; in my opinion she would have wanted to remain a child for ever. Responsibility frightened her, and as for anything ugly or unpleasant, she shrank away from such things. She was enchanted by the idea of being a bride, but being a wife was not so much of a pleasure to her. Poor Ronan, I fear he had to be very patient with her. When she found she was with child she was most distressed. With my own ears I heard her cry many times that she was too young, that she should not have been obliged to endure such a thing. And I know she would not let her husband near her; her old nurse slept in the great bed with her, while Ronan had to make do with one of the guestchambers. He blamed himself sorely for having given her the child.''

"Perhaps she would have become more mature had she been given the opportunity. She *was* very young. How old? Fifteen? Sixteen?''

"She was turned nineteen—older than you. And I tell you this, she never touched the hearts of the people the way you have— Just look at this! What have you brought this time, Catell?''

The maid had entered bearing a tray piled high with small gifts for Sabina.

"You may well ask, *ma dame*." Catell set the burden down carefully. "You'd think folks would have eased off by now, but everyone in the parish wants to send an offering to *ma dame*. See what the Widow du Crann sent!'' Gingerly she held up a mandrake, its roots twisted into a form that was undeniably male. "*Le Bon Dieu*, we can do without this just at the moment!''

"Mandrake powers are said to be very potent,''

observed Dame Morgan with a smile. "Maybe you should put it aside for some future date."

"And if I don't need it I will let you have it," said Sabina to Catell, smiling.

"Poof! Why should I need such a thing?" Still holding the root between finger and thumb Catell opened one of the oak chests and dropped it in.

Sabina was still smiling as she settled down to rest. For the first time since she had lost the baby she felt her misery lift a little, not because of Catell's joking, but because of Dame Morgan's comments. Never for one moment had she thought she could compare with Marianne. Now, though, it seemed that the previous Dame de Plou-Aven was not quite as perfect as time and Ronan's fond memories had made her seem. It was an encouraging thought.

As Dame Morgan had predicted, Sabina's powers of recuperation proved to be excellent. Before long she was out of bed, and in a remarkably short time she ventured down to the great hall.

"Are you sure this is wise?" asked Ronan.

"Very wise," stated Sabina. "Any more lying in bed thinking dismal thoughts and you will find that you have got a mad woman for a wife!"

"Perish the thought!" Taking her hand, he led her to the dais. "I have missed you by my side at high table. I'm glad to have you back in your rightful place."

His smile was one of true pleasure. It made Sabina happy to see him smile so, his face lighting up, his eyes glowing with genuine delight. Hopefully she looked into those dark eyes and saw warmth and affection, but nothing she recognised as love. Purposefully she quelled her regrets and smiled back.

Chapter Nine

As she grew stronger Sabina found the confines of the château restricting. Ronan was adamant in forbidding her to resume her duties in helping the sick. He issued equally strict orders that she was not to visit the Englishmen either, not until they had recovered from a bout of sore throats that had afflicted them.

"What am I to do?" she demanded. It was a crisp autumn day with air like wine and a sun which still held a last, lingering warmth. She was desperate to be out and about, but Dame Morgan considered riding imprudent.

"Then can we not walk?" Sabina suggested. "If we take our time..."

Her pleading won over Dame Morgan. Ronan, however, only agreed if a litter followed behind in case she felt tired.

"And don't declare it will make you sick!" he replied to her protests. "If you are going the short distance you claim, the swaying of the litter cannot possibly affect you."

Sabina gave in. It was a small price to pay for a

walk abroad. She was only sorry that Ronan could not accompany them.

She meant to be prudent, she really did, but the beauty of the day had intoxicated her, and the joy of being out in the fresh air at last. Dame Morgan began to suggest they had gone far enough, but Sabina would have none of it.

"If we go a little further we might see Yannick. I've had no news of him of late," she said. They went a little further, and a little further—then the weariness hit Sabina suddenly. She felt limp and shaken and faint.

"There, I feared it would be so," said Dame Morgan, fanning her with her kerchief.

"What ignominy! We'll have to return by litter after all," said Sabina with a wan smile.

"You will, *ma petite*. I cannot abide those things. I am going back on my own two feet!"

Dame Morgan was obstinate, and so she and a couple of servants took the short cut on foot, while Sabina rode in the litter, with Catell and Cudenec to attend her. Within minutes she began to feel better, and to her surprise she found she enjoyed the gentle swaying of the litter on this occasion. To accommodate the width of her transport they had to take a broader, more devious track, and she hitched up the leather curtains the better to see the brilliant golds and reds of the autumn woodlands. Her pleasure diminished somewhat when after a while she realised where their path was leading them. Past Ty Lannion!

The last thing she wanted was another encounter with Louise de Lannion! After her illness she was not confident she felt strong enough to win a second battle of words. There was another reason why she wanted to avoid Ronan's mistress; after their last confrontation and the ensuing quarrel with the Seigneur, he had spent more time at Plou-Aven; now, since losing the baby, it had been her secret fear he would once more start paying attention to Louise. Her still fragile nerves dreaded the prospect. She could not bear to look at the house where Ronan had found such solace, and she lowered the curtains as they began to pass.

She did look, of course. The temptation to lift the curtain was more than she could stand. At her first glimpse she drew in her breath sharply. "Stop!" she called urgently. "Stop!"

"Help me out!" she commanded when they came to a halt.

"*Ma dame—*" Catell began to protest.

"Out!" she insisted, extending her hand.

She descended from the litter and regarded Ty Lannion. An unnatural silence hung over the house. Cautiously she approached the gate. It hung drunkenly on one hinge. The garden was littered with sticks and stones and other debris—splintered shutters and shattered slates showed where they had found their target. The place was deserted. To judge from the trail of domestic items strewn on the path the inhabitants had left in a hurry.

"What has happened here?" demanded Sabina.

"What can you mean, *dame?*" Catell's eyes were innocently wide, but a tell-tale flush was already staining her cheeks.

"You know what I mean. Come now! The truth!"

"The woman who lived here has gone," muttered Cudenec.

"I can see that! Where has she gone? And why?"

"How am I supposed to know where and why?" complained the groom. "She's gone and there's an end of it. I care nothing about it, just so long as she doesn't come back."

"Amen to that!" Catell chirped up. "Good riddance, we all say!"

Sabina eyed the pair of them, her suspicions aroused. "Louise de Lannion left in a hurry, and probably unwillingly by the looks of things. I want to know about it. And don't pretend you know nothing. A chicken cannot sneeze in this parish without you two knowing the details before anyone else—so tell me!"

Catell and Cudenec exchanged looks, then the maid spoke up. "The folks of the parish got tired of having a strumpet like her in their midst. So they told her to leave."

"It wasn't right, her breathing the same air as honest, sober God-fearing folk," Cudence stated.

"Honest? Sober? God-fearing?" Sabina raised a quizzical eyebrow. "Can this be Plou-Aven you are describing?"

"I suppose we'd best tell you, or we'll be here all day," muttered Catell. "I've no wish to earn the Seigneur's wrath for keeping you out overlong! Very well, *dame*, if it pleases you to know—the people drove away the trollop because she ill-wished you!"

"She did what?"

"Ill-wished you! How else did you lose your babe! You were fine! I've never seen anyone look so well in their early months. And you say yourself you never ail. So it had to be the evil forces which killed your unborn babe, and near enough killed you too."

"You cannot mean it!" Sabina went cold to think of herself as a target of the Black Arts.

"We do!" said Cudenec. "And the whole parish goes along with us. The Widow du Crann saw an owl flying over the château in broad daylight the very day you miscarried. And the gatekeeper swears he saw a hare jump over the bit of wall beyond the moat. You were ill-wished, *dame!* Never doubt it."

"But why Louise de Lannion? It could have been anyone…"

"No, it couldn't, *ma dame,* begging your pardon," said Catell. "She had reason to wish you harm for…for being who you are. And who else here-abouts had cause to hurt you? Would anyone in the parish wish you bad luck? Of course not! It was that de Lannion woman! It had to be!"

Sabina was touched that the people of Plou-Aven should have gone to such lengths to support her. None the less, she was uneasy at being the cause of what must have been a near riot.

"No one was hurt, I hope?"

"Not they! A few stones against the shutters and they ran like scared coneys," chuckled Cudenec.

"That they did!" confirmed Catell.

"So you were both there?"

"We—er—happened to be passing," said the groom warily. An uncomfortable suspicion was be-ginning to grow in Sabina's mind. "You two didn't stir up the people, I hope," she said.

"Oh, no, *dame!*" Cudenec and Catell answered in unison.

Sabina was not convinced. Their replies had been a little too prompt and a little too emphatic. As they continued their journey back to the château she could not help feeling shaken. It was gratifying to learn that the people of Plou-Aven were so loyal to her, and she did not regret the departure of Louise; however, the outcome of the fracas could have been more serious. Accusations of ill-wishing could lead to condemnation for witchcraft and the punishment for that crime was death in the flames. She was relieved that she had not been the cause of the other woman meeting such a terrible fate.

She was so shaken by what might have been that it was some time before another implication of Louise's departure occurred to her—her chief rival for Ronan's affections had gone! At least, her chief mortal rival—the ghost of Marianne still stalked their marriage. Yet even her powers were diminishing a little. The affair reflected on her miscarriage, too; if the loss of the babe had been because of supernatural forces and not because of some defect within herself, surely that meant she was capable of having a healthy child in the future? Especially since the cause of her misfortune was now out of the way. With such encouraging thoughts in her head and a new determination in her heart Sabina entered the Château de Plou-Aven feeling happier than she had done in a long time. Ronan would love her eventually! He would! He would…!

Now that Sabina had recovered there was no reason for Dame Morgan to stay. She watched her go with real regret, for she had grown very close to the plump, kindly lady during these last few weeks.

Left to herself she felt restless, and her thoughts dwelt more and more on gaining Ronan's love. Her hopes suffered a prompt set-back when an accidental glimpse of herself in the mirror reminded her most cruelly that she was plain. She regarded herself with critical dismay. As ever, her gown was shabby. The soft bloom which had touched her during pregnancy was gone. Her eyes seemed doe-like in her pale face, and she had lost weight, so that her already slender figure had become even more slight. Remembering the voluptuous curves of Louise de Lannion, she winced. Ronan clearly preferred his women with meat on them, which left her at a sorry disadvantage.

"Do what you can with me!" she instructed Catell despairingly. "Make me less of a scarecrow!"

Catell's skills as a tiring-woman had increased tremendously. It was incredible to remember her beginnings as a menial servant. The way she washed and dressed Sabina's hair was most expert, and she added subtle touches of face paint to give colour to her mistress's complexion. The flattering white frill of the veil with which she framed Sabina's face bore witness to backbreaking hours spent with the tiny goffering iron.

"Is this really all I have to wear?" asked Sabina as garment after garment was held up and dismissed as too worn, too thin, or too ancient.

"There are the bolts of stuff the cloth merchant brought. They've been here three weeks or so, waiting your instructions." Catell observed. "That peacock-coloured velvet would make a lovely sideless surcoat, over a white worsted kirtle, say, and edged with ermine."

"Very grand it sounds, but, as you point out, it's still wrapped in its bolt and is therefore no help to me at the present moment. Talking of velvet, where is my pink gown? I will have to wear that."

"Your pink gown, *ma dame?*" repeated Catell in a vague tone.

"Come, you can't have forgotten it. My clothes chest is not *that* ample."

"Of course not, *dame*. It's just I can't recall seeing it of late... Oh, now I remember where it is. It's in the closet."

"What on earth is it doing in there?" But Sabina was talking to the back of her maidservant. When the girl returned her face was flushed with excitement and apprehension.

"Here it is, *ma dame*," she said, holding out a gown.

"What jest is this? That's not my gown, as you well know. Whose is this, and where did it come from?"

Although the garment on Catell's arm was velvet, it was of a rich crimson, trimmed with dark miniver.

"Your pardon, *ma dame*, it *is* yours." Catell was holding back her laughter with difficulty. "You did say I could do what I liked with it, didn't you? Well, I took it to Yves Bouvier, down by the river. He's very skilled with dyestuffs."

"But this is incredible!" Sabina held up the gown and examined it. "The new colour is a definite improvement, without doubt."

"I altered the neck and took it in, too. And retrimmed it. Let me help you into it, *dame*, please!"

Even if Sabina had not been delighted by the transformation of her old gown, she would have found it hard to resist the pleas of her maid.

As Catell did up the laces an expression of awe crossed her face as she regarded her mistress. "*Ma dame!*" she breathed. "You look beautiful!"

Sabina turned to the mirror, about to retort, "Don't talk such nonsense!" but the words died on her lips. It was a stranger who looked back at her from the mirror, a stranger whose fragile beauty was emphasised by the flowing lines of the elegant cote-hardie and whose delicate colouring was enhanced by the crimson of the velvet. Half bemused by the transformation, she held out the wide skirts and let them fall, feeling the rich material with its border of dark fur swing seductively about her thighs.

"Where did the miniver come from?" she asked.

"From an old chest in the storeroom, *ma dame*. It may have been Dame Yolande's or Dame Marianne's. Anyway, it seemed a shame to leave it to the mice and moths."

"Well…! I thank you for your hard work."

"It wasn't all mine, *dame*," admitted the maid. "My sewing's still not up to a lot of stitchery. Widow du Crann, who mends the linen, gave me a hand. She said it made a nice change from darning sheets."

"Then I thank you both." Sabina turned back to the mirror with growing delight.

Catell beamed. "I knew you would look beautiful, *ma dame*. It's very virtuous not to care about your outward appearance, but it's good to look comely, isn't it?"

"I'm afraid my shabbiness owed more to carelessness than to virtue," Sabina confessed.

"Now, *ma dame*, if you would only—"

"I know what you are going to say," she laughed. "You can start on the new cloth as soon as you please."

When Sabina entered the great hall the hubbub

that usually accompanied mealtimes died away into a stunned silence. She ought to have been gratified, instead she felt acutely embarrassed. The temptation to run back up the stairs and tear off her new finery was great, but behind her the solid little body of Catell blocked the way.

The look of astonishment on Ronan's face would have amused her if she had not been so discomforted.

"Ma dame!" He stepped down from the dais, his hand outstretched, to lead her to the high table. Hesitantly she went with him, conscious of his eyes upon her. *"Ma dame,"* he repeated, when they had sat down. "You—you are in splendid looks today."

Sabina's awkwardness found relief in a touch of her old asperity. "From the tone of your voice I deduce it is something of a surprise," she retorted. "Well, look your fill now, for you will probably never see such a show again. In a weak moment I gave way to Catell's persistence, and now I regret it. I feel most uncomfortable, quite unlike myself!"

"But you sound like yourself," grinned Ronan. "It's a relief to hear you. I was beginning to fear my wife had been stolen away."

"Don't mock me, sire. I am ill at ease enough as it is. And stop staring at me!"

"I cannot help it. Some magic has been afoot here."

"Oh, nonsense!" Sabina said rudely. She pretended to be occupied with ladelling meat on to her trencher of bread, but she could not help glancing at Ronan under her lashes. He was continuing to gaze at her, open admiration on his face. It delighted her, yet at the same time it increased her embarrassment. She knew she should take advantage of the situation in some way, but how? Flirtatious behaviour and coquetry were quite foreign to her, she had never learned such arts.

"So you approve of my fine feathers?" she asked at last.

"I do. You look most beautiful."

"Oh," murmured Sabina, desperately searching for words to express her delight. "Then since it pleases you, Seigneur, I will endeavour to keep myself dressed becomingly—or rather Catell will, for the skill and artistry are hers. I have already given her leave to start fashioning the fine cloth you bought for me, and Widow du Crann will be glad to help her, she gets so tired of darning sheets, poor woman. And I must play my part, too, and not rip the hems, or drip things down myself. And I will try to remember, when I go into the herb-room, not to bend too long over the cauldron, for the steam will melt the starch in my veil and it must take Catell an age to get it in this new fashion... Ooh!" She finished with a wail, for the Seigneur was convulsed with laughter. "Oh, sire, I was not joking. I was being most serious!"

"I know you were," he answered, gasping for breath and mopping his eyes. "But, oh, *ma dame*...you are unique! What other lady, being complimented upon her loveliness, would promise not to steam the starch out of her veil?"

Laughter overtook him again, and Sabina turned her gaze away, to stare miserably at her trencher in front of her. So this was how she intended to earn his love—by talking too much, and talking foolishness at that! For all her months of marriage and her fine resolutions she had learned nothing.

"No, be not so glum." Ronan's laughter faded as he looked at her with concern. "I did not mean my words to make you unhappy. I was not criticising you. I only meant it is refreshing to find a lady so completely frank and devoid of artifice. No man would complain at having such a wife."

He lifted her hand and kissed it. As always, his touch brought a warmth tingling through her. His head was bent low as his lips softly touched her skin, and as she looked down on the thick dark locks of his hair she felt her heart ache with tenderness for him. How idiotic her earlier thoughts had been! Of course she had learned something in these last months. She had learned to love him more than life itself.

That night she hoped he would come back to her bed. Since the miscarriage he had slept in one of the guestchambers, a poignant echo of his life with Marianne. As she lay listening for his step outside the door she remembered every warm, approving word he had spoken to her that day. She recalled, too, his look of blatant admiration when she had entered the hall. No man who was indifferent could have looked like that, could he? Surely he would not leave her to lie alone in the great bed any longer? But as the night slipped by without Ronan she tried to tell herself it was his consideration that kept him away. He was reluctant to come to her until she had fully recovered her health, that was it! So successful was she in her arguments that by the time she fell asleep she had almost convinced herself. Only in a very small corner in her heart did she fear Ronan was staying away because he did not want her.

* * *

Trying to maintain her newly acquired elegance proved harder than Sabina had expected, but she did her best. If ever she was tempted to wipe her grubby hands on her gown or wrench at a snagged hem instead of disentangling it, she remembered the way Ronan had looked at her. The image was enough to spur her on.

Gradually she picked up the threads of her life again, and her thoughts turned once more to the Englishmen locked in the north tower.

"Catell says the sore throat has completely gone from them, Seigneur," she said one morning. "Surely I can visit them now?"

"Very well, if you wish it."

"I regret to admit it but I had forgotten about the letters that were to be sent to England. Were they despatched?"

"Letters?" Ronan looked blank for a moment. "I suppose the messenger came but I had no word of him. You will have to ask the Englishmen what messages they sent with him."

"I'll go as soon as Père Martin is fetched."

"There is no need to trouble the good father. Catell will suffice as chaperon."

"Thank you, sire. In that case I will go at once."

The warmth of their welcome proved how much the Englishmen had missed her visits.

"What a sight for sore eyes you are, my lady!" cried Dick. "And looking so well. We've prayed hard for your recovery, haven't we, lads? And to judge from the looks of you our prayers have been answered."

"I am grateful for those prayers," smiled Sabina. "But what of you?"

"The fear was that we had the putrid sore throat among us, but the Devil was cheated of his dues," grinned Kit. "It turned out to be an ordinary cold. Nay, not so ordinary, it silenced Ned for two whole days."

"What do you expect? It was a Breton cold," retorted Ned. "Aught that comes out of this God-forsaken land has got to be cursed!"

Sabina was shocked by the deterioration in the red-haired Englishman. He had become gaunt and stooping, and after being in his company for only a few minutes she recognised there was a profound change in his manner.

"Now, tell me your news," she demanded. "What message did you send to your Master Gilbert, Dick? And how long ago was it despatched?"

Ned gave a groan and buried his head in his hands, while Dick, Kit, and Jack stared at the floor, not meeting her gaze.

"Well?" she demanded. "Will no one tell me what happened? It was naught good by the looks of you. Did the messenger fail to come?"

"He came, my lady," said Dick quietly.

"Or so we were told!" Ned's voice was bitter.

"Then you did not see him? You sent your letter, though, didn't you?" asked Sabina with increasing anxiety.

"No, my lady," replied Dick even more softly.

"Why ever not?" she cried.

"The messenger came when you were sick unto death, my lady," said Kit. "How could we trouble the Seigneur at such a time?"

"But surely the chaplain…the seneschal…?"

"No one else has the authority to despatch letters,

my lady, so the messenger left for England empty-handed.''

"Oh, no!'' Sabina's groan almost matched Ned's for despair. "Because of me you lost your chance!''

The men protested vehemently, begging her not to blame herself. Ned was jolted from his dark lethargy to say, "You couldn't help it, lass.''

Their words were useless. Sabina was consumed with guilt.

"We will send one of our own men,'' she said at length. "I will persuade the Seigneur—''

"You needn't bother yourself, lass.'' Ned raised his head, his eyes blazing with sudden enthusiasm. "We've worked out a better way.''

"What is it?'' she asked eagerly.

Again Dick, Kit, and Jack, exchanged uncomfortable glances.

"We've been talking of escape, my lady,'' said Dick.

"And you're going to help us!'' stated Ned, as though there was no doubt of it. "You promised you'd get us home somehow, didn't you? Well, now's your chance.''

Sabina swallowed hard. She had never considered escape as a way to get them home, perhaps because such a course was fraught with dangers and difficulties.

"Surely it's too perilous a scheme?'' she declared. "How would you avoid the guards? Not to mention getting through the gates of the château. They would only be the first obstacles. Then you would have to get yourselves to the coast and thence across the Channel. Your chances of success are perilously slim.''

"So we are aware, my lady," agreed Dick. "We've given it much consideration."

"Having nothing better to do," put in Ned sourly. "Getting out of this room is no problem. I've picked harder locks in my time. The guards will be the stumbling block. They will be your responsibility. We'll need sleeping draught to put in their drink to render them unconscious."

"I'm not sure I have one strong enough. And such a measure is unreliable. What will render one man drowsy will kill another."

"Then let him be killed." Ned was unconcerned. "Let's kill the lot of them! Slit their throats!"

"Nay! Nay!" exclaimed Sabina. "I will see what I can do." She felt uncomfortable at the whole proposal, but Ned's bloodthirsty fervour was alarming.

"If we can also beg your assistance in the matter of a map of the countryside, my lady." After Ned's outburst Dick's request sounded incredibly reasonable.

"That will present no difficulty," said Sabina. "The Seigneur has one I can copy. But how will you get out of the château?"

"We plan to go at the New Year," said Dick. "The people hereabouts call it the Feast of Eginane, and the whole parish comes up to the château for the merrymaking. Once out of our tower we can mingle with the crowd. We won't be noticed."

"In midwinter! The weather will be harsh!" Sabina pointed out.

"We can endure the hard weather," said Kit eagerly. "The important thing is that the château gate stands open far into the night. We can't let such a chance slip by. Never fear, my lady, we'll succeed.

Dick can do our speaking for us, knowing the tongue."

Sabina looked surprised. She had not realised Dick spoke Breton.

"My mother comes from Bodmin, my lady," he explained. "There is little difference between the Cornish language and the Breton."

"You seem to have given your escape much thought." Sabina tried to keep the unease out of her voice. She was wondering how the Seigneur would react when he learned that his wife had aided the prisoners to escape. There was no avoiding the facts, however. She had given her word to these men, and she would have to stand by it.

"I think I had better go and start on my contribution to your plans." Sabina stood up. And immediately Catell also rose. "Ah, I had forgotten my tiring-woman."

"The wench is devoted to you, her tongue will not clack," said Ned.

"No, it won't, because I'll not have her involved!" Sabina was adamant. Ronan's wrath towards her was going to be bad enough; she was not going to allow Catell to suffer too.

"As you wish, my lady." Dick moved to the door and signalled to the guard to let her out. "And our thanks for your aid."

As soon as she could she began copying the map of the region, drawing small portions by stealth whenever the coast was clear. She suffered sorely from divided loyalties as she crept in and out of the room where it was kept. Every line she traced seemed a betrayal of Ronan. She hated to deceive him this way. But what else could she do? She prayed that the Seigneur's understanding would be greater than his anger.

Ronan still slept in the guestchamber, much to her disappointment. One night as they were about to part company on the stairs, in desperation she summoned up enough courage to say, "The guestchamber must be cold in this east wind."

Unfortunately shyness and modesty kept any hint of encouragement out of her voice, making her words sound more like a comment on the weather than an entreaty of love. At any rate, that was how Ronan seemed to interpret them, for he replied, "I pay no heed to the cold, and I fancy the wind will veer by dawn."

So much for her feeble attempt at seduction. She wished she had paid more attention to the behaviour of her sisters. They seemed to be able to enchant men with a soft word or a downward sweep of their lashes. Of course, they were all beautiful, and Sabina had always thought that such artfulness came naturally to beauties. However, these days her mirror told her she was comely, so why did she not know how to be alluring to Ronan? She wondered if a love-philtre might work. But the monks at the abbey at Brézel were hardly likely to have included such a concoction among their recipes.

Then she remembered the mandrake root given to her by the Widow du Crann. It was said to have magical properties; but what did one do with it. The person to ask was Catell.

"Mandrake root, *ma dame?*" the maid asked cautiously. "Why do you want to know about that?"

"I am just curious."

"You don't want to meddle with such things, *dame*. Dangerous, they can be when tampered with."

"Oh," said Sabina despondently.

"Were you wanting something special, *ma dame?*"

"I was just interested where one went for certain things... A good-luck charm, for example."

"Oh, you need the wise woman at Sainte Anne in that case, *ma dame*."

"She's good?"

"So folks say."

"Very well, we'll go to see her tomorrow, while the Seigneur's away hunting."

A look of understanding crossed Catell's face. "Maybe you would be prudent to visit her, *dame*. A bit of protection against being ill-wished again wouldn't go amiss, would it?"

"Exactly!" said Sabina, grasping at this ready-made excuse. She suspected her maid knew the true motive, especially when the girl added, "We'd best have Cudenec come with us, *ma dame*. We don't want a lot of tongues wagging, do we?"

Cudenec disapproved of the idea and said so volubly. "Daft idea!" he muttered gloomily as they rode out. "That's no place for a lady to be going. There's bound to be trouble, you mark my words, *ma dame!*"

Sabina took no notice of his rebellious murmuring. Despite his irascibility the old groom was completely trustworthy. She concentrated instead upon enjoying the ride, her first long ride for many weeks. In time weariness and stiffness overcame her, however, so that she was relieved when Catell said, "There's the wise woman's house, *ma dame*."

"Are you sure," asked Sabina in surprise, regarding the neat stone-built cottage set back from the track. "I expected some squalid hovel, yet this looks very tidy. Did you ever see such fine fowls pecking round the door?"

"How do you know they *are* fowls and not disappointed customers?" muttered Cudenec. "By your leave, *dame*, I'll take the horses into that spinney over there, away from prying eyes and off her property. If she's a mind to turn me into a toad she'll have her work cut out at that distance."

Sabina experienced a frisson of unease as she prepared to knock. This unease increased when the door flew open before she had touched it, and a pleasant voice said, "Ma Dame de Plou-Aven, welcome. I've been waiting for you. Come in, if you please."

The figure before Sabina was small and rotund, with rosy cheeks and uncomfortably observant eyes. Iron-grey locks peeped from under a spotless white cap. In her equally immaculate apron and trim homespun gown the wise woman looked like a prosperous farmer's wife, rather than one who dabbled in magic. Yet she knew Sabina's name and was expecting her—the table was spread with a linen cloth and set with wine and a dish of butter-cakes.

"How—how…" stammered Sabina.

The wise woman laughed. "I know many things. Else, why would you bother to come all this way to speak with me?" She turned her attention to Catell. "Doubtless your mistress wishes to speak in confidence. Here's cake and a jug of cider. I suggest you go and share it with the gloomy old fellow who guards your horses. You'll find him skulking in the trees yonder, sitting on a fallen elm."

At this demonstration of the wise woman's all-seeing eye, Catell, whose nervousness had been struggling with her curiosity, grabbed the provisions and ran.

"There, now we're alone. You can speak freely," smiled the wise woman, pouring wine into two earthenware bowls and passing one to her guest. "I've long wished to meet you. I hear you are my rival."

"From what I've seen, there's more than enough work for us both," replied Sabina briskly, determined not to show her nervousness.

"Well said." The wise woman seemed pleased. "There must be gaps in your knowledge, none the less, for you have come to see me. How can I help you?"

"I need—I want—" Suddenly the whole idea seemed silly. "I should not have come," Sabina said, rising to her feet.

"Pray, stay a moment… You have come on no frivolous errand. The help you seek is of tremendous importance to you," said the wise woman, "something you feel you cannot achieve alone. You have greater powers than you realise, but I am happy to aid you if I can. I heard that not long since you miscarried a child, so it would be easy to guess you are here for a charm to make your womb fruitful. But that's not the whole reason you are here, is it?"

"No." Sabina sank down again. "It is a lovephiltre I seek," she said in a barely audible voice.

"For your Seigneur, or has your eye strayed?"

"For my husband, of course," replied Sabina indignantly.

"You managed to get rid of the de Lannion woman very well by yourself, so I've been told. I suppose it's a harder matter to oust the ghost of his first wife, eh? Tell me, do you want the philtre to bring the Seigneur to your bed, or do you wish to reach his heart also?''

"To reach his heart!" cried Sabina, then added awkwardly, "Well, perhaps, both."

"You should have more faith in yourself. These are both things you can achieve alone if you try."

"But I cannot. That's the trouble! I have no artifice! No skill in enticement! I am too plain!"

"I do not see you so and, unless he is blind, nor does your Seigneur. Still, I can tell this is important to you, too important to give you a simple charm as I would do for a lovesick milkmaid."

The wise woman rose and disappeared into the inner room of the cottage, leaving Sabina anxiously nibbling her cake. When she turned she was carrying a leather thong to which was attached a small bag.

"You must take something of your Seigneur's and something of your own," the woman instructed. "Metal for preference, but not a knife—a sharp blade might sever his love instead of binding it to you. Tie both objects firmly together with the thong then drop them into Merlin's Foundation, in the deep part."

"Is that all?" asked Sabina, looking at the little bag and the strip of leather as they lay on her palm.

"You would have done something more difficult?"

"Of course I would!"

The wise woman smiled. "Love can be surprisingly simple, *ma dame*. Now you had best get home before the Seigneur returns from hunting."

"You know that my husband is hunting?" Sabina stared at her. Then she began to smile too. "You are right, I must go. Many thanks." Her hand went to the pocket on her belt to take out a coin, but the wise woman waved her away.

"Only when the charm succeeds do you pay me," she said.

"You look weary," was Ronan's first comment when he saw her. Sabina feared that he might suspect something, but he accepted her explanation that she had been riding. "Take care not to overtax yourself," was all he said.

Sabina woke next morning feeling decidedly stiff and aching after her exertions.

"Is this wise, *ma dame?*" asked Catell when she ordered he mare to be saddled.

"The way to throw off my aches and pains is to get back on my horse," Sabina said, unwilling to admit the true reason why she wanted to leave the château. When they set out she had the ingredients of the wise woman's charm securely tucked in her pocket.

"Where are we going, *ma dame?*" asked Cudenec as they mounted up, with Jester in ecstatic attendance.

"I thought a ride to Merlin's Fountain would be pleasant," Sabina said casually.

Catell and Cudenec exchanged glances, and the groom mumbled something uncomplimentary about women in general and those who claimed to be wise in particular. Nevertheless, when they reached the pool in the forest it was he who said, "There, off you go, *ma dame*. I'll keep watch to make sure no one disturbs your nonsense."

"You can stay here, too, if you wish, Catell," said Sabina, already striding along the narrow track.

"Not I! I'm coming with you, *dame!*" puffed the maid, hurrying in her wake. "You never know who's abroad these days. Oh, the saints have mercy!" she finished with a shriek as a figure burst out of the undergrowth.

"Never fear!" shouted Cudence. He came lumbering up, his sword drawn, only to groan, "Oh, it's only that plaguey Yannick! I thought we were being attacked!" Sheathing his sword, he stamped back to the horses.

Yannick's joyous welcome showed that he had been disturbed by Sabina's absence. It took a lengthy show of mime for her to explain she had been ill. Giving inarticulate grunts of pleasure he accompanied her and Catell, and when they reached the pool he crouched contentedly at the waterside with Jester.

"Whatever it is you're putting into the pool give it a hefty throw, *dame,*" advised Catell.

"How do you know I'm putting anything in the water?" demanded Sabina.

The maid gave a shrug. "Everyone does. That's why most folk come here, to get the magic of Merlin to work for them."

"Oh…" Feeling rather self-conscious, Sabina withdrew the bound articles from her pocket. Her first throw was a failure. The love-charm fell into the shallow rock basin instead of the deeper pool beyond. Catell had already begun to kick off her shoes to fetch it when Yannick stretched his long arm and fished out the small bundle. Beaming proudly, he handed it to Sabina.

Drawing back her arm, Sabina let fly the charm again and this time her aim was true. It fell right in the deepest part of the pool. She watched until the last ripples had ceased to disturb the mirror surface of the water. Then, and only then, did she allow herself to hope. With the powers of Merlin and the wise woman behind her, Ronan was bound to love her now.

In the next few days she had to admit that there was no change in his attitude towards her. He was amiable, courteous, even affectionate in a brotherly sort of way, but he gave no sign of being consumed with passion for her. Not with a passion which matched hers for him. Sabina made herself be patient; the wise woman had given no time limit for the charm to work. In the meantime she kept busy. Gradually she resumed more and more of her old duties, but mostly she was occupied with helping to plan the escape of the prisoners.

Already December was upon them, cold and wet. She was thankful that the four Englishmen would not be cooped up much longer. Whenever she looked at Ronan it hurt to know that she was deceiving him. It also hurt to find no sign of a growing love in him and she wondered how long it would be before the charm began working.

She was taken completely by surprise one night when the chamber door opened and there he stood.

"Seigneur?" she greeted him questioningly.

"Will you listen to that wind, *ma dame!*" he said.

Obediently she listened. A gale had been raging for days, accompanied by torrents of rain, but try as she might she could not hear any difference in the shrieking of the wind as it swept about the draughty château.

"Seigneur?" she repeated, even more puzzled.

"You were right! The guestchamber *is* freezing cold when the wind is from the east!"

Catell, who had been about to settle down in the *couchette,* gave a giggle, picked up her things and departed.

The truth dawned on Sabina. He wanted to share her bed. The charm was working. Confident in the power of the magic, she gave him a smile bright with welcome.

"I thought you said you did not feel the cold," she teased.

"I lied," he said shamelessly.

"Such a pity! I'm so comfortable here."

"Then out of the kindness of your heart will you let me be comfortable too?"

By way of an answer she turned back the coverlet. The heavy bedcurtains closed, enshrouding them in an intimate darkness as she held out her arms to him. He *was* cold. After he had divested himself of his nightrobe his skin struck chill against her, and in an urgent need to give comfort she entwined herself about him, letting her warmth seep into his icy limbs. She had so much faith in the love-spell that she let her instincts have full rein, nestling closer to him and caressing the cold smoothness of his skin with her lips. Ronan began to respond with obvious pleasure. Giving a contented sigh, he pressed against her.

"We've been apart a long time," he whispered. His hands began to explore the soft curves of her flesh. "And I have such need of you."

Sabina did not reply that her need was as great as his. Such words were unnecessary. Her willing body answered far more potently, cleaving to him in a way that made him gasp. There was no holding back now.

Why should she? She was confident he would respond to her, just as she knew she could assuage his hunger. It was as if some ancient knowledge, latent before, had come to life in her, telling her what to do, how she could make him desperate for her as he had never been before. Her hunger fed his in a passionate conjoining that rose to a sensual crescendo that left both of them breathless.

Stunned and drained by the force of both her emotion and his Sabina permitted herself only the briefest remembrance of Marianne—this time she had been the one Ronan had wanted, not as a substitute for his dead bride, not as a mother for his child, but as his wife!

Lazily Ronan pulled her toward him and rested his cheek against her hair. "You smell of roses," he said drowsily, twisting one of her dark locks gently around his fingers. "Roses in December! How delightful!"

"Catell has taken me in hand," admitted Sabina. "She's forever anointing me with creams for this and lotions for that. I fancy she is bitterly ashamed of me at times."

"The poor girl must have a hard life of it. I wonder if she ever wishes she was back scrubbing tables."

"Wretch!" Sabina pretended to be indignant and turned away from him. But he caught her and held her tightly.

"No, you are not to move," he instructed. "The night is cold and you are keeping me nicely warm."

"Shall I get Catell to heat a stone for you and wrap it in a soft cloth to keep you even warmer?" suggested Sabina mischievously.

"No, thank you. You will do well enough." He gave a contented sigh. "They are wrong, you know."

"Who are?" she asked.

"The minstrels and the troubadours. Those fashionable ballads they sing about courtly love—it's all nonsense. A knight sighing and languishing for a lady he can never have. So-called love flourishing when the so-called lovers never touch. It's ridiculous, I say!"

"Oh, and are you an expert on love?"

"Of course I am! I'm a red-blooded Breton. Who else can talk on the subject with greater authority?" He pretended to be haughty. Then he gave a laugh and hugged her tightly. "No, loving is being warm and close, it is comforting each other. Yes, and giving pleasure, too, as we have done tonight. What joy is there in mere looks and sighs to compare with that, eh?"

Sabina did not reply. She could not find the words. She raised her head the better to kiss him. He had not actually said he loved her—but he had spoken of her and love in the same breath. That meant the same, surely? She could hardly believe it! The ghost of Marianne had finally gone! Ronan's love was hers alone now!

Chapter Ten

Sabina feared that once Ronan awoke the mood of tenderness would be broken, but when they rose to go about their daily duties he stopped her at the door with a kiss.

"I would have you spend time with me today," he said softly. "I grow envious of the folk with their boils, their rheumatism, and their bellyaches, who claim so much of your attention."

"You could always say you have boils, rheumatism, or a bellyache," she said with a smile. She was astonished with herself, that she could laugh and tease him so easily, when she had always found such gentle flirting difficult. It was the love-charm's doing.

"I have no wish to stand in line with your other admirers," Ronan replied. "Especially not in this rain. It would be much more agreeable to play backgammon and drink wine by the fire, would it not?"

"It would be a close-run thing." She pretended to consider. "But upon careful thought backgammon by the fire does sound very pleasant."

Outside, the rain continued to fall; no one could remember such a prolonged spell of wet weather.

Dampness seeped into everything, making the servants and the dogs in the great hall quarrelsome and irritable as they jostled for the best places by the huge log fire. But in the solar each day, alone with Ronan in blissful contentment, Sabina was oblivious of everything else. Her world was perfect.

She was careful to honour her debts. Cudenec was despatched, cursing volubly, to pay the wise woman, though Sabina wondered how she could ever truly repay her for all she had done.

Christmas was fast approaching, bringing with it a full week or more of merry-making. The knowledge that during the festivities the Englishmen would make their escape did not dim Sabina's joy. Ronan would be angry, but he would forgive her, because he loved her.

She climbed up the stairs to the solar, humming to herself, then she came to a halt. Through the thick oaken door she could hear Ronan's voice, and he was very angry. Angrier than she had heard him in a long time. The door flew open and a man ran out, almost knocking her over. It was Ronan's body-servant.

"*Ma dame,* I didn't do it! I swear I didn't! Please tell the Seigneur!" cried Markiz, tears flowing down his cheeks.

"You didn't do what?" she asked, surprised to see the quiet, unassuming man so agitated.

"I didn't steal, *ma dame!* I'm not a thief! I've served the Seigneur since he was a boy. Never once has he had to question my honesty!"

"Of course you're not a thief!" she said consolingly. "I'm sure this is a misunderstanding. What are you supposed to have stolen?"

"A pin, *ma dame!* A small, base metal pin! And I haven't even seen it…"

Sabina's heart sank. She had been so sure Ronan would not miss the pin, and certainly never dreamed that Markiz would be accused of taking it. "You have no need to worry," she said. "I borrowed it. I will speak to the Seigneur about it immediately."

She entered the solar to find Ronan throwing things out of one of his chests. His face was flushed with fury, his brows angrily drawn together, yet there was more than temper in his expression, there was distress too.

"The thieving rogue!" he muttered. "The rouge…!"

"Markiz is no thief. You should know that," Sabina said, keeping her voice calm with a great effort. "This pin you say is missing—a little grey metal thing, is it? Roughly fashioned like an ear of wheat?"

"It is. Have you seen it? Do you know where it is?"

"Yes, to both your questions. I borrowed it."

"You did what!" Ronan stared at her.

"I borrowed it. I had need of a pin, so I did not think you would mind if I took one of yours." She hoped her words sounded casual.

"Did it never occur to you to ask my permission?" Ronan spoke in a low whisper.

Sabina sought defence in attack. "No more than it occurred to you to ask if I had seen it, instead of accusing poor Markiz in that heavy-handed way. The fellow was in tears when I saw him. You know there is no one more honest or trustworthy—"

"*Ma dame!*" broke in the Seigneur hotly. "We

are not discussing my relationship with the servants! We are discussing your taking one of my possessions!''

''I thought that at our wedding you vowed your goods were my goods,'' put in Sabina quickly.

The remark was a mistake. Ronan's eyes glittered dangerously. ''Don't try to prevaricate, *dame*. Why did you take it?''

''I had need of a pin, that's all.'' Sabina was alarmed that he should be so angry with her.

''If you had asked me I'd have gladly given you a dozen pins of silver or gold—but never that one.''

''Why not?'' she demanded.

Ronan did not reply to her question. Instead he said more calmly, ''I would be grateful if you would give it back immediately.''

Now what was she to do? She could not tell him the pin rested in Merlin's Fountain, bound to a ring of her own as a love-charm.

''There—there are difficulties, sire,'' she said.

''What difficulties? Where is it? What have you done with it?'' The calm had gone from his voice, and he spoke with mounting fury.

''It's...it's... At the moment I do not have it...''

''Then where is it? For heaven's sake, *ma dame*, let me have a sensible answer!'' he shouted at her, taking a step forward.

''Such a fuss about a worthless pin!'' cried Sabina.

''It is not worthless to me!'' Ronan roared, equally incensed. ''I would sooner lose a chest of gold than that little keepsake. Marianne gave it to me. Do you not understand? It was a gift from my wife!''

Sabina recoiled as if he had struck her.

"*I* am your wife!" she cried. "Though you only seem to acknowledge the fact when it suits you!"

With that she turned and ran swiftly from the room, her head bent so that he would not see her tears.

"Catell," she said, encountering the maid in the passageway. "Order my horse to be saddled. I am going out."

Catell took one look at her mistress's tear-stained face and replied, "Not alone, you're not!" Adding belatedly, "By your leave, *ma dame*."

"Very well, come if you must." Sabina wiped her eyes on her sleeve, not caring about the damage she was doing to her new peacock-velvet surcoat. "But no groom, mind. Not even Cudenec!"

The pair of them rode in silence; Sabina was too concerned with painful thoughts for speech. Time and again she went over the tender moments she and Ronan had spent together of late. They made no difference. In his heart he was still married to Marianne, no matter how many sweet words he spoke to her or what intimate caresses he gave. In the midst of her misery, anger stirred. She had tried everything she knew to gain his love and still he rejected her! If that tawdry pin meant so much to him she would get it for him!

"Your pardon, *dame?*" Catell asked.

Sabina realised that she had spoken her thoughts aloud.

"We're going back to Merlin's Fountain," she said brusquely. "The objects I threw in—the charm didn't work and I intend to retrieve them."

"*Ma dame!*" Catell's jaw dropped. "How will you do such a thing? It's bitterly cold."

"I do not know," snapped Sabina. "I only know I've got to get those things back. And there's an end to it!"

Casting off her shoes and stockings and hitching up her skirts, Sabina plunged into the icy waters of the pool. The chill took her breath away and spread a dull ache through her limbs, but she did not care. Despite her protests Catell joined her and, together, they waded thigh-deep, searching. The iciness of the water even robbed Catell of speech, so that when she heard someone coming all she could do was to give a harsh cry. It was only Yannick, and his eyes grew large with astonishment at finding them splashing about in the pool. He would have joined them but Sabina deterred him. She reasoned that two of them dying with cold would suffice; he would be more useful keeping a lookout.

There was no knowing how long Sabina would have continued if she had not noticed Catell's face had turned an ashen grey. Stricken with remorse at having made her servant endure for so long she took the girl by the arm, and together they made their way stiffly out of the water. As they rode off, their sodden skirts flapping damply about their legs, they were watched by Yannick, his face still puzzled.

Once back at the château, after they had changed into dry clothes, Sabina insisted that Catell sat with her beside the fire in the solar to thaw out. Ronan would not disturb them. He, too, had ridden out. There would be no cosy sipping of wine and playing backgammon today, or any other day. As they both sat, their skirts turned back to their knees, their numbed hands and feet held out to the flames, Sabina worried over what excuse she could give for not returning the pin. She even toyed with having a replica made, but she could not remember the design well enough.

Later, throughout supper, she sat in trepidation, waiting for the vital question.

"Well, *ma dame,* and have you deigned to find the missing pin for me?" Ronan asked at last.

"I hope to have it for you before long, Seigneur," she replied. It was a lie. She had no hope of returning it. But she did not know what else to say.

The atmosphere at the high table was almost as chilling as the waters of Merlin's fountain. Sabina considered a dozen different explanations she might give, all of them fabrications, not one of them feasible.

It took an uproar at the far end of the hall to jolt her out of her stupor. Several servants were grappling with a solitary figure. Far from trying to escape, the man seemed to want to enter the hall.

"What *is* going on!" bellowed Ronan testily.

Suddenly the man broke free from his captors and, dodging and waving, he headed for the dais.

"It's Yannick!" cried Sabina in surprise. "Let him come!"

"Now what's amiss that we cannot eat supper in peace," growled Ronan.

Yannick collapsed before the high table, out of breath and soaking wet, but with a smile of triumph on his face. Rising unsteadily he held out his hand to Sabina. On his palm lay a sodden little bundle, entangled with green pondweed.

"You have found it!" Sabina could have wept with relief. "Oh, Yannick, you have found it!" She took the charm, then, eager to give some immediate

reward to him she pushed her trencher laden with
slices of roast mutton towards him. Greedily he
seized it, and sitting on the edge of the dais, proceeded to wolf it down.

"What the devil have you there?" demanded
Ronan.

Sabina had no option but to uncurl her fingers and
show him. The colour drained from his face.

"Are you mad!" he hissed in a low voice. "To
show such a thing openly? Come with me!" Stuffing
the charm swiftly out of sight into his pouch he
seized her arm and all but dragged her out of the
hall. As she went Sabina's concern was still for the
cold and soaking Yannick.

"Catell," she called over her shoulder, "see he
gets warm dry clothes...and some mulled cider...oh,
and he's to have the best place by the fire..."

By this time she and Ronan were out of the hall
and heading towards the solar. Once inside he
slammed the door and shot home the bolt.

"What is this?" he demanded, thrusting the wet
charm towards her.

"It—it is the pin you set such store by, and a ring
of my own," she faltered.

"I can see that! But what is this? And this?" He
pointed to the leather binding and the small bag attached to it. "You have been dabbling in witchcraft!"

"No," protested Sabina. "Never that. I only went
to the wise woman. Lots of people do it if they need
help."

"But you are not lots of people! You are the Dame
de Plou-Aven! All eyes are upon you. Once it is
whispered that you are calling upon supernatural

powers it is but a short step to being accused of witchcraft." Taking his dagger, he cut away the thong and the bag and threw them into the fire. "That could be your fate too, don't you realise it?" he exclaimed.

"No, I was doing no harm!"

"I am sure you were not." His voice became gentle, as he took hold of her shoulders. "Oh, Sabina, how you frightened me! You must give me your promise never to do such a thing again."

"I promise," she said quietly. "It's no great thing, the charm didn't work anyway."

"But why did you need it? What were you trying to achieve?"

"Nothing important." She pressed her lips together stubbornly.

"Nothing important? Yet you journeyed to the wise woman for the charm, and risked a burning at the stake for it! What was it?"

"I cannot—will not say."

He tilted her head up, the better to see her face. "I know the charm involved me, or you would not have needed the pin. You did not wish to harm me, I think."

"Never that!" She was aghast at the very idea. In a sudden burst of honesty she cried. "I wanted to please you!" It was the nearest she could bring herself to admitting her need for his love.

"Oh, Sabina!" he groaned, pulling her to him. "You risked so much just for that. It wasn't necessary, you know. I'm not displeased with you. I know how much you grieve for the babe. And I do, too; we will have plenty of bonny children in good time, just have patience and a little faith. I will not have you putting yourself in danger to give Plou-Aven an heir.''

He had misunderstood. He thought she had got the charm to make her fertile. Sabina did not enlighten him. What was the use? Instead, she buried her face against his chest and wept. He enfolded her in his arm and held her so tightly she could feel the beating of his heart. He talked softly to her, saying comforting words. But she would not be comforted. She knew that, close as she was to him now, the ghost of Marianne still stood between them, as strong and as impenetrable as a barrier of steel.

Sabina awoke next morning to find Catell laying out her clothes.

"Ah, you're awake, *ma dame!*" The maid hitched back the heavy bed-curtains and held out Sabina's chamber-robe. "Such excitement! Part of the outer wall has collapsed! All this rain must have weakened it. The Seigneur's had men out there through the night working by torchlight. They're afeared the north tower will go too."

"Was anyone hurt?" asked Sabina, alarmed.

"No, thanks to *le Bon Dieu!*"

"Dress me quickly, then, and get my thick mantle. I must go and see what has happened."

It was bitterly cold as she crossed the bailey, and heavy white flakes fell intermingled with the rain. Quite a crowd had gathered, braving the freezing weather to share in the drama. They fell back to let her through. There was a sizeable gap in the thick stone wall where it adjoined the north tower. The tower itself looked unscathed until she drew close, then she saw a great crack had developed down one side. Ronan was there, supervising the small army of men who were working to repair the damage. He was caked in mud and looked cold and tired.

"How do things progress?" Sabina asked.

"We are winning," he said wearily. "I do not think any more will fall now."

"No one was hurt?"

"No, that's one thing we must be thankful for."

"And the English prisoners?"

"I have housed them in the apple-store."

Sabina frowned. "But you cannot put them in there!" she protested. "It's too dark and cold."

"Where else have I to put them?" snapped Ronan. "Back in the north tower, where they might fall to their deaths at any moment? Or in the old dungeon that is running with wet after this rain? Never fear, with luck they will not have to be there above two or three weeks."

Two or three weeks! That would be long after the New Year festivities. It was not the Englishmen's comfort Sabina was worried about, it was their chances of escape. Then Ronan rubbed wearily at his eyes with the back of a muddied hand and her concern was for him.

"I am sorry," she said contritely. "I know you have done your best for them. Will you not come and rest now, and take some food? You've a long day ahead of you."

"You are right. It's time I called a halt. Tired men make mistakes and this is no place for anyone to grow careless."

"There will be food for all of them in the great hall. I will go and see to it now," she said.

As Sabina made preparations to feed the men her

mind was occupied with plans of escape for Ned and his friends. But how? The apple-store window was too small, and its only door opened into a guardroom occupied by a dozen or more men-at-arms. It seemed impossible.

An atmosphere of muted excitement pervaded the great hall. The meal had begun silently, for the men were too cold and tired to talk much, but as they consumed the food and the mulled cider the noise level grew.

The pinched look had gone from Ronan's face, too. "I was sharp with you, out there at the wall," he said. He nodded to Markiz to pour him more spiced wine. "I'm sorry. I had much to occupy me."

"And I troubled you about where the prisoners should be lodged. It is I who should be sorry," replied Sabina. "I know you have done your best for them."

"I'm glad you realise it. I don't like putting the poor fellows in that hole, but at the moment I fear it's the best hole we have got." He smiled at her and she smiled back. "There is one thing which will severely displease you, though," he went on. "Your visits to the prisoners must stop while they are held in the store. It's not seemly for you to enter the guardroom."

Sabina's mouth formed an O of protest, then she restrained herself. He was right, of course. He had already shown remarkable forbearance in letting her visit them at all.

"If that is your wish, sire," she said regretfully.

Ronan regarded her steadily. "Such meekness does not become you, *ma dame*," he said. "Oh, very well, if it will please you, make one last visit to the prisoners to see if they need aught. Go this morning. The guardroom will be empty. It's to be brief, though. And definitely the last until they return to the north tower!"

"Thank you," said Sabina, smiling gratefully, thinking how few men in his situation would have shown such compassion.

Ronan rose to his feet, a signal to the other men to move also, and for a while the great hall seethed with movement. Sabina went, too. She was eager to get to the prisoners. Poor souls, what could she say to comfort them?

The storeroom smelled sharply of ripe fruit when she and Catell entered. It was below ground level, the only light coming from a wide, shallow grille near the ceiling which gave directly on to the cobbles of the inner bailey. Even as she looked Sabina saw the familiar plumed legs of Jester wander past. She shivered. The iron brazier in the middle of the room was too recently lit to give off much heat.

Dick came to greet her. "Thank you for coming, my lady," he said, his customary good humour absent. "Come and take what cheer we have."

"Cheer? That's a laugh!" said Kit.

As for Ned, he just kept staring at the floor, not even acknowledging her presence.

"I'm sorry things have gone so badly," Sabina said.

"Thank you, my lady," replied Dick. "Did you ever know such bad luck?"

"What's to be done now?" she asked.

"What can we do? Escape from this place seems impossible. We've racked our brains until our heads ache, but we can find no solution. Not unless you have a plan, my lady?'' Dick looked at her hopefully. But she shook her head.

''I fear not. I only wish I had. And I must tell you, this must be my last visit until you return to the north tower, the Seigneur was most firm on the matter.''

''We were so close!'' cried Kit in despair.

''Aye, and the plans so carefully laid,'' said Dick.

''There *must* be a way!'' Sabina exclaimed. ''Could you not tunnel?''

''We're on solid rock here, my lady,'' Kit said. ''It would take an age to chip a space big enough for us to get through, even if we could hide our work from the guards.''

''There must be a way!'' repeated Sabina vehemently.

Outside, hearing the sound of her voice, Jester pawed frantically at the grille. He could hear her but he could not reach her. Frustrated, he sat down on the wet cobbles and threw back his head and howled. The sound echoed eerily through the courtyard, stirring a memory in Sabina's head.

''The shaft!''

''Your pardon, my lady?''

But she ignored Dick. Her eyes searched the room until she saw something which gave her hope. At one corner the ceiling sloped inwards at an angle, forming an alcove beneath it.

''What is...'' she began, then remembered the presence of her maid. ''Catell,'' she said, ''go and fetch Jester, for pity's sake, before his howls disturb the Seigneur.''

After the girl had gone she said urgently, ''Over the alcove there, is that where the stairs run?''

"Yes, but there's no door behind the sacks, We've looked."

"Try the ceiling! Quick!"

"Right! Up you come, Jack lad!" Dick was perplexed but he was willing to humour her.

They crowded in the corner while he hoisted the boy onto his shoulders.

"Now, push upwards!" ordered Sabina.

"It gives!" cried Jack "It gives!"

"That's your way out!" Sabina was triumphant. "Above there is a shaft going up parallel to the stairs. You can escape that way!"

"Are you sure, my lady?"

"How do you know?"

"Where does it lead?"

The questions poured from the men. But Sabina's sharp ears heard Catell's voice out in the guardroom.

"Wait!" she said. "My maid is returning!"

Fortunately, when Catell entered towed in the wake of an enthusiastic Jester, she did not notice the hope in the men's faces, nor the sudden bright enthusiasm that had come to their eyes. She also had a message to deliver.

"Your pardon, *dame*, but the Seigneur wishes your presence urgently in the great hall," she said.

"I must go." Sabina rose to take her farewell.

"But what's to be done? How are we to know the plan of escape, my lady?" Dick asked anxiously.

Sabina's brain had been working at a feverish pitch. "Be ready just as we arranged before, when the festivities are at their height," she replied. "I will give you a signal… Oh, I know, I'll drop some stones or something down the shaft. That will be your signal to push up the trapdoor. You will have a fair climb. Can you scale a rope?''

"My lady, we're all seamen." Dick's tone was gently reproving.

"Of course! How foolish of me...!"

"By your leave, *ma dame,* will you come swiftly." Catell was hovering at the door. "The matter is indeed urgent. One of the workmen is injured."

"Why didn't you say so at once?" Sabina made to hurry after her. As she was leaving she turned to the prisoners for a last time. "Trust me," she said. "The first part of the escape is my responsibility."

The injured man proved to be only the first of a string of casualties, as the men working on the wall grew tired and the conditions underfoot deteriorated. It was very much later before Sabina could examine the closet where Jester had spent his first, noisy night. She discovered that she could lift out the floor quite easily, but as she gazed down into the profound darkness she wondered how she was going to be able to get the men up the shaft. By rope, of course, but there was no suitable point for tying it. Then she noted the post-holes in the masonry for fixing scaffolding. A stout wooden beam slotted in would solve the problem—though the acquiring of such an item and carrying it unseen up the closet would be problems enough in themselves.

The damaged wall proved an unexpected Godsend in one respect: ropes and beams in abundance were left for the taking in the outer bailey. When she tried, surreptitiously, to take a suitable length of rope, however, she was appalled by the weight. She had to settle for shorter pieces, which she appropriated and coiled round her body concealed under her mantle—not an easy task to perform away from prying eyes.

It was as she made her way across the outer bailey one day, the last length of rope wrapped round her waist, that she encountered Ronan. She had seen little of him of late. True, he had been fully occupied repairing the wall, but ever since the incident of the pin he had seemed to grow more remote from her. It was ironic that, eager as she was for his company, she should meet him at such an inconvenient moment.

"Ma dame," he greeted her. "You should be indoors, it is too bitter to be out today."

"I am comfortable enough, I thank you," she replied.

"You are? From the way you grasp your mantle to you I thought you were feeling the cold."

Sabina did not know what to answer. An uncomfortable feeling round her middle warned her the rope was slipping.

"How goes it at the wall? I suppose you cannot be spared from it for a moment," she said, hoping he would take the hint.

"Not at all. We are making such good progress I thought to have an hour or two's rest."

To her horror he took up his place beside her and began to walk with her. Her rope girdle had sunk a little further, and she tried to restrain its descent by pressing her elbow against it.

"That is good news," she said, putting on a smile she was far from feeling.

"Yes, it is. I've a fancy to sit peacefully by the fire for a spell, and maybe sip some wine." He paused, clearly expecting some response from her.

But Sabina's panic-stricken thoughts were occupied with the wayward coil of rope which had now sunk to her hips. She pressed her cramped elbow harder to her side. Perhaps if she sagged a little at the knees the rope would slide no further...

"Are you all right?" asked Ronan. "You seem suddenly to walk with a limp."

"A limp?" she gazed up at him in horror. "Oh no, sire! These cobbles are so slippery!"

"And cold. Come with me now. Keep me company in the solar? I found those hours we spent playing backgammon and talking together were very pleasant. I would spend another afternoon thus, if you are willing."

The pleading in his voice was undeniable. At any other time such an invitation would have delighted her. Why did it have to come now, with her unconventional girdle threatening to impede her completely?

"No!" she said, her voice harsh in her desperation to get away from him before disaster struck. "No! I am too busy."

He flinched at the brusque rebuff. "As you wish, *ma dame*," he said, the coldness of his tone betraying his hurt.

Without another word he strode away, leaving Sabina near to tears in her distress and frustration. She longed to call after him, but dared not; the rope had given way to gravity and lay in coils about her ankles. Stuffing the unwieldy bundle under her mantle she hurried up the stairs to the closet eager to hide the rope quickly, and then go to Ronan in the solar. First, though, she would have to change her gown, for the rope had been muddy—and since Catell was nowhere to be found she had to struggle with her laces by herself.

Presentable again, she dashed down to the solar with unseemly haste. She flung open the door, and could have wept with disappointment; Ronan was not there. When she encountered a servant and asked where his master was she got the answer "In the great hall, *ma dame,* playing cards with the captain of the men-at-arms." Sadly she turned away. The Seigneur no longer had need of her company, it seemed.

Christmas passed in a blur for Sabina. The midnight mass on Christmas Eve, the burning of the great Christmas log, the feasting and the fun, hardly touched her at all. Her thoughts were focused on the last day of December and the escape. She was consumed with nervous dread and it seemed incredible to her that signs of her inner turmoil were not more evident.

She awoke on New Year's Eve, her stomach a knot of apprehension. The morning was not half done when the beating of *tambours* and the wail of *binious* drifted up from the *bourg.*

"I thought you said this Feast of Eginane celebrated the New Year," she protested to Catell. "It cannot have begun yet!"

"Oh, but it can, *ma dame!*" Catell's head was on one side to catch every sound, her face bright with anticipation. "Oh, now you'll see some fun, *dame.* The procession, will already be going round the parish."

"Then, surely, they will be here before long? And we're not ready!" cried Sabina, in a panic for the outcome of the escape rather than the merrymaking. She feared she had made a mistake in the timing.

"Don't fret, *ma dame*. They come here last, and that won't be until about midnight," chuckled the maid. "Those who can still stand, that is! Every household gives something, food or money and there's usually a cider-jug at every door, too. The money is divided among the poor and the food provides a feast for the whole parish."

Sabina was still not convinced the procession would not reach the château until after dark. All day long she was on tenterhooks lest the merrymakers arrived early, in the daylight, and ruined her plans. Several times she crept away to check her preparations, making sure the beam was in place and the rope tied securely.

Eventually it grew dark, and the night was hours old before the sound of the *tamours* and the bagpipes—now somewhat off-key and hesitant—began to grow louder. She had intended to wait in her bedchamber, close by the closet, until the vital moment, so she was horrified when Ronan himself entered the room.

"The revellers are nearly here," he said. "Come, we must go down to the door to greet them."

"Greet them?" She stared at him stupidly. It had not occurred to her that she had a part to play in the festivities.

"Yes, as *dame* of the household you must be here. Come, it's great sport."

He did not wait for an answer, but snatched up her mantle that lay on the bed, slung it round her shoulders, and grasping her hand firmly led her downstairs.

The servants and other occupants of the château were crowded round the main door, chattering excitedly.

"Is the gate open? Can they get in?" asked Sabina, from her vantage point on the steps.

"Certainly. All gates and doors are open to them, otherwise the household is doomed to ill-luck." Ronan was peering over her head for the first glimpse of the procession.

Sabina thought of the prisoners, fraught with waiting. She wondered how long it would be before she could slip away.

"They're coming!" a cry went up, and then a hush fell upon the onlookers.

As Ronan had said all the gates stood open. Sabina could see through to the outer gatehouse. The steep slope and the alcohol had silenced the bagpipes, so the procession approached to the beat of a single *tambour,* its dull throb reverberating in the frosty air. Behind the drummer came the fool, a man decked all over in bright ribbons, a crown of green leaves round his hat. In one hand he brandished a beribboned stick, his wand of office, with the other he led a horse, its grey flanks covered by a white cloth, and with two large panniers slung across its back. Behind, followed a procession of men; their torches flared in the darkness, glinting on the evergreen garlands bedecking their hats and the bright hues of their ribbon favours. On they came, singing a repetitive refrain which sounded unearthly in the cold night air, a mass of light and colour and song advancing like some brilliant mythical reptile.

Sabina felt a shiver run down her spine. This was more than a country frolic—this was pagan, and eerily mysterious. Ronan felt its power, too, she could tell.

Just then the men gave a great shout: *"Eguin an eit! Eguin an eit!"*

"What do they mean?" whispered Sabina, alarmed.

"It is a plea for a good harvest," Ronan whispered back. "An old cry, just as the whole rite is old!"

The procession came closer and entered the more brightly lit inner bailey.

Ronan moved forward to greet them.

"A blessing on you, Seigneur, on your good *dame,* and all your household," called the fool. "Have you an Eginane offering to give us, to ensure a good harvest?"

"I have indeed!" Ronan replied, producing a tiny bag of meal.

This was a familiar joke, and the meagre offering was greeted with a derisive cheer.

"We thank you for your generosity, Seigneur!" The fool bowed. "But have you not a little more you could give?"

Ronan pretended to consider. "Perhaps I can spare more, now I think on it." And at a signal from him the servants moved forward to put bread into the panniers, while across the bailey came pack-mules laden with meat, game, and, most important, cider.

"The jesting is over," cried Ronan. "I entreat you all to sup before you go, to bring good fortune to this place!"

Taking Sabina by the hand, he led the cheering, laughing crowd to the great hall. On the advice of Seneschal Le Godet, the veteran of a score of such festivities, Sabina had made sure that ample food and drink was set out. Even so, it disappeared at an astonishing rate as more and more people crowded in.

From her seat at the high table she watched in fascination despite her anxiety about the prisoners. Her stomach began to contract sickeningly with nerves as she thought of all she must do that night. As her tension grew she wondered when she could decently make her excuses and leave. It was Ronan who came to her aid.

"The celebrations can become very boisterous," he said, his mouth close to her ear because of the din. "If you wish to withdraw soon none will take it amiss."

"Thank you, sire. I think it wise if I left now." She rose to go, and immediately Catell made to come with her. "You stay and enjoy the fun," she told her maid. "I can manage alone for once."

"Thank you, *ma dame*," Catell replied gratefully.

Sabina hurried out of the hall up to the closet. It took her only minutes to clear sufficient space. The wooden floor lifted out with ease and she let fall the rope. She had even remembered to snatch up a handful of pebbles to drop down as a signal. She heard them patter on the wooden hatch far below her. There was a creaking, then a bang, as for one heart-stopping moment the bottom hatch refused to budge and had to be thumped. Immediately after, the rope went taut, and the unmistakable sounds of someone climbing echoed up the shaft. Young Jack, as the lightest, had come first. Then came Kit, then Ned, and finally Dick.

"Being a prisoner certainly weakens the limbs," he puffed as the others hauled him over the edge.

"Here!" Sabina thrust a bundle at each man. "Put

these on to make you look more like Bretons. Ned, you pull your hat well down to hide your red hair. There's food, too, and money—not much, but I hope it will pay your passage across the Channel."

"My lady, what can we say…" began Dick.

"Say naught! Just get ready. I've brought things for you to carry—a tray of bread, a couple of jugs of cider—they'll make you look less conspicuous. Are you ready?"

"Just about, my lady." Dick finished tying an apron round his waist and picked up the bread tray. "Which way do we go?"

"Down the stairs and through the door at the bottom. It leads straight into the great hall, which you must cross and go out of the door at the other end. Come and see."

Sabina led them to a small alcove in the bed of the stairs. There was an opening in it through which it was possible to gaze down on the great hall below.

"Holy Mother!" breathed Kit, looking at the sea of bodies below. "What a crush! You could get a whole army through that lot and not be noticed."

"Getting four men through will suffice for now," said Sabina. "See? At the far end is the door through which you must go. It is much used, for it leads to the kitchen and the buttery, so you will not be remarked upon. I understand the procession must return to the *bourg* before long. If you hide in the shadows outside you should have no difficulty in joining the throng without being noticed. Now, who will go first?"

Kit picked up one of the cider-jugs. "This smells good," he said, sniffing appreciatively. "What say you and I share it as we go along, eh Jack?"

Jack, silent as ever, only nodded his head. They set off, and the others listened to their footsteps as they went down the stairs, then the door creaked and they were gone.

"I see them!" said Sabina, gazing down into the hall. She spoke softly, though there was no chance of anyone down there overhearing her.

Through the pall of smoke from the log fire and the rank tallow torches the three of them watched as Kit and Jack wove their way unsteadily through the hall, their arms about each other's shoulders as if for mutual support, taking alternate swigs from the cider-jug.

"They're through!" Dick heaved a sigh of relief, "Now it's our turn, Ned, my friend."

Ned had been unusually quiet so far. Now he spoke for the first time. "You go on your own," he said. "You'll stand a better chance by yourself, you speaking the local tongue."

"Nay, friend," protested Dick.

But Ned gave him a gentle push. "Go!" he said. "We'll come after you, never fear."

"We?" queried Dick and Sabina together.

"I thought that, if the good lass here has no objections, I'd go through the hall as her servant, clearing the way for her. That way, all attention will be on her, the good Dame de Plou-Aven. No one will notice me."

"I like it not!" Dick's face shone troubled in the lantern-light.

This time it was Sabina who gave him a gentle push. "It's an excellent scheme," she said. "Go you now, before the procession begins to leave."

Dick's progress through the hall was agonisingly

slow, as he held out the tray of bread to importunate hands at either side of him. Eventually it was empty, and he made his way nonchalantly through the far door, the tray tucked under his arm.

"And now it's our turn," Sabina said to Ned with a cheerfulness she was far from feeling. Too late she remembered she would have to walk past Ronan on her way through the great hall. What excuse would she give for her return? What would she do if he stopped her? Ah, well, there was no going back now. "Come, Ned," she said. "We must go."

But Ned did not move.

"Aye, lass," he said. "It's you and I together now. All the way to England and none shall hinder us!"

"What are you talking about? I'm not coming to England!" exclaimed Sabina, puzzled.

"Yes, you are! That was why you engineered our escape, wasn't it? So that we two could be together?"

"Nay! You've got it wrong!" She looked at him with sudden unease. His face was pale, his eyes glittered with unnatural brightness.

Ned did not seem to hear her protestation. He stretched out and took her in his arms, his hold on her hard and relentless.

"What a life we'll have when we're back home, my pretty!" he breathed, his dry mouth nuzzling at her neck. "Once we get there you'll know what it is like to be loved by a proper man, not some puny Breton weakling! Just you wait and see!"

"Ned!" Sabina tried to pull away from him. At her struggles his grip tightened, his breathing quickened. She was frightened now. His voice, his manner, his words—everything told her that Ned's brain had snapped. She longed to scream for help, but that would betray the others. Instead she forced herself to stay calm.

"Ned," she repeated, her voice trembling slightly. "I will go with you through the hall, but no further. It was never part of the plan for me to go to England. If you misunderstood then I am very sorry, but you must believe me, my place is here. I am married to the Seigneur. I will not leave him."

He moved back from her enough to stare her in the face, a puzzled desperation in his expression.

"But you're mine!" he cried. "You will come with me! You will! You care naught for that poxy Breton!"

"I do! He's my husband! I will not leave him!" She spoke kindly but firmly.

"You will!" Ned's voice rose to a shrill scream. "You must!" His hold shifted, and an edge of cold steel was pressed to her throat.

"Kill me if you must! Much good will it do you!" Sabina did not know how she managed to sound so calm. Her whole body was one throbbing mass of fear. "And if you shout so someone will come, and that will be the end of your escape."

Her words seemed to reach him, for he released her and gave a chilling laugh. "You're right," he said, slipping the knife back into his belt. "Dead, you'll give me no pleasure—and believe me, I mean to have the pleasure of you! I know another, better way to make you come with me." He snatched up the lantern and one of the cider-jugs. "That Breton who seems to delight your heart! How do you fancy having him burnt as crisp as a sucking-pig?"

Sabina backed away from him, relieved to be free from his grasp. "What harm can you do with cider?" she asked, rubbing her throat where the feel of the knife-blade still lingered.

"A deal of harm with cider of this vintage." He laughed again, a macabre sound, as though he cherished a sinister secret.

He thrust the cider-jug under her nose. Its neck was corked with a rag, but the resinous smell was unmistakeable.

"Turpentine!" exclaimed Sabina in astonishment. "But I didn't..." She looked more closely at the jug and realised that it was not one of hers. "Where did it come from?" she asked.

"The apple-store. Yon Breton guards were a mite slack in their clearing out. I found it behind a barrel... Have you ever seen turpentine burn?" he asked gleefully, wafting the lantern flame perilously close to the rag stopper.

"No," Sabina said, licking her lips which had suddenly gone dry.

"I have." He stared at the jug and the lantern flame as though fascinated. "At Dartmouth it was, on board ship. A tub of this stuff spilled down on to a fellow working in the dark of the lower deck. It caught his candle and whoosh! Four days a-dying they say he was, and in agony for every minute of them..." Ned paused to give his words their maximum effect. "I haven't enough of this stuff to do that much damage." He swilled the turpentine round in the cider-jug. "But I've enough to maim your pretty Seigneur. All I've got to do is light the rag then..." He made as if to drop the jug down into the hall below.

Directly underneath them was the high table were Ronan sat.

"No!" cried Sabina in horror. "For pity's sake, no!"

She tried to snatch the jug but he was too quick for her, holding both it and the lantern out of reach.

"That's not the way to serve your lord," he said. "You know how. Come with me to England."

"No!" she protested. Then, "Yes! Oh yes!" as he dangled the jug over the narrow parapet once more.

He meant what he said. She was not sure if the turpentine would burn in the way he described, but she knew that she dared not take the chance. The vision of an agonised and scarred Ronan was too dreadful to contemplate.

"I will come," she said quietly.

"Then, let us go, my lady!" With a bow and a flourish he held the lantern before her to light the way downstairs like a well-trained servant. At the bottom, however, he turned, his eyes glittering even more than before.

"I hope you have no little scheme simmering in that pretty head of yours to cry for help as we move through the hall," he said. "If you have, remember I still have my jug here and I'll not hesitate to throw its contents over someone. Maybe not your Seigneur, more's the pity! But someone, nevertheless—perhaps even you…"

Their progress through the hall was ridiculously simple. People greeting her at either side took no notice of the servant who cleared a way for her. In no time at all they were going through the door at the other end and out into the fresh air. The inner bailey was nearly as thronged with people as the hall had been, and Sabina peered desperately through the patchy gloom for a sign of Dick, Kit or Jack, without success. Of course, they would be keeping out of sight as much as possible. However, they were bound to meet up before long and she knew that the other men would come to her aid. At least, she had some hope to sustain her.

From somewhere inside the château the *tambour* began to throb again and scores of voices took up the refrain of the Eginane song. The procession was preparing to go on its way for the final celebrations back in the centre of Plou-Aven. Sabina greeted the reappearance of the fool and the revellers with relief. In the chaos of the journey back to the *bourg* she might be able to give Ned the slip. Barely had the thought come to her than she felt his grip on her wrist tighten and he held the jug of turpentine before her eyes. Even out here in the open air the scattering of inflammable liquid among so many torches and lanterns was bound to be catastrophic.

For Sabina the procession with its jostling bodies, flaring torches, and insistent *tambour*, became one long nightmare. Fear for herself and fear for those about her stretched her nerves to breaking-point. Worse was to come. When they reached the outskirts of the *bourg* Ned suddenly tugged at her, pulling her down a small side-lane.

"We've turned off too soon," she protested. "This is not the route we planned!"

"This is the route *I* have planned," he said with sinister emphasis, dragging her along the rutted track.

"But this goes nowhere! Only to a boggy marsh," she cried.

"You lie! This is the road I have chosen. It will

get us to the coast more quickly! Let the other fellows take the long route if they wish. They're fools!'' There was arrogance in his voice now, and she knew that there was no use in arguing.

She tried to block her mind to all but the moment—to think of what lay ahead was too terrifying. Despite the darkness she was aware of the bushes and trees thinning out into open moorland. Here and there, patches of snow glowed luminous against the sombre light, while beneath her feet the ground grew steadily softer. The sounds of the festivities were becoming fainter, drifting on the wind. After a long time something else caught her ear. Ned heard it too. He paused, tense as a wild animal.

"Horsemen!" he said. "We're being followed."

Without another word he began to run, pulling her along with him, so that she had no choice but to run too. It was no easy task keeping upright in those miry conditions and Ned fell full length, dropping the lantern and the jug. Sabina was forced to her knees, but she recovered swiftly. Scrambling to her feet, she began running back towards her rescuers.

"Help me! Help me!" she screamed.

But running in a skirt that was becoming increasingly sodden was difficult. In no time Ned was in pursuit of her, and his long legs easily caught up with her.

"You don't want to go that way!" he hissed, clutching her to him. "You're coming with me, remember! We're going home."

"Let me go, please! Please!" begged Sabina, trying to pull away. But it was no use. His grasp was stronger than ever. As he dragged her onwards she cast a despairing glance over her shoulders. The

sound of horses' hoofs still came to her but she could
see nothing.

Without warning a group of horsemen emerged
from behind some rocks, charging towards them. The
leader was galloping towards them at full speed, re-
gardless of the darkness and the rough terrain. Even
in the darkness she recognised him.

"Ronan!" she screamed. "Ronan!" But her cries
were cut off by Ned tugging at her with painful force.

They were running again, through deeper and
deeper mud which clung to Sabina's skirts and
dragged her down. Every step became an agonising
effort.

"I can't—" she sobbed, her lungs heaving. "I—
can't—go on!"

She collapsed half-conscious, heedless of the mire.
She knew only that the iron grip on her wrist had
gone. Horses' hoofs splashed about her, men
shouted. Then arms lifted her up and wrapped her in
a cloak, and she was being carried back to the château on horseback, her head resting against Ronan.
The nightmare was over!

Catell it was who undressed her, put her to bed
with hot possets and much sympathy. Sabina sub-
mitted to her ministrations gladly, too weary to help
herself, and too relieved to care.

"Where is the Seigneur?" she asked at last.

"Gone out after the Englishmen! He'll be back
soon." Catell tucked the coverlet around her with
brisk efficiency. "Who'd have thought it, eh? I never
did trust that red-haired one! Too saucy by half, in
my opinion. The others, though, I never thought they
would do you harm, *ma dame.*"

"They did not... It was Ned..."

Weariness overcame Sabina. She fell asleep, her
words unspoken.

Chapter Eleven

Sabina awoke feeling surprisingly refreshed and ravenously hungry.

"You're in a better state than many this morning, *ma dame*," chuckled Catell, bringing her some food. "There are some sore heads, I can tell you. Oh, and the Seigneur's just come back."

Sabina had barely finished her bread and honey when she heard Ronan's familiar step outside, and the door opened.

"Sire," she greeted him happily. Then her smile of welcome faded. Ronan's face was white, not with weariness but with intense emotion.

"You will be happy to know, *ma dame*, that your paramour escaped," he said, his voice low and chilling.

"Paramour? What can you mean?"

"Your bewilderment is most convincing. What a pity I already know the truth!" He glared at her with burning contempt in his eyes.

"What truth! I don't know what you are talking about!"

"Come, *ma dame*, you are not going to try to convince me that the red-headed knave really abducted you, are you? That is the story I have circulated abroad, but please don't think me so simple that I believe it!''

"But I didn't go willingly! You've got to believe me! He threatened me—"

"What! After you had engineered his escape? And that of his comrades? You don't deny it, do you?"

"No. I admit I helped them. But Ned had become crazed—"

"With love for you, no doubt? Did he say he could not live without you? That you had to accompany him or else he would pine away? Did he play on that well-known tender heart of yours, so that you felt you must go with him? Oh, save your breath and spare me such nonsense!"

"But it's true…! At least, in part." She could not believe this was happening. How could Ronan think such things? It was like a continuation of the nightmare.

"I will not ask which part. I've no wish to hear the sordid details. In fact, I've no wish to remain in your company. You will stay here until I order otherwise. The household understand you are overcome with shock after your distressing experience. Catell alone will attend you. You are to have communication with no one else!"

Ronan turned towards the door.

"Where are you going?" cried Sabina. "You cannot leave so!" She half scrambled out of bed to stop him. "Listen to me—"

"I have heard all I wish to hear!" He swung round and strode towards her, only to stop just beyond her reach. She flinched. His features were set as though carved from the Breton granite. A beating pulse in his jaw betrayed the maelstrom of emotion he was concealing—that, and the hurt look lingering behind the anger in his eyes.

Suddenly he flung himself forward and, grasping her by the arms, almost lifted her from the bed.

"I trusted you!" he said in a low voice that was half a sob. "And you betrayed me."

In one violent motion he flung her from him and hurried from the bedchamber.

Sabina lay sprawled across the pillows where she had fallen, too shocked to think of moving. She was even too stunned for tears. Dry-eyed, she went over the events of the last few minutes. His words whirled in her tortured head, making her giddy. Particularly the last ones—he *had* trusted her, and she *had* betrayed him by helping the Englishmen escape. Her conscience was sore, and she was ready to beg his forgiveness for that, but she was guilty of naught else!

"I am innocent!" She cried the words aloud. Then she fell back on the pillows, trying to organise her thoughts into some sort of order. There had to be a way of persuading Ronan that she spoke the truth, if only she could think of it. The unexpectedness of his accusations, coming on top of all else seemed to have befuddled her wits.

"I will go to him!" she said, flinging back the bedcovers. "Catell, help me to dress."

"Oh, *ma dame,* best not! Stay here, pray!"

"Dress me, I say!"

"The door is barred, *ma dame,*" said the maid apologetically. "The captain of the men-at-arms is outside. He has instructions to keep you in."

"I see..." Sabina's indignation ebbed as swiftly as it had arisen. She sat down on the edge of the bed. "So, I am to be kept prisoner, am I? What am I to do?"

"Let the Seigneur cool down a bit, *ma dame*. You know what he's like. All noise and temper one minute, then desperately sorry the next. You'll see, tomorrow when some sort of sense has got into his brain he will be in here begging your pardon on his bended knees. Now why not get back into bed and have some rest?"

Obediently Sabina slipped back under the covers.

"I did betray the Seigneur, you know," she said morosely. "I helped the prisoners escape."

"I guessed as much, *ma dame*. And who's to blame you? They are your own folk."

"The Seigneur blames me. He said he trusted me..." She paused, her thoughts still confused. "What happened here after they—after we had gone?" she asked. "Who raised the alarm?"

"Yannick, *ma dame*! He came running into the great hall, grabbed hold of the Seigneur and made a fair attempt at dragging him to the door."

"Yannick did?"

"Indeed! Some thought he had gone raving mad and tried to drive him off. But I saw his face... And so did the Seigneur. He was frantic with worry, certainly not mad."

"There were enough madmen abroad last night, heaven knows!" said Sabina shuddering.

"The red-haired Englishman?" asked Catell.

"I should have seen it...been prepared..." In her mind Sabina relived the awful moments when she had feared Ned would drop burning liquid on Ronan.

Then she took a deep breath to calm herself. "I would talk of something else. Finish your tale."

"When the Seigneur looked at Yannick he guessed something serious was amiss. 'We'll go with the wild man and see where he takes us,' he said. Then he and some of the men mounted up and followed Yannick. One of the men said they found you out at the reed-cutter's marsh."

Sabina nodded, remembering the mud and the cold, icy water. "Yannick must have seen Ned dragging me along..." Her voice trailed away. She really did not want to remember it... "The Seigneur said he must decide what to do with me. What do you think he meant by that?" she asked tremulously.

"It was just his temper talking," said Catell.

But Sabina did not believe her.

All the next day and the next Sabina paced back and forth across the bedchamber floor waiting for Ronan to come. She wrote him innumerable letters, but the fate of each one, Catell regretfully informed her, was to finish up on the fire unread. By the third day of imprisonment Sabina's emotions had settled into a calm despair.

On the morning of the fourth day a familiar tread outside brought her to her feet. There was the sound of the bar being drawn back and Ronan entered. She meant to greet him with hard words but the sight of him tore at her heart. He had the look of a man who had not slept in a long time. His face was pale and drawn, dark circles ringed his eyes, and there was an air of despondency about him which had been absent at their last meeting. He stepped into the room, not speaking.

"Catell, you may go," said Sabina, her eyes not leaving his.

"You continue to give orders with authority, *dame*," Ronan said curtly.

"That is because I am still the Dame de Plou-Aven. Have you forgotten?" Sabina said evenly.

"I wish I could!" He spoke with fervour. Then he sat down, regarding her coldly from the great carved chair. He sat stiff and proud, his mouth an uncompromising line. His shoulders beneath the tawny wool of his gown were set square and the folds of the long garment fell to the floor. He looked impressive and fearsome, the embodiment of avenging justice.

"I have made my decision on your future," he said.

"Oh…!" A sick dread clutched at Sabina. But, as ever, when she was afraid a spark of anger started to burn within her—at Ronan for being so unreasonable and at herself for not fighting harder.

"Wait!" she said, as he opened his mouth to speak again. "I have done nothing wrong! I refuse to stand before you like a naughty child!"

Seizing a stool, she slammed it on the floor in front of him and sat down hard upon it, her eyes still holding his. She knew that it must look ludicrous, the pair of them sitting face to face. At any other time she would have expected to see his lips start to twitch and his eyes sparkle with the sudden laughter which delighted her so. But not today! Today there would be no laughter!

"So!" she said as haughtily as she could, "You have decided on my future, have you? May I ask why such a step was necessary?"

"You can ask that? After all that has happened?"

"I know I am accused of some misdemeanour, but of what exactly I am not sure. Nor do I know why I should be so accused, or on what evidence?"

"I accuse you of being unfaithful to me. Is that plain enough?"

"I would know with whom and on what grounds."

"With the red-haired Englishman, Edward Prettyjohn."

"Well, that is a clear accusation, right enough. What I would know is how I managed to dally with Ned. Until the Eginane festival I had never been alone with him! Or are you saying that I committed adultery with all four Englishmen, including young Jack? *And* with Catell looking on, not to mention Père Martin? Either you think me a most depraved creature, or the whole thing is nonsense!"

"Infidelity can take many forms. You freed the prisoners. Do not deny it! You were caught fleeing with the Prettyjohn fellow. Do not deny that, either!"

"I have already admitted helping them to escape. I have never tried to avoid taking the blame for that."

Their voices had been rising, the hard edge of anger creeping more and more into their words. Sabina caught her breath. This was no way to reach Ronan, by increasing her fury.

"Seigneur," she said, in a voice that was suddenly quiet, "you are a just man, and have ever been. Hear my version of the events. You would grant that much to a common thief."

"A common thief would not have dishonoured my

name!" snapped Ronan. Then he, too, seemed to recollect himself. "But I will listen," he said.

Sabina took another deep breath, considering her
words with care.

"I helped the English prisoners to escape because
I was concerned for them, and because I felt my family owed them much. The first plan was to escape
from the north tower, but after the wall collapsed we
had to alter things. I remembered the builders' shaft
which runs up with the stairs. We used that as the
escape route. The Feast of Eginane had been chosen
as a time when there would be many people about
and much confusion. Things went well at first. Kit
and Jack went together, then Dick, which left me
alone with Ned. Imprisonment had not been kind to
him, it had turned his wits. I had not appreciated how
much until he started talking of us going back to
England together. Where he got such an idea from I
do not know. When I tried to explain that my place
was here he became angry, frighteningly so, and
threatened..."

"He threatened to harm you?" prompted Ronan
as Sabina's voice faded.

"No—he threatened you."

"Me?" The Seigneur looked astonished. "You
need to think up a better story than that!"

"Hear me out!" cried Sabina. "You said you
would! We were in an alcove on the stairs, the one
which looks down into the great hall. Ned had some
turpentine he had found, he said he would set it on
fire and drop it on you if I did not go with him. I
still do not know if it would have burned as fiercely
as he said, but I could not take the chance. I went
with him."

"And you found no other opportunity to escape?"

"No. Even after we were beyond reach of you he still would have used the turpentine. Can you imagine the terrible hurt it could have caused among all those people? And afterwards, when we were making our way alone across country, he swore it would be me who would burn if I did not keep with him... And, I confess I have an awful dread of flames, so I went."

"The other Englishmen, did they not come to your aid?"

"We did not see them again, or I'm sure they would have helped me. I swear I was never unfaithful to you, either with my body or my thoughts. I beg forgiveness for assisting the prisoners to escape; other than that I have no cause for remorse."

"You wish me to believe that you had no longing to return to England?"

"I do... Because my place is here with you."

"You would play the devoted wife now, would you?"

"I pray you, do not sound so scathing," Sabina protested. "It is the truth! Would I ever wish to leave you or do you harm when I love you so dearly—?" The words were out of her mouth before she could stop them. She waited, scarcely daring to breathe, for his reaction.

Ronan rose swiftly to his feet, his fists clenched.

"I fear you added one embellishment too many to your story, *dame*," he said, his voice icy. "Until that moment I was inclined to believe you, you tell a very convincing tale. But a protestation of love—that is too incredible to swallow."

Sabina closed her eyes in humiliation and pain,

wincing at the scorn in his voice. Slowly opening her eyes, she saw that Ronan was pacing the floor with thoughtful measured steps.

"What I have heard has done nothing to alter my decision, save to wish the business done with even more quickly," he said. "There are three courses open to me. I can put you away, either by sending you back to your father's house or to a convent. The first I consider unsuitable," he went on, ignoring her horrified gasp. "I would not have my good name mocked in England for being cuckolded... In truth, I blame myself for this misfortune!" For the first time his voice shook, and she saw that he was controlling his feelings with great difficulty. "I—I permitted you too much licence, foolishly so. I made no allowance for the fact that you are so young... I sowed the seeds of my own misery. But it is too late to remedy that now." He paused, his back half-turned to her as though he were reluctant to betray his emotions. "No, to return to your father would serve no good purpose. As for sending you to a convent, it is a course of action which has its points. In its favour is the fact that you would be out of my life and away from the world. Against...against it is your youth and your lively spirit. The cloistered life would be a torment to you, and I feel I owe you something, you have been good to the people of the parish, you have worked hard for them. Also, as my wi—" He stopped, unable to bring himself to call her his wife. "Also, our life together has not been without its pleasures. I grew so fond... I could have grown fond of you if things had been otherwise. So I cannot bring myself to treat you harshly. Therefore,

I will take the third course of action open to me—you will remain here as the Dame de Plou-Aven.''

Hearing his words, Sabina felt her senses spin with relief. She had to clutch the sides of the stool to prevent herself from falling.

''Thank you, Seigneur.'' She whispered the words.

''There are conditions, of course. Things cannot be as they were before. In the eyes of the world you will still be my wife. You will share my board, sit with me at high table, entertain our guests, and behave as is proper for the Dame de Plou-Aven. You will share my bedchamber also, but not my bed. Up to that door yonder, you will be my wife, with all the rank and privilege which is your due. Once inside this room, however, we will be as strangers.''

''No! No! You cannot mean it!'' cried Sabina horrified. ''Is that your idea of not being harsh? It is the most cruel thing you could do to me!''

She tried to imagine a life with Ronan where there was only coldness between them, future days, weeks, months, years, when he treated her with nothing but frigid hostility, when there was no hope of ever gaining his affection. It was like the prospect of Hell itself.

''Sire,'' she said, rising to her feet. ''If you would have me beg and plead for your forgiveness, then I will do so. I am innocent, but I will do anything you say, only please do not treat me thus! Give me another chance—''

''There is no hope of anything between us ever again. Pray do not ask it, *ma dame*. It serves only to distress us both.''

''Then if you are distressed you must have some little fondness for me—''

"Enough, *dame!*" His voice was harsh. "Enough... I will hear no more."

He made to leave.

"What of the heir? Plou-Aven has no heir!" cried Sabina to his retreating back.

He came to a halt but did not turn round.

"Your one obligation will be to bear me an heir," he said.

To conceive his child with no love, no warmth! Sabina gave a shudder at the thought. She could have done so once, in the early days, before she had come to love him. But now she knew that duty was a pitiful substitute for love, too pitiful for her to contemplate...

"If you please, I will enter the convent," she said in a tense voice.

Ronan turned. "You only say that in the heat of the moment. You will change your mind tomorrow."

"I will not. If you offer me only a hollow sham of an existence as your wife then I would prefer to take the veil, and gladly."

"To renounce the outside world can be very hard for someone so young." Genuine concern sounded in his voice, nearly destroying her last shreds of self-control.

"That depends on what the outside world has to offer, does it not? Under the circumstances the convent is infinitely preferable. And you forget, I have some experience of the cloistered life."

"Ah, yes. You were 'a disruptive influence' were you not?" A brief smile flickered across his face, a smile touched with such sadness that Sabina almost cried aloud.

Instead she said, very quietly, "You will permit me to enter the convent, Seigneur?"

"If that is your wish. I will make arrangements."

Ronan left the room, closing the door behind him.

Sabina wished that she could weep. All she could do was sit huddled beside the burning hearth, a blanket wrapped round her, staring into space. Even when night fell she had no wish to stir.

Catell gave up all pretence of cheerfulness. "You can't go to the convent, *ma dame!*" she exclaimed. "What will happen to us, to the folk of the parish?"

"Hold your tongue!" snapped Sabina, too bowed down with unhappiness to cope with her maid's entreaties. "If you have naught else to do get my boxes packed. I leave for the convent in the morning."

"So soon?" The maid was aghast.

"If I wish to be with the good sisters before the ways are completely blocked with snow, yes!"

Sabina awoke next morning with the knowledge that this was her last day at Plou-Aven. Worse by far was the thought that she would never see Ronan again.

It was nearly time to go.

"The Seigneur entreats you attend him in the solar before you go, *ma dame,*" sobbed Catell. She had wept unceasingly since first light.

Sabina could think of no words of comfort, so she embraced her maid, then hurried to the solar.

Ronan was standing with his back to the fire. She was reminded of her first morning at Plou-Aven, seemingly centuries ago. He had been standing in exactly the same manner then. At the sight of her he gave a slight bow in greeting.

"You are ready for your journey, *dame?*" he asked. "You have everything you need?"

"Yes, thank you, Seigneur."

"Do you wish me to accompany you?"

"I would prefer not." Deliberately she kept her answers brief and impersonal.

"As you wish. Cudenec will be in charge, he knows the way well. I have ordered six menservants to protect you on your journey. Will that suffice?"

His voice was dry and abrupt. She wondered if he was sharing her thoughts—that this was such a bleak, passionless way of ending their marriage—a marriage which at times had promised so much.

"Yes, thank you—" she began, when she was interrupted by an excited servant entering.

"I said we were not to be disturbed!"

Ronan's sudden blaze of fury betrayed just how precariously his emotions were balanced.

"Yes, Seigneur... B-but three of the Englishmen have returned, and are most pressing to see you."

"Englishmen? Are you drunk?" asked Ronan.

But even as he spoke the door pushed open and Dick entered, followed by Kit and Jack. They looked cold and tired, but otherwise well. At the sight of Sabina their faces lit up with relief.

"My lady! You're safe!" Dick cried seizing her by the hands.

"We feared—we feared—we don't know what we feared," gabbled Kit. "But you're safe and well and that's all that matters!"

"Will you be kind enough to tell me what these fellows are jabbering about?" Ronan demanded.

"We captured them in the *bourg!*" declared the servant proudly.

"The devil you did!" cried Dick, speaking Breton. "We were nearly here at the château!" Belatedly he remembered his manners and bowed low to the Seigneur. "Your pardon, sire. We have forgotten all courtesies at seeing the Dame Sabina is safe."

"What did you think had happened to her?" asked Ronan, silencing Sabina, who had been about to speak.

Dick looked puzzled. "Do you not know, Seigneur? That our companion, Ned— But perhaps it is we who are wrong, and our fears were unfounded..."

"Tell me about your fears, nevertheless," ordered Ronan.

"As you wish, sire. It was after our escape..." Here Dick paused and looked questioningly at Sabina.

"The Seigneur knows about my part in your escape," she said.

"...After our escape at the feast we saw no sign of Ned Prettyjohn. We waited for him until near dawn, then in the end we had to go without him. It wasn't until we were almost at the coast that we encountered him. For some time we had been concerned for him; some men take ill to being locked-up and we had begun to fear for his wits. Now, it seems, the excitement of the escape turned his brain completely. It was hard to make sense of him, but he seemed to be saying that he had brought Dame Sabina with him but he'd lost her on the way. He rambled on, cursing and shouting. One minute he said he had killed you, Seigneur, the next he had killed Dame Sabina. He even claimed to have burned down the château. We grew ever more anxious, so when he ran off we decided to come back. We feared, from what he said, that he might have forced you to come part of the way with him, *ma dame,* and that you were now wandering lost on the moors, or lying injured, or even dead..."

"And so you returned to your place of imprisonment?" said Ronan.

"Of course. We wish to be free and to go home very much—but not if Dame Sabina is hurt in the process. Now we see it was just the ravings of poor Ned."

"Not quite." Ronan's voice was quiet. "Your companion did abduct Dame Sabina. Fortunately the alarm was raised and I was able to fetch her back safely."

"He thought I was going back to England with him," said Sabina.

"You say so, *ma dame?*" Dick's face, beneath his unshaven stubble, registered surprise. Swiftly he translated for the benefit of the other two, then he turned his attention back to the Seigneur. "How Ned could have got such a worm in his brain I do not know. There was never any question of you coming with us, was there, *ma dame?* Why should you. Your home is here, and your Seigneur. It's different for us, we have families back home in Devon, but you are a Breton lady now."

"Yet the Dame Sabina helped you escape," said Ronan.

"That she did, the kind lady." Dick shot her a grateful smile. "She knew how we were fretting. And there was Kit's cough not getting any better, not to mention Ned's moods. But to come back to England with us..." He shook his head at the preposterous idea.

"And now I feel even more beholden to you!" cried Sabina. "You would have been home by now if you had not come back to see if I was all right."

"An uneasy homecoming it would have been, too, worrying ourselves in case you were lying dead in a ditch somewhere, my lady. Now we'll just have to wait until someone finally decides to exchange those Breton boys to get us home."

"There will be no need for that," said Ronan, his voice growing ever more quiet. "I will give you horses to take you to the coast, and a letter of passage to one of my captains. But we will talk of this later." He turned to the servant who had been listening agog to everything. "Take the Englishmen down and see they are treated as honoured guests."

Dick and the others tried to thank him but he waved them away.

After the three Englishmen had left the only sound to disturb the silence of the room was the crackling of logs in the hearth.

"What of your Bretons?" Sabina asked to ease the tension.

"Perhaps the fellow who speaks our tongue—Dick was his name?—will take letters to that Master Gilbert of his. Let us not speak of it now. I have more important things to say. I did not believe you...and I was wrong. I beg your forgiveness."

"What is there to forgive? It does not matter," said Sabina dully. She felt drained of emotion, empty, as she had done when she had lost the child.

"I should have trusted you..."

"So you should. If only you had thought, or had a little faith in me, you would have seen how stupid the whole idea was. What is there for me in England now? Why could you not have seen the stupidity of your accusations?''

"Because I did not want to... I think I wanted to believe that you had been unfaithful."

"But why?" asked Sabina in astonishment.

"To punish myself—to stop me thinking kindly of you. So often I drew close to loving you and I did not want that. I fought against it—oh, how I fought against it!"

"But—what was wrong with loving me. I am your wife!"

"Marianne was my wife before you."

"Marianne is dead!"

"Yes. Dead of the child I gave her! I loved her and I killed her. The least I could do was to be faithful to her memory! I did not mean to care for you! I needed a wife to get me an heir, and I thought that was all. But I found myself softening towards you. You made me laugh—even when you did not mean to—and you were always so kind, so compassionate to anyone or any beast that needed help. Again and again I hovered on the brink of loving you, yet always something happened to bring me back to Marianne, to remind me that I was still hers. Even this last time—"

"Surely you did not accuse me of unfaithfulness just to ease your conscience?"

Angrily Sabina walked to the window and gazed out at the snowflakes slowly falling.

"Your involvement with the escape of the prisoners...then finding you with that Prettyjohn fellow... It all seemed to indicate how wrong I was to love you. It sounds so foolish when put into words, does it not? But I feared being unfaithful my-self...being unfaithful to Marianne.''

"Well, she can rest content. She has got rid of me most effectively. She has you all to herself now." Sabina could not keep the bitterness from her voice. "Marianne is dead, and she still has so much love from you. I am living, and I longed above all else to hear you say words of love to me. Now you have come close to it, and it is too late."

"I did not know how you truly felt." Ronan had moved behind her now. She could feel him close to her. "Always I kept remembering how unwilling you were to be my bride. You gave me so few signs, no outward signs as..."

"As Marianne used to?" she finished for him. "How could I? She knew what it was like to be loved. I did not! I did not know how to show you my love. For a long time I held my feelings back, fearing that if I betrayed my true emotions you would mock or scorn me."

"You thought that of me? I would never do such a thing!" cried Ronan.

"But you did! You did!" she cried in answer. "Not a day since I told you I love you and you flung that love back at me unwanted. And you wonder why I say it is too late for aught between us!"

"I suppose I deserve no better." Ronan's hands came up to hold her arms briefly, for a second, then he let her go.

Below in the courtyard the grooms were bringing out the horses ready saddled for her journey to the convent.

"It is time for me to leave," said Sabina... She tasted salt on her lips and realised she was crying.

"There is no need. This is your home. You do not have to go." He spoke with hesitancy and hope.

"Why should I stay?" she asked flatly. "To share the château and you with Marianne? No. I prefer the peace of the cloisters to that. At least, my heart will not get broken at the convent."

She picked up her mantle and drew it round her.

"The place will be empty without you," he said. "No laughter, no flea-ridden dogs, no disasters befalling me. I do not think I can bear so well-ordered a life any more."

She said nothing. She had reached the door and her hand was on the latch.

"Do not go! Sabina, I need you! There is no life here without you!" His voice shook as he spoke. "'If you would have me beg and plead for your forgiveness then I will do so.' You said those words to me not long since and I treated you roughly. Now it is my turn to say them. I implore you, be more generous than I was. Do not discard my love as I seemed to discard yours—for that is what I am offering you now—my love and my heart, shared with no one living or dead. Sabina, my dearest, do not leave me, for without you..."

Sabina heard his voice break under the force of his unhappiness, and she felt her own heart would break too. She could bear no more... Never to see him again or to hear his voice, never to feel his warm body against hers. How could she suffer it? She turned, the tears still flowing freely.

"Ronan—" she said, half-choked with sobs. "Ronan—my love..."

And she ran into his waiting arms.

* * * * *

...there's more to the story!

Superromance.
A *big* satisfying read about unforgettable
characters. Each month we offer *six* very different
stories that range from family drama to adventure
and mystery, from highly emotional stories to
romantic comedies—and much more! Stories
about people you'll believe in and care about.
Stories too compelling to put down....

Our authors are among today's *best* romance
writers. You'll find familiar names and talented
newcomers. Many of them are award winners—
and you'll see why!

If you want the biggest and best
in romance fiction, you'll get it
from Superromance!

Emotional, Exciting, Unexpected...

HARLEQUIN®
Makes any time special ®

HARLEQUIN®
INTRIGUE

WE'LL LEAVE YOU BREATHLESS!

If you've been looking for thrilling tales of
contemporary passion and sensuous love stories
with taut, edge-of-the-seat suspense—then
you'll love Harlequin Intrigue!

Every month, you'll meet four new heroes
who are guaranteed to make your spine tingle
and your pulse pound. With them you'll enter
into the exciting world of Harlequin Intrigue—
where your life is on the line
and so is your heart!

THAT'S INTRIGUE—
ROMANTIC SUSPENSE
AT ITS BEST!

HARLEQUIN®
Makes any time special ®

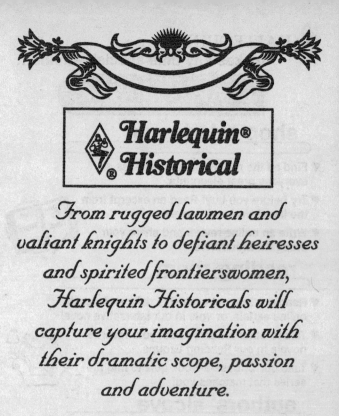

Harlequin® Historical

From rugged lawmen and valiant knights to defiant heiresses and spirited frontierswomen, Harlequin Historicals will capture your imagination with their dramatic scope, passion and adventure.

Harlequin Historicals . . . they're too good to miss!

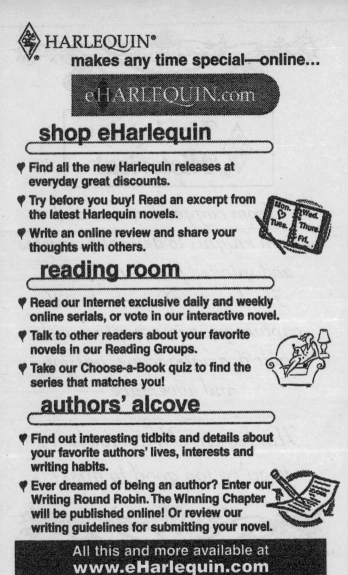